THE SPEAKER OF CLOVIS CREEK

ALSO BY C. K. CRIGGER

Ault's heir

Black Crossing

Double Deal and Other Western Stories

Hereafter

Letter of the Law

Liar's Trail

Lost Girl Lake

Madame's Daughter

Rebel Hearts Anthology

Yeggman's Apprentice

Yester's Ride

China Bohannon Series

The Gunsmith Series

Hometown Homicide Series

The Woman Who Series

THE SPEAKER OF CLOVIS CREEK

C. K. CRIGGER

WOLFPACK
PUBLISHING
— EST 2019 —

The Speaker of Clovis Creek
Paperback Edition
Copyright © 2023 C.K. Crigger

Wolfpack Publishing
9850 S. Maryland Parkway, Suite A-5 #323
Las Vegas, Nevada 89183

wolfpackpublishing.com

Paperback ISBN 978-1-63977-147-9
eBook ISBN 978-1-63977-865-2
LCCN 2023946614

THE SPEAKER OF CLOVIS CREEK

"Sheriff Welburn's comin'." A youngster up well past his bedtime darted through the café's double doors to announce the news in an excited shout. "He's comin', and he's got that damn murderin' Russkie in handcuffs."

A man seated on one of the counter stools raised his head to respond. "Should've shot him down where he stood. Save the taxpayer's money on a trial and a hanging."

To Ocean Galliard, wearily shuffling dirty dishes to the kitchen, he sounded very certain of the trial's outcome. Whatever happened to innocent until proven guilty? Being Russian didn't necessarily mean one was a murderer.

Only one table in the place still had customers occupying chairs. They emptied as the two men in for a late supper rushed over to gawk out through the open door. Sheriff Early Welburn, his full-time deputy Ash Jones, and another man, a stranger, slumped in their saddles as they rode down the street.

Even the cook left his kitchen long enough to have a look. That allowed Ocean Galliard time to sweep crumbs from the oilcloth covering the newly emptied table into her hand and give it a thorough swipe of her cleaning cloth. She wished she could hurry those last men into finishing their meal and leaving. It had been a long day, one already half an hour past closing time. Her feet ached, and she had a painful cut on her forefinger from a broken glass.

"They're stopping out front," Ollie, the cook, called to her over the men's raised voices as one opened the door to shout out something to the sheriff. "Aw, hell. Looks like they're coming in."

They exchanged a tired glance. They didn't dare deny service despite the sheriff's late arrival. Butch Seibert, the cafe's owner, or more likely his wife, would fire them on the spot if they did, and in a town the size of Clovis Creek, jobs were scarce as hair on a snake. Even Ollie, whose reputation as a cook had no peer, not even in the hotel down the street, walked on tenterhooks around Elsie Seibert, the old shrew.

As for Ocean's job, well, most any girl could wait on tables if she had to. Or was desperate enough. And she was, always subsisting an inch away from sleeping in a barn somewhere. But her main trouble was with Elsie. The woman was jealous of any younger, prettier female and always on guard against perceived competition for her husband's regard. Not that Ocean ever had given the slightest provocation. Nor had Butch, as far as she knew.

Who'd want to get close to Butch, anyhow? A question she asked herself nearly every day. Sweaty, a bit rotund what with all the food there to sample, and sadly, a bit stinky.

She'd just shoved the chairs under the table when the chatter ceased. Outside, bridle bits jangled, and saddle leather squeaked in the abrupt silence.

"Get down," she heard Sheriff Welburn say, cold and stern, and adding impatiently only seconds later, "Hurry up if you want to be fed. This place is about to close for the night, and I, for one, don't feel like going to bed hungry."

There was a mutter, the words indistinguishable at this distance.

"Ash, get him off his horse," Welburn said. "What the hell is the matter with him? He so stupid he can't understand plain English, you suppose?"

Ash Jones, as far as Ocean could tell, made no reply. Could be he was too busy manhandling the prisoner off the very large horse he was riding since when Welburn pushed the so-called Russkie into the cafe ahead of him, the man could barely walk. Clearly, his capture had included a tussle. The fellow's hands were shackled, his cheekbone bore a great darkening bruise, and his shirt was torn. One leg limped, and he had no coat. Ocean figured he must be freezing. The calendar might say April, but they'd been having a cold spell with nightly frosts.

"I'll take Ranger and Buck on over to the livery," Ash said from the doorway. "That big plowhorse of his, too."

"Later," Welburn said, steering his prisoner to where Ocean stood at the newly cleaned table. "Get in here. You haven't eaten either. I reckon the county can afford a decent hot meal."

Ocean flicked a glance at Ollie, who didn't try to hide his displeasure. "Dang, Sheriff." He scowled mightily. "I got the grill cleaned, and the fire's almost out. All I got is either chili or stew. Take your pick."

"Chili," Welburn said, not bothering to complain, "with plenty of crackers. How about you, Ash?"

"Stew."

"You?" Welburn asked the prisoner. "Chili or stew? Sit down and mind your manners."

But the prisoner neither sat on the chair Ash pulled out for him nor made his wishes known as to his supper.

To Ocean's astonishment, he burst out weeping. And talking, though judging by the blank expression on their faces, none of the men understood what he was saying. Listening, wishing she could put a plug in her ears to block out his repeated protests, her mouth tightened.

"Great guns, he's going off on us again." Welburn looked at Ollie. "Bring him whatever you got the most of. He'll eat it and like it."

"Stew." Ollie nodded and trod off to his kitchen.

Meanwhile, Sheriff Welburn made a short speech about the murderer's capture, even as he tried to ignore the questions being pelted at him by the remaining customers. One of them was the newspaperman, Horace Freeman, and going by his avid expression, he wanted answers.

"By the looks of your prisoner, you had quite a scuffle. Put up a fight, did he?" Horace Freeman asked, grinning.

A sly way of accusing the sheriff, or maybe the deputy, of playing rough. "Sure he put up a fuss. He's tougher than he looks. Don't think he was expecting us to come down on him so fast," Welburn said easily. "But nothing Ash or me couldn't handle."

The deputy frowned. "He acted mighty desperate," he reminded the sheriff in his deep, soft voice. "Kept trying to go back to his cabin. Funny he didn't make a try for the woods."

Welburn shrugged. "Who knows what he had on his mind—if he has a mind. Hard telling with all the chitter-chatterin' he does. I'm beginning to wonder if he knows any English at all. What I do know is we got our man. Case closed."

Toting eating utensils, a coffee pot, and cups on a tray, Ocean's lips tightened as she laid the table. The man kept talking, his tone, as Deputy Jones had said, desperate. Frantic. Terrified. Ocean heard all those things in his speech.

The men ignored him.

"Order up," Ollie called and, her feet dragging, Ocean went to fetch the bowls, a basket of crackers, and half a pan of cornbread. She added a flagon of honey. The cornbread, left from this morning, was getting a trifle dry.

"That poor man," she whispered to Ollie. "I wonder if he really did murder that rancher. He doesn't seem like he would've. He..." She stopped and started over. "I don't think he knows what they say he did. Or why he's being held prisoner."

No. She didn't think. She knew.

Ollie gave her a stare out of bleary eyes. "None of our business, girl. Just get them folks out of here. I'm tired and gettin' mighty thirsty."

The cook truly did like his drink. The Seiberts

didn't complain as he never missed a beat when it came to getting tasty food to the customers.

Ocean looked back at the three men, her dark eyes worried. "But none of those men can understand what he's saying, Ollie. He can't defend himself."

Ollie put a heavy hand on her shoulder. "Welburn'll do what's right, missy, depend on it. He's a fair man. The feller will get whatever is coming to him. Guilty or not guilty. You'll see. Now you go do what you can to hurry them along."

Nodding, Ocean cleared dishes from in front of the man at the counter in a pointed sort of way. With a final look at the sheriff's group, he took the hint, paid, and left. Evidently inspired, and maybe with his nose put a little out of joint by Welburn ignoring more questions, the newspaperman and his friend soon followed.

Shades pulled over the windows at last and the door locked, Ocean went over to the table when the sheriff called to her. "Got any more of this chili?" he asked. "And maybe another helping of stew for Ash?" He eyed his prisoner's bowl with only a few bites eaten. "Don't look like this one is hungry. Well, don't blame him, I guess. Hard to eat when you're accused of murder."

The prisoner looked up, his eyes filling with tears.

Ocean couldn't bear the misery on the man's face. "I'll get refills," she said over her shoulder as she hurried away.

In the kitchen, Ollie had finished washing the dishes and was glad enough when she used the rest of the chili and stew. "I drained the dishwater. Just stack their things before you go. Morning shift can take care of washing up. I'll lock the back as I leave. Good luck getting out of here before midnight, missy."

Not for the first time, she had to smile. Ollie never used her name but always called her either girl or missy. "On account of ocean ain't a name," he had said once. "It's a whole lot of water."

Carrying in the refilled bowls, she placed them on the table. "You should eat," she told the prisoner and made signs of lifting the spoon to her lips. "It's good." The prisoner glanced at her, then away.

The sheriff nodded, swept his mustache out of the way, and lifted his spoon. Ocean liked that he avoided soiling his facial hair like that. So many of her customers didn't bother, which she found distasteful.

Deputy Jones, who preferred a clean-shaven face—although he had quite the dark stubble at the moment—looked up and spoke a simple thank you.

Stepping back, Ocean smoothed her soiled apron over the black and white gingham plaid skirt she wore, feeling self-conscious as he regarded her. "You look tired, Miss Galliard. Don't worry, we'll be out of here soon." He cocked his head at Welburn. "Glom it down, Sheriff. It's long past quittin' time for this lady."

It seemed to Ocean that her heart stopped for a minute. Or maybe just a few seconds. Hard to tell. But her ears had a definite buzz.

Deputy Asher Jones knew her name? Ash Jones, whose name got bandied about by every single woman in town—and several married ones, too—every time he was sighted going about his rounds? Though not a large man, he had presence and exuded an aura of strength and honesty. Plus, she found him quite handsome with his regular features, nice hazel eyes surrounded by eyelashes as long and dark as a girl's—and all his teeth.

But, she realized a few seconds later, it wasn't really

on Ash Jones' account—or his fault—her ears were buzzing. Or, more accurately, reverberating.

No. Blame that on the prisoner who'd started talking again. Loud, shouting. He banged his spoon—apparently, the sheriff had removed the fork from his place setting—on the table hard enough to leave a dent visible through a slit in the oilcloth.

Abruptly, taking them all by surprise, he leapt to his feet, his chair toppling backward. He almost went down with the chair until he gripped the edge of the table with his shackled hands, dragging the cloth and the bowls to the floor.

Anger flashed for just a moment. More mess for her to clean up. But even as Sheriff Welburn and Deputy Jones reached for him, he was backing away. Crying, shouting, cursing.

"*Cholera!* Dammit! I must get home," he yelled, his voice high-pitched with anxiety. "Let me go. I did not kill anybody. You. You are the ones killing, not me."

Ocean stared at him. Was that an accusation against the sheriff?

"Please. Oh, God, please let me go," he wept. "I have to get home. He will die. He's just a baby. He doesn't know how to care for himself. I must go to him."

Welburn and JonesAsh both got hands on the man's arms, yanking him backward and not being particularly gentle about it.

"*Prosze.*" he said. "Please."

"Get the chair upright," Welburn said.

Still processing the man's shout, it took a moment for Ocean to decide the sheriff meant for her to do it.

Skittering cautiously out of the way as the men

wrestled, she got the chair onto four legs. "Done," she said.

They forced the prisoner into the seat. He never stopped talking. Never stopped begging. "I have not done anything wrong." He looked sincerely into Welburn's eyes. "I have not. You have the wrong man. Believe me. Please, believe me. I do not know this man you say is dead."

The sheriff stared at him blankly.

He shifted his gaze to the deputy. "I do not know him!"

Next, he looked at Ocean, as if she had anything to say about anything, his eyes dilating as he begged. "I do not know him. I do not."

And she said, "I believe you."

Only she said it in Polish, same as he'd been speaking all along. Nobody else had understood a word he said.

Just Ocean.

Which was when Welburn, Ash Jones, and, it must be said, the prisoner, all fell into a shocked silence. The quiet didn't last long.

The prisoner, despite having the sheriff hanging on one arm and Ash on the other, almost succeeded in regaining his feet. "You hear me," he said. "Thank God, you hear me."

She nodded. "I hear you. What—"

He cut her off, his eyes beseeching. "You must tell them, Madame. You must tell them I did not do what they say. They are saying I killed a man. Murdered a man. I did not. I swear, I did not. They must let me go. I must go home. Quickly. Quickly."

Welburn watched her with bugged eyes. "You

understand this gibberish?" He seemed astonished that anyone could.

"Understands and speaks the language, too, from the sound of things," Ash said. He gave a short huff of laughter. "This could get interesting."

"It could," Welburn said dryly. "If we didn't already have that cowpuncher from the Sleeper ranch saying he saw this man shoot Roy Sleeper dead."

"Hmm." Ash's grunt was noncommittal. Eyebrow arched, he smiled at Ocean. "What's he saying now?"

"He's saying he didn't kill anybody. No, *insisting* he didn't kill anybody." She listened a moment as the prisoner spoke, then nodded. "He says he doesn't recognize the name you're saying. He says he swears by all he holds holy."

Welburn's eyes narrowed. "He understands us?"

"Some. Not well enough to speak. He says he's lost his English, that he can't remember how to say it." Ocean's lips compressed. "He's afraid. Wouldn't you be scared in a strange land where no one can understand you, and you truly can't understand them?"

Ash Jones quirked an eyebrow. "Guess he's in luck then, Miss Galliard, since you do."

The sheriff nodded. He smoothed his hair and put on his hat. "I'd say so. If you'd come over to the jail with us, Miss, we'll get this man settled for the night. Maybe you can help us talk to him in the morning."

Ocean shook her head. "I'm sorry, but no. I don't want to be mixed up in your business. If Mrs. Seibert heard about it, she'd likely fire me. She doesn't care for me, you see, and she doesn't like foreigners. I don't want her to know I was able to speak with this man."

"I'll talk to her," Welburn said. "And to Butch. I'll see she don't fire you."

Somehow, Ocean doubted anything the sheriff said on her behalf was apt to change Elsie Seibert's made-up mind.

"Huh," Ash added. "We don't even know this man's name for sure. We could use your help."

"Oh. Easy enough." At this, she turned to the prisoner again. "What is your name, sir? These men," she indicated the lawmen, "don't know your name."

"Artem." He looked up. "I am Artem Dzik."

She opened her mouth to translate as Ash said, "I got it. Artem Dzik." He managed the first name well. The last turned into an approximation.

Ash muttered something to Welburn that Ocean didn't get when the prisoner began weeping again. He begged as he looked into her eyes.

"Repeat that," she said, hoping against hope she hadn't heard what it sounded like he'd said. It had been a while since she'd heard or spoken her very old grandmother's native language. Five, no, six years at least. When she'd been fourteen. Long enough, it had taken her some time to understand Mr. Dzik at first. But now—

Artem Dzik tried again to gain his feet until the sheriff told him "sit," as if he were a dog, and he had to obey. Shaking, Artem stared at Ocean, attempting once again to explain.

And she, well, she listened closely this time. Until blood pulsed hard through her veins, and all thought of being tired disappeared. Until something Sheriff Welburn said got through to her.

"You can't do that," she said, her eyes opening wide.

"You need to let him go home. You *have* to let him go home."

Welburn's eyebrows went up. His face turned red. "You ain't giving the orders here, little lady. I'll do what I got to do."

Slowly, as if sensing a puzzle to be solved, Ash looked from one to the other of them. Especially at Ocean's dark eyes which were blazing pure fury.

"You men!" she said. Her voice rose. "Shame on you. Shame!"

Welburn startled. "What? What are you talking about? You mind your—..."

Ocean interrupted. "Mr. Dzik has a son. A two-and-a-half-year-old son. And you two have left this child, a mere baby, out at Mr. Dzik's homestead by himself."

———

MAKE NO MISTAKE. Ash Jones liked to take his meals at Seibert's café for only one reason, and that didn't necessarily include Ollie Sullenberg's cooking. Contrary to the cook's own belief, along with a loyal following, Martha's Place at the other end of Main Street served food every bit as good. What Martha didn't have was a waitress by the name of Miss Ocean Galliard.

Ash had to admit he enjoyed watching Ocean trip around the restaurant as lightly as though she were dancing. He even liked her deceptive strength as he knew a tray of those heavy crockery plates filled with spuds and steaks would put muscles on a bulldogger.

Put together with her brown hair hanging down her

back in a thick, shiny braid, a trim waist set off by the bow of her apron strings, and the flash of her fine dark eyes, well, what wasn't to like?

He even enjoyed listening to her talk, although she didn't do a lot of it. But when she did, she used precise words, clear diction, and a better vocabulary than most of the ladies around this little northwest town. Ash could tell she'd had an extended education. He'd had one himself, or at least enough to recognize hers, though he'd buried the remnants of his somewhere between here and there.

So, he figured, had she, or was making the attempt. He couldn't help wondering why.

Little Miss Galliard had been a bit of a mystery from the time she stepped off the stage last fall and went to work in the café.

He felt bad about the sheriff, their prisoner, and himself showing up to eat tonight just as the café was closing. Or, more accurately, he and Early demanded dinner. The prisoner didn't demand anything, nor did he touch more than a bite. With a few breaks of silence, he kept up his infernal yapping in a language without a single word intelligible to either himself or Early. Same as he had non-stop from the time they left the fellow's ranch.

Sheriff Welburn, pausing to slather butter and honey on a generous chunk of cornbread, scowled at the talkative prisoner. "What do you suppose he's yammering about now?" he asked Ash. "And bawling. What grown man cries his eyes out right in front of people."

"Wish I knew." To tell the truth, Ash couldn't help worrying about the man's reaction to the arrest. Not too often a man who'd shoot someone down in cold blood cried about it afterward. In his experience, most of them turned even more belligerent. Guess this one knew that wouldn't work. Not when there'd been a witness to the killing. "Maybe he's making his confession."

They both chuckled. It didn't seem likely.

"Got anymore of this chili?" Early called to Miss Galliard.

Afterward, it seemed like those words were a code as to what happened next. Ocean brought the refills, and all seemed well. Until the prisoner started a new round of what Ash called 'lamentations' in his own mind. But it didn't end there. The Russkie jumped up, pulled everything off the table onto the floor, and started shouting.

Which was when little Miss Galliard began talking that difficult-sounding language right back to him.

They apparently understood each other well. Well enough that when she translated the gist of it on them, it was like dynamite exploded right over the top of him and Early.

A bitty kid left alone on a ranch? Lord have mercy.

2

"Baby? What baby? What are you talking about?" The sheriff's mouth gaped like he'd never heard the word before. He looked, Ocean thought, as though he'd swallowed a frog. Sounded like it, too.

"His baby." She pointed at Dzik. "His son. At least, that's what he's saying. Although I think the child is not quite an infant, he's not old enough to care for himself, either." She glared at Deputy Jones, impervious to his authority, his good looks, or anything else she'd previously gotten gooey-eyed over. "Didn't either of you think to check his house before you hustled him off to town? What if there'd been a pan on the stove and his house caught on fire?"

Neither man spoke, perhaps because they didn't think it mattered if the house got reduced to ash and charcoal chunks.

Hands on her hips, Ocean's voice rose to soprano heights. "Or, mercy me, what if the man had a child who somehow got left behind?" The sarcasm came on strong and didn't exactly suit her usual meek demeanor.

"Oh, no matter," she replied to her own question in that same squeaky tone.

Welburn blew a snort strong enough to fluff his mustache. "What if he's lying? He's accused of murder, you know. Story about a kid," he blew again, "probably not true. He wants to soften us up, right Ash?"

Ash didn't answer directly. He studied Dzik with narrowed eyes. "Quick," he said to Ocean, "ask him the kid's name."

Finally, someone who had a brain. She turned to the prisoner. "What is your child's name?"

He didn't need time to stop and think. "Fedor. My son is Fedor Dzik." He said it with pride.

"Fedor," Ocean said to the deputy. "It means Theodore. And I believe him."

Ash had watched the prisoner closely as he answered. "So do I. Wish I didn't." He turned to Welburn. "You'll have to send somebody to check. Bring the kid, provided there is one, into town."

Slowly, Welburn nodded. "First thing in the morning. I'll have to think who'll do it without complaining. Some folks won't care much about seeing to a murderer's kid. More particularly, a Russkie's kid."

Ocean, hands on hips, glared at the sheriff with enough disdain to make him hesitate. "What?" he asked her.

"In the morning? You're saying you're going to leave a small child in a deserted house with no heat, no food, and no protection for however many more hours?" She stamped her foot. "Bad enough you left him in the first place when you didn't know any different. To leave him longer when you do know is a crime."

Part of her attention slid to Dzik who, aware of the

tension, kept asking, "What does he say? My son, miss? What about my son? Please? I must go to him."

Then there was Deputy Jones, who eyed Ocean as if he'd never seen her before, even though he ate in the café nearly every day and she served the food. He turned to the sheriff. "Think she's got you there, Early."

Welburn's jaw stuck out pugnaciously. "Yeah? You volunteering, Ash?" He took off the hat he'd just put on and swept it across his pant legs in a useless gesture of frustration. "How about you, Miss Speaker on Behalf of Murderers? You want to ride out in the dark on the off chance of a kid that ain't just a figment of this man's lying tongue?" His face had turned an unbecoming shade of puce.

At this, Ocean took a step back. "I do believe that's your job, Sheriff Welburn. Not mine." She couldn't avoid seeing the way Artem Dzik's reddened eyes shifted back and forth between her and the sheriff, and once to Ash Jones. She figured he'd guessed the way the discussion was headed, and his bound hands clutched at the table's edge once again. He looked ready to leap up and throttle the sheriff. Ocean hoped he wouldn't. The action would not help his case.

"Don't you get smart-alecky with me, young lady," Welburn said, though he sounded more weary now than mad. "Ask me, I wish you hadn't understood Dzik's jibber-jabber in the first place."

To tell the truth—and to her shame—Ocean was thinking almost exactly the same thing. But she had, and now she couldn't abandon the stance she'd taken.

"I'll do it," Ash said, breaking the stalemate. "Two, three hours there and back."

Welburn huffed out a great sigh. "Thanks, Ash.

And you..." He pointed at Ocean. "You'd better ride out with him, seeing as how you're so all-fired set on the story being true. I don't suppose the kid, if there is a kid, talks anything but Russkie. It's more likely to cooperate if it can understand what somebody says."

"Me?" Ocean sort of squeaked. "Three hours?" She was already so tired she figured the next thing anyone knew she'd be asleep standing up. "Anyway, the boy is not an it, but a he. And, for your information, neither Mr. Dzik nor I are speaking Russian. We're speaking Polish with a smattering of Ukrainian border dialect."

The two lawmen looked at her like she was touched in the head. As, she suspected, she was. Especially when she said, almost triumphantly, "Furthermore, I don't have a horse."

It was Ash Jones who grinned at her, winked, and said, "That's all right, Miss Galliard. I've got a spare I can loan you."

At that point, Ocean saw nothing at all handsome or charming about the deputy. Even though twelve hours earlier she would've reveled in borrowing his spare horse for a ride in the country with him.

"Get your coat, missy. It's cold out there," Sheriff Welburn said, brusque as could be. He hefted Artem Dzik to his feet. "I'll take care of this one. And I'll explain to the Seiberts first thing in the morning about the place being a mess. I'll say it's my fault. Mine and the prisoner's. I'll tell 'em I sent you out on a special mission. Ought to settle them down some."

Ocean, who begged leave to doubt his confidence, gave in. What else could she do? She'd instigated this midnight rescue mission, after all. The sheriff and deputy were doing as she'd insisted. But first, she had to explain to Mr. Dzik what was happening, whereupon he fell to the floor right in front of her and gripped her around her knees.

"*Dziękuję*," he said, repeating it over and over.

"Hey there, you." Welburn pulled him to his feet. "None of that."

"He's just saying thank you," Ocean informed him.

"Go ahead, Early," Ash said, "I'll help Miss Galliard lock the restaurant. Mrs. Seibert strikes me as a spiteful woman, so we don't want her any madder than she's gotta be."

A faint hope, in Ocean's opinion.

ASH JONES STUCK CLOSE to her as they tidied the cafe, turned out the lights, and locked the front door, almost as if he suspected she might try to renege on their adventure. He insisted she accompany him while he saddled a small black mare for her to ride. The mare's name, he said, was Daisy, which for some peculiar reason she found hilarious. Then, at her insistence, they stopped at her rooming house, where, tiptoeing to her room, she bundled up, making sure to take an extra blanket, then quietly raiding the kitchen larder for a few comestibles she believed a two or three-year-old might eat.

"It'll be daylight before we get back at this rate," Ash grumbled.

He didn't try to stop her, though, which she took to mean he trusted these preparations to be necessary. Ocean hoped they were. What a right fool she'd feel if Artem Dzik had managed to hoodwink her.

Within twenty minutes of closing the restaurant door, she and Ash had left Clovis Creek and started northward, toward where the rolling hills turned into the rougher foothills of the nearby mountains.

They rode under a starlit sky, a crust of white frost crackling under the horse's hooves. They didn't talk much. After what seemed a long, silent while, Ash stopped his long-legged brown horse and allowed the black mare to come alongside. They were at a wide spot in the road, just before an uphill climb onto a narrower trail. Wind whistled down a draw at the hill's base, cutting through their clothes and chilling them—or Ocean, at least—to the bone.

"You all right?" Ash asked.

Ocean, who'd had her chin tucked into her coat collar, nodded. Unfortunately, the motion allowed cold air to rush inside her coat. Even at its best, the shabby, second-hand garment hadn't been a good one. Tonight, it failed completely. She shivered, her nose so cold she had to touch it every once in a while to make sure it hadn't frozen off.

"How much farther?" Her teeth clacked together.

"A couple miles." Ash, who apparently didn't feel the cold like she did, studied her. "The trail widens again at the top of this hill. You keep up when we get there. Ride beside me. We'll talk. It'll help take your mind off the cold."

Ocean nodded, though she wasn't so sure. What did he want to talk about, anyway? She didn't like to talk about herself. An out-of-the-way place like Clovis Creek had seemed just the right town for her when she stepped off the cross-state stage last fall. She'd made herself small and meek, so folks didn't pay the new waitress at the Seibert's cafe much mind. All good until she slipped up just now.

But what else could she have done tonight? She couldn't allow a child to be abandoned in the wilderness and live with herself. She'd had to translate Mr. Dzik's words. Let his concerns be known. Why, the man had barely fought against the charge against him. She still wasn't certain he fully realized why the sheriff had scooped him up and put him in handcuffs. His only concern had been for Fedor.

It shouldn't matter that he was Polish. People, immigrants from all over the world, came to this country for a new life. Many different languages were spoken. Why should this one instance be noticed? When they got back to town, she'd simply fade into the background again. Those who'd heard she spoke Polish would soon forget. Someday, so would she.

Even with her cold hands clinging to the saddle horn, by the time they got to the top of the hill, Ocean's knees shook with the effort of gripping Daisy's rather plump middle. She saw Deputy Jones hadn't been lying. The road ahead straightened out into a flatter, wider way, what she could see of it through the inky darkness. She sighed and, at his direction, toed the horse up beside him.

No choice, she supposed.

He started with the questions, just as she'd known he would, beginning with, "How is it you speak Dzik's language? Polish, with a smattering of Ukrainian border dialect." He copied her description exactly.

So. It began. She had a simple answer. Not too much and not too little. "I learned Polish as a child. My father's mother was Polish, and she lived with us until she died." The truth. And she'd ruled the roost, as Ocean remembered, imperious to the end. "Russians, by the way, speak a different language. Similar in some ways, but not completely compatible." Watch it, she warned herself. You don't have to be this man's teacher.

"Interesting. Guess I wouldn't have known." Ash chuffed out a short laugh. "Probably nobody else around here would, either. I'd say Mr. Dzik is real lucky to have met up with you in Seibert's cafe tonight."

"Mmm." Ocean didn't know what to reply. Lucky for everyone but her.

Ash turned to look at her and motioned her forward again as she'd allowed—encouraged—the horse to lag behind.

"We've got a couple Frenchmen who've set up a still in these mountains." He waved northward in an off-hand way toward Canada. "Also got some God-fearing sect of Germanic folks who've taken exception to them and their still. They won't, or can't, talk to each other, nor to us, in any meaningful way. Don't suppose your Polish would be of any help? They're suing each other."

"Not unless they each speak Polish." She sucked in a breath.

"Not much alike, eh?"

"No." She supposed he actually knew that. Drop it, she willed him. Please, just drop it.

But he didn't. "So it has to be French or German. I don't suppose you can talk in either of those languages."

What should she say? "Do you want to know if I speak French or German?"

He didn't answer with a yes or no. Instead, he said, "Galliard is a French name, isn't it? Sounds like it might be."

"I don't know. I'm American, if that's what you're asking. Though I can't imagine why you would."

An eyebrow arched, a grin quirked. "You're a whole lot more snippety than you let on when you're rushing from table to table in the café, Miss Ocean Galliard." The smile faded. "I just wondered, with you having a French name, and being as you speak Polish with a Ukran—"

She interrupted. "Get on with it. I know what I was speaking."

"Snippety, like I said." Ash twisted in his saddle, said, "Hup, Daisy," and grabbed the black mare's bridle to hustle her up even with his taller horse again. "Do you speak French?"

Glaring at him, for some reason, Ocean refused to lie. "Yes. So what?"

"And German? Do you speak German?"

"Maybe."

"Maybe? What does that mean? Seems you either do or you don't."

"For your information, there are many different dialects of German, depending on what area they're from. Most are quite a bit alike, but probably not the same." There she went again, apparently unable to stop acting like a prissy-faced teacher.

"Huh. And what variety do you speak?"

She hesitated long enough for him to peer at her between horses and through the dark.

"I can probably make myself understood to most," she admitted, then immediately wondered why she had. She could have lied about that much. Or just remained silent.

"Four languages. I don't guess I ever knew anybody who could do that before." He sounded admiring.

Ocean shrugged, refusing to volunteer that there were a couple more languages stored in her brain. She didn't know how she did it either. She just did, all of them learned when she'd been a child from a wide range of family members and acquaintances. Adding to her repertoire of languages was of benefit to her papá's business enterprises. Enterprises that had more often than not run contrary to the law.

And probably still did, somewhere, knowing her papá. Unless somebody had killed him by now. Not everyone survived incarceration.

THEY REACHED the top of yet another steep hill, upon which the road immediately meandered downward again, coming to a series of large meadows. The starlight was brighter here in the open, allowing Ocean to spot the dark humps of cattle scattered about in the new grass. Some lay chewing cuds, others stood and grazed.

"I believe these are your friend Dzik's cattle." Silently, the deputy made a quick count of the cattle. One of the cud chewers abruptly scrambled to its feet in front of his horse, which shied. So did the black mare, nearly unseating Ocean.

Ash eyed the scrambler and a couple other cows critically. "They look in fine shape for this early in the spring. We're near the house. Keep a look out for..." He trailed off without finishing.

Ocean knew. Any small lump lying out in the grass that might turn out to be a little boy, frozen to death.

The horses plodded on. A few minutes later, she glimpsed the peaked roof of a low barn. Set fifty yards away on a slight rise, she spotted a shabby little log cabin with a privy behind it. Prosperity, from the look of things, seemed to have passed Mr. Artem Dzik and his son by.

The whole place, except for a coyote yipping like a demented housewife higher up on the hill, struck her as preternaturally silent. As if all but the single coyote was holding its breath. Or maybe that was her imagination working overtime.

She let the air out on a gust, steam blowing ahead of her. The horses' hoofbeats seemed loud.

"I don't see anything," she whispered. "Anything out of place, I mean."

Ash turned to look at her. "No. Me either. Looks just like when the sheriff clamped his handcuffs on Dzik and we took him away."

They pulled up in front of the house. Quickly, Ocean slipped from Daisy's back. "Did you leave the door open?" It hung open now, an easy entrance or exit for small children or wild animals.

A guilty look suffused the deputy's face. "I don't remember. We'd had a struggle taming the Russk...the Polack enough to get the manacles on him. We might've left it open."

"Might've." Stepping up onto a low-cut stump serving as a stoop, she repeated the word so softly as to be inaudible.

"Wait." Ash's warning came a bit late since she'd

already pushed the door wider and gone on through. He followed in a rush.

Going by touch, Ocean found a barn lantern hanging from a peg set in the wall beside the door. Ash reached it down, gave a shake to check for kerosene and, scratching a lucifer to life, held it to the wick. Though far from bright, enough light shone for them to get a better view of the interior.

The cabin, a single room, held a bone-shaking chill, not a surprise considering the weather and the open door. The dark interior left her barely able to make out a cast iron stove at one end that appeared to serve for both cooking and heating—when there was a fire. Right now, it was stone cold. A table with two normal chairs and one set on taller legs, obviously built for a small child, took up the center of the room. A shelf containing a few dishes hung alongside a wooden apple box cupboard nailed to the wall. At the opposite end of the shack, a low bed with a tussle of blankets had a steamer trunk positioned at the foot.

Ocean pointed at the high chair as Ash came even with her.

He swore. "You were right. Dzik wasn't lying."

"I don't see the boy." Ocean's heart thudded with dread.

"We'll find him." So Ash said, though not in a convincing sort of way. "First, let's make more light. There must be another lamp in here somewhere. Or even a candle."

"He's not here," Ocean said.

"Maybe there's a crawl space. Some of these old cabins had a hidey-hole left over from the days when settlers worried about bandits or Indian attacks." Ash went over to the stove, setting his hand on the cold top. He shook his head.

Ocean stood in the middle of the room and spun a slow circle. "Fedor?" she called softly.

Just then, her stomach rumbled. At least, she thought her stomach growled, although she didn't think she was all that hungry.

"Fedor?" she said again.

Another soft rumble answered. She noticed that Ash heard it as well and was looking around with narrowed eyes before he pointed toward the bed.

Ah, not my stomach then.

Funny, those blankets didn't strike her as thick enough to conceal even a small child. She took a couple steps forward, thinking to check anyway, when this time, an altogether more serious growl sounded a keep-away warning.

A small, white-furred head poked out from beneath the bed. Two black button eyes glared at her as toenails scratched the floor. A set of tiny white fangs gleamed.

Behind her, Ash chuckled. "Is this Fedor? I hope we didn't make a trip out here to rescue a dog."

Ocean, while not seeing a thing wrong with rescuing a dog, still had to agree. "No. Mr. Dzik said his son. I doubt he's that deluded."

With something of a struggle, the dog emerged. It had fluffy white fur, rather matted at present, a black nose and eyes, and a little tail curled tightly over its back. She'd never seen a real dog of its breed before. Just some pictures.

"*Witam, maly pies.* Hello, little dog." She smiled. The dog was cute.

Just then, a small, thin arm reached out, grabbed the

dog by a hind leg, and tried to pull it back under the bed. The dog yelped a protest.

Ocean kneeled down to peer under the low bed and spoke in Polish. "Hello. I see you, Fedor. Your *tata* sent me to get you. You and your dog. Will you come out? I have food if you're hungry." She spoke slowly, unsure if Fedor was old enough to understand all she said.

The boy didn't answer, only buried his face in the dog's fur.

She looked up at Ash, who wisely remained silent. He shrugged and made reaching-in and pulling-out gestures. She shook her head and tried again.

"Fedor, your *tata* told me your name. My name is Ocean." It occurred to her he might have a difficult time translating ocean as a name and be confused. Well, no time to worry about it now. "This man with me is Ash. He wants to help you. Are you hungry?"

"*Tata?*" She glimpsed a dirty, tear-streaked face asking the question. "*Glodny!* Hungry!"

Progress, Ocean thought, relief flooding through her. Progress, at last. Her knees were getting cold here on the floor. And if she was cold, the poor child must be nearly frozen.

3

SLOWLY, VOICE SOFT AND COMPELLING, OCEAN talked the child into scooting from under the bed. Frankly, she didn't see how he'd gotten under there in the first place, as it had very little clearance. He'd dragged in a blanket and made room for the little dog, as well. She imagined the dog had been a great comfort and helped keep in enough body heat to save him.

The odor accompanying the youngster as he emerged had Ash gagging and plugging his nose. "Phew. Ain't that kid housebroke?"

Ocean, wondering if she'd turned as green as Ash, answered in a stifled sort of way, "Evidently not. Although, by this age, I think he should be. Maybe he was just frightened, and with no one to help him, didn't know what to do."

"Maybe." Ash stayed as far away from the source of discomfort as possible. "Can you get him cleaned up so we can start back?"

"Me?"

"Yeah, you."

"Why don't you, you and him both being boys and all?"

Ash almost cracked a smile. But then he held up one finger, stopping her. "Do I look like I know anything about babies?"

"Do I?" She asked in her turn, glaring up at him.

He studied her a moment. "But you're female. Babies come naturally to women."

She gulped. "Do they? I always heard it takes—"

Ash held up that one finger again. "You hush, Miss Ocean Galliard. Being here is at your instigation. Now there's a problem, I figure it's up to you to take care of it. I've got other business that needs attention."

Most likely, seeing the set of his mouth, this was an argument she'd never win. "What other business?" she demanded.

"I'm gonna take a more thorough look around. Sheriff Welburn and I, when we arrested Dzik, didn't do much investigating. The Sleeper cowpuncher said what happened, and we took him at his word. Looking around, it strikes me we might've been a little previous."

Ocean sat back on her heels and waited for the boy to move toward her. The dog acted first, coming over to nose her hand and give a little whine.

"You mean Mr. Dzik might be telling the truth when he says he didn't shoot Roy Sleeper?" She gave the pooch a quick pat. "Hello, you," she said to it.

Ash didn't answer one way or another. "I'll get a fire started in here and put a bucket of water on to heat. It's too cold to wash that kid with water fresh from the pump, and I ain't taking him nowhere stinking like he is. Maybe you can warm up some of those victuals you brought for him while I'm away. For the dog, too."

"Yessir," she said smartly, just as if those weren't the first items on her list anyway. She got busy and hardly noticed when he left.

***

ASH HAD BEEN GONE for half an hour before Ocean deemed the water, while not overly hot, warm enough to wash the child without sending him into convulsions. The interior air of the cabin, as long as they kept near the stove, likewise was tolerable. She made short work of bathing the boy, feeling inadequate as she did so. Ocean hadn't been lying to Ash. She probably didn't know any more about dealing with children than he did. She'd been an only child herself, and they'd moved too often for her to make any friends. But she did know about being clean. And about feeding people.

As for Fedor, though his skin puckered against the lingering chill, he didn't cry and didn't protest the bath. The dog, head cocked, watched everything as though to make certain the boy didn't leave his sight. Ocean couldn't help being impressed.

Finished with her preparations and finally able to sit down, weariness drained all the starch out of Ocean's spine. Aggravation scraped at her. At this rate, it would be daylight before they got back to town, and she had to work the morning shift. Mrs. Seibert would have a fit otherwise, even though Sheriff Welburn claimed he'd make everything right.

Softly, she muttered under her breath. Where on earth had Deputy Jones gotten to? Why was it taking such a long time to complete a simple look around? Had something happened to him? God knows that's all she'd need. Then, before she realized, her eyes drooped shut.

She didn't go under all the way. Daisy nickering a welcome to Ranger roused her, and she jumped to her feet just as Ash, casting a final look over his shoulder at the surrounding dark, entered the cabin in a tearing hurry.

If relief was Ocean's first reaction, worry came a close second. Very close. And maybe a bit of temper.

"What—" Ocean started to ask, then stopped as she noticed the grim look on his face.

The little boy, clean and dressed in warm clothes with his belly full, lay asleep on the bed with the dog beside him. The dog, awakened a bare second before the door opened, growled a soft warning. Apparently, he intended to defend his young friend come hell or high water. He'd also eaten a share of the provisions Ocean had brought, gobbling them down like a starving miniature wolf.

"Get the kid ready," Ash said, sharp as a knife. "We're leaving. Now."

Ocean could tell something had him in an uproar besides the lingering smell. Figuring the discoveries she'd made could wait a few minutes longer before she told him, she kept her voice low. "What is it? What's wrong?"

"Maybe something, maybe nothing." He went to warm his hands over whatever heat the stove retained. Knowing they'd be leaving soon, she not only hadn't added any wood to the fire, but had scattered the embers. She wanted it to die out as quickly as possible.

She stood rooted to the spot. "What do you mean?"

"I mean, I didn't find anything that points to Dzik

being a rustler or a killer. I took a good look around and made a circuit around the meadow, counting cattle and checking brands."

"And?"

"Not one of those cows has the Sleeper brand. Not a one has a fresh brand, for that matter. I didn't find any branding tools in the barn, either. Unless he buried them under the manure pile, he plain doesn't own any. And that means someone set him up."

Ocean nodded. She took a breath as if to speak, but Ash wasn't done.

"We need to clear out of here. Right now. Gather the boy and his stuff and get back to town right away."

A frisson of panic swept through her. Ocean didn't argue. The way he spoke, a tone she'd heard in the past from her father, struck her as ominous. Shrugging into her coat, she looked around, then at Ash. "I'm ready. I already bundled up what I thought he'd need."

Sure enough, a neat packet wrapped in a blanket sat waiting on the table. The room itself, although it still smelled some, was tidy.

Ash nodded. "Bring the kid." He snatched up the packet to tie on the back of his saddle. "And hurry. I'll wait for you outside."

Easy for her to guess he'd seen something. Or someone. Someone who had him spooked. And if Deputy Jones was spooked, then so was she. "You take the dog," she said.

"The dog?" Ash wasted a moment staring down at the little fellow.

"He'll fit in your saddle bag," Ocean said in a tone indicating she'd brook no argument.

After putting Fedor down on the bed after his bath,

Ocean had done some poking and prying of her own. She'd gone through the cabin, looking for clothes to change the boy into, a small boy she'd discovered could speak pretty well, although it was all in Polish. In the midst of her search, she'd found more than clothes. Bundling those things separately, they resided now in an inside pocket of her coat.

She was glad she'd taken precautions as she wrapped the sleepy child in the blanket and carried him out. "Take him," she told Ash before she blew out the lantern and closed the door.

Mounting the black mare, she held out her arms for Fedor.

EARLIER, when Ash set out to make a quick inspection of Artem Dzik's property, he'd already made up his mind the ranch hand who said he witnessed Roy Sleeper's murder needed further questioning. From the time the fellow busted into the sheriff's office to report the death, Ash had sensed there'd been something off about the story. Everything too pat. Too detailed. Too...rehearsed.

He hoped to find something to back up this decision. Sheriff Welburn wasn't going to like him taking on an extra inquiry if he didn't have something obvious to base his suspicions on.

The second purpose of the inspection he hesitated to admit even to himself. It was a question dating from when Early and he had arrested Dzik. They'd plopped him onto the first horse they spotted in the corral. A workhorse, as it happened. But thinking back, something felt off-kilter about the horse.

Mounting Ranger, he nudged him into a trot over to the barn and the corral behind it. Poking around, he found only another draft animal, a gentle creature smaller than most of its ilk he'd seen, but still large. A twin to the one they'd put Dzik on for the ride to town.

"What kind of rustler rides a plowhorse to steal cows?" he muttered half-aloud. He stored the information in his mind and rode on. It was something both he and the sheriff should've cottoned to earlier.

The night gathered around him as he took a circuitous route in passing through the cattle. A grove of trees near a small, noisy creek struck him as a prime spot for cattle to gather, and thinking some might be hiding in the shadows, he rode over for a second look. He didn't find any. Only the ones he and Ocean had already seen on their way to the ranch.

If Dzik had rustled any of the Sleeper cattle, he'd sure enough hidden them well away from his home ground.

Ash was about to turn his horse back to the homestead when he heard noises from a short distance away. Men talking, cows mooing, and a horse whinnying. Why would men be moving cattle in the middle of the night? Especially cattle on another man's land? Yet another strange incident he didn't figure to let pass without investigation.

Dismounting, he hitched Ranger to a tree branch and hiked through the woods toward the sounds, staying careful where he stepped and moving as silently through the dark as he knew how. Presently, he came to the road. Two riders and three head of cattle were stopped only a few yards away. They blocked the road.

He huffed. Two men to herd three cows? Not very efficient.

"Goddamn it, Aaron," one said. "Chase that other cow back here. You sleepin' or what?"

Ash recognized the voice, nasal and high-pitched, and certainly distinctive, though not in a pleasant way. It belonged to Peck Peckham, the same ranch hand who'd reported Roy Sleeper's murder.

His nerves thrummed.

"Get 'er your own self." The other man sounded a surly sort and none too happy at being ordered around like a Chinese coolie. "This is all your idea anyhow. Welburn and that deputy took the Russkie in. The thing is done. They'll hang him sure. Hell, he don't even talk American."

At this, the first man offered up a more conciliatory explanation. "Maybe, maybe not. I ain't leavin' anything to chance. We need these critters planted here in case Welburn or that damn deputy decides to come back. Public opinion. String the Russkie up, and everyone will forget what happened to Sleeper."

"Well, yeah. That's what I said." A pause. "Say, you suppose the Russkie has any money hidden in his shack? I hear some of them immigrants got lots of money or jewels and such."

"Dunno. We'll look when we get there. Now go get the cow afore I get mad and shoot you."

Yammering something about being too damn gun-happy, and look what happened with Sleeper, the man spurred his horse and headed off into the brush. The bossy one lit a smoke and dismounted to unbutton his britches and utilize a tree. The horse held the other cows in place by itself.

It didn't take any kind of education to decipher what they'd just admitted to. Ash figured he'd heard enough. Ignoring his first inclination to arrest them right then and there, he started back through the woods to where he'd left his horse. Ocean and the child came first. A fine decision, until he stepped on a dry stick. It snapped, making enough noise to disturb a couple birds high in a tree above him.

Ash froze. A full minute ticked past, until figuring he couldn't wait all night, he crept away. His most important job right now was to get back to Ocean and the boy and get them out of the cabin and onto the road to town. They'd have to take to the woods and side-step the rustlers.

———

AT THE CABIN, he found Ocean had been as quick and efficient in getting the kid cleaned up and ready to go as she was in performing her job at the cafe. Didn't even ask too many questions. It was almost as if she had experience in packing up and moving on at the drop of a hat.

"Stay quiet," Ash said as he helped her onto the black and settled the boy in her arms. "Keep the kid quiet too, even if you have to muzzle him."

Her big dark eyes widened. "Muzzle him? What's happening, Deputy Jones? What's got you in a frazzle?"

"Nothing." He felt, rather than saw, her frown as she stared at his back when he turned away to stuff the dog in an empty saddlebag per her orders. A short struggle ensued. "You be good and settle down," he whispered to the pooch.

The dog reached up and licked his chin.

Ash led off, urging Ranger into a trot as they crossed the meadow to the shelter of the trees. He'd have kept on, trusting the horses to see in the dark, until Ocean called out, "Stop. I'm going to drop this child if this horse's gait doesn't even out. He's heavier than he looks. Maybe you'd like to carry him?"

"Ssh," he snapped a low reply. "Be quiet. Don't talk until I tell you it's safe." But he slowed Ranger to a walk, the black following suit. Her indrawn breath came clearly to his ears, kind of like she didn't care for the way he'd spoken to her. Or maybe it was the word "safe" that worried her. Wisely, she didn't speak again.

A couple hundred yards farther on, a cow lowed mournfully, along with the sound of a rope slapping flesh. A man whistled a shrill note and called out, "Hie there, move along, cow." A horse's hooves thudded with a hollow sound.

At that, Ash dismounted and grabbed the black's bridle, holding her still. Ranger's head lifted as he quaffed the odor of strange horses on the breeze, and Ash got ready to pinch his nostrils to stop a whinny. As for Ocean, she froze in place, the black's reins taut, listening to the commotion on the road.

Presently, the sounds faded as the rustlers put distance between them. Ash figured they'd have an easy time getting away now, considering the rustlers intended to ransack the house and steal anything of value from the Russkie. The Polack, he meant. He thought he wouldn't mention their intentions to Ocean. She'd probably insist he stop them.

And if he'd been alone, he would've.

He led them back onto the road where the going was easier, and finally, said to Ocean, "Speak soft so you don't wake the kid. If he howls, they'd most likely hear him. What do you want to know?"

"Who are they? Why are we hiding?"

He didn't see any reason not to tell her, and several reasons why he should. "You heard the one with the high-pitched voice?"

"Yes. Who is he?"

"He's the ranch hand who reported seeing his boss murdered by Mr. Dzik."

She was silent a moment, then said, "But he lied, didn't he?"

"Yes. He did. We believed him at first, Sheriff Welburn and I. Even when we found out about the kid, we had to hold Dzik in custody."

"But now?"

Ash sighed. "The evidence don't add up. I'm not going to name everything, but the accusation is shaky."

She toed Daisy's ribs to bring her level with Ash. "Right now, these men are driving those cattle onto Mr. Dzik's place. That's proof, isn't it? Because if they were retrieving stolen cattle, they'd be going down this mountain, not up."

He admired her quick understanding. "I'd say it proves they're rustlers, anyhow. And until I know different, it's my guess since they're rustlers, they most probably killed Roy Sleeper when he discovered them stealing his cattle."

She gave a little gasp. "And those men, they're not going to like what we have to say about seeing them."

He snorted. "No, they're not."

Ocean paused a moment as that sank in, inhaled and exhaled a deep breath, then brightened. "Here's some good news. Turns out Fedor is housebroken. After his bath, he knew to use a pot."

Surprised, Ash broke into a laugh. "I guess that's something," he said.

4

To Ocean, the night dragged on in an interminable manner until they finally reached the edge of town. The streets were still, their horse's hoofbeats a soft thud breaking the silence. The only signs of life were a yellow tomcat sitting outside the butcher shop cleaning its face, and a flickering lantern marking the entrance to Dobby's Hotel.

Ocean, fighting to stay awake, was sure her arms were about to disconnect from her body, benumbed as they were from shoulder to fingertips from the weight of the sleeping child. Only fear of dropping the boy kept her conscious and the numbness at bay.

"Finally," she murmured to Ash. "I thought we'd never get here."

"Mmmm."

She took it for agreement and shifted the boy's position for what must be the hundredth time. Daisy, obeying the inadvertent nudge of Ocean's knee, took her closer to Ash.

He put out a hand to steady her. "Don't fall off," he

said, a smile in his voice. "Where do you want to take the kid? To your rooming house? Will Mrs. Bothell care for him?"

At this, Ocean woke up fast. "Where do *I* want to take the kid? Deputy Jones, I don't want to take him anywhere. I'm not responsible for him. You are. Where do *you* want to take him?"

"Me? I dunno," Ash faltered. "I haven't given it a thought."

Tired as she was, Ocean had been thinking hard about nothing else for the last two miles. "Well then, I may have a solution."

"You do? What?" Utter relief swept over the deputy's face. Ocean thought he would've agreed to any suggestion she made right about then.

"We should take him to the jail and put him in the cell with his father. That should satisfy Mr. Dzik and comfort his son at the same time."

Ash stared at her. "Are you serious? Put a kid in jail? I doubt Sheriff Welburn would agree with that."

"Why not? As long as the two are in a cell by themselves, what can it hurt? It's not as if he'd be a prisoner, for goodness sake. I'm sure Mr. Dzik will only become more docile if he's got his son to care for. I'm not saying the boy should be put in a cell with a bunch of drunken cowboys or loggers. Besides, his father should be released soon. Hopefully, tomorrow."

Gradually, Ash's frown lines smoothed. "You may be right." Suddenly, he smiled, bright and sunny, charming Ocean with its flash of warmth. "Not sure I want to be there when Early comes into the office in the morning and finds he's got a new guest though."

Ocean, on the other hand, wished she could. Sheriff

Welburn's reaction might be amusing. "Two new guests." She grinned. "Don't forget the dog."

The sheriff, after all, had steamrollered her into this night's excursion, and she felt somebody owed her for her time. Especially, she thought darkly, if Mrs. Seibert intended to fire her as the woman so often threatened to do. Ocean wasn't so sure Sheriff Welburn, regardless of what he said, could convince the boss to do otherwise. Still, whatever happened, happened, she guessed. The time for second, possibly wiser, thoughts had passed.

Sweeping Daisy and her riders along ahead of him, Ash turned Ranger toward the sheriff's office and jail situated in a cul-de-sac beside the small courthouse.

They found the office deserted, as was usual after midnight on a weeknight. On Saturdays, when men came to town to blow off steam in one of the two saloons or the creek-side brothel, either Ash or Ned Hazenberger, the part-time deputy, might stay the night. Or both of them, depending on who or how many troublemakers they'd hauled to jail.

Ash helped Ocean, who still held the boy, from Daisy's back and fished the wiggly little dog from his saddle bag before producing a key to unlock the jail-house door. The dark inside was intense until he got a lamp going.

Ocean glanced around curiously. She'd been in a jail more than once, not as a prisoner herself, but on a mission to have her father released after one of his con jobs went wrong. Those had been big city jails and much, much larger than this place. There, the front room had bustled with hardened criminals, harlots, drunks, and opium eaters all mixed together in a waiting area until they were locked into cells. It had stunk to the point of nauseating her. She'd only been fourteen the first time and looked younger. She'd been terrified of both the place and of losing her father and him never coming back.

She sighed. In the end, it had been she who had left in hopes of him never finding her again.

This jail was a two-room building with four chairs lined up against the outer wall, plus two more chairs fitted with wheels behind each of the desks. A couple filing cabinets, a cast-iron stove, and a gun cabinet pretty much completed the furniture. A log wall separated the front room from the back with its three cells, each with a heavy door and a glassless window with vertical iron bars set well above the lock.

Ash retrieved an iron key ring from the bottom drawer of one of the desks and beckoned Ocean and her burden forward. With the dog beside her, they stood aside while he opened the cell door. The cell's occupant didn't move.

"Go ahead and call out to Dzik." Ash straightened up. "I want to see his face when you hand him his son. I'll know then if this was all worthwhile."

She nodded. She'd had the same idea. "*Pan Dzik, wake up*." She spoke softly, so as not to startle either the man, in case he came up fighting, or the child sleeping in her arms.

He lay on the cot with a single blanket pulled over him. A thin, dirty blanket.

"They'll need another blanket or two," she told Ash. "And give them clean ones. That thing is filthy." Then, louder, "*Pan Dzik, wake up*."

The man stirred, rolled, and opened his eyes. They widened as he stared. Ocean felt sure Deputy Jones learned what he needed from the change of expression on Artem Dzik's face. He smiled and held out his arms. If a man could look radiant, he did.

Relieved of Fedor's weight, Ocean's arms felt like dead sticks and shook uncontrollably when she'd handed over her burden. The dog pattered into the cell, taking three tries to jump onto the cot.

"Fedor," Dzik whispered, holding his son as if he were the most important thing on earth. And, Ocean suspected, he was, to this man.

"Tata," Fedor murmured as first Ocean, then Ash backed out of the cell.

There was a storage shelf on the wall separating the cells from the front room. Ash rummaged until he found a pair of moderately clean blankets and a recently washed sheet.

"This do?" he asked Ocean.

She took a sniff, nose wrinkling only a little. "It'll have to, I suppose."

OUTSIDE AGAIN, the deputy boosted her onto Daisy and prepared to see her to her rooming house. They plodded through the dark, empty streets, at peace.

"Are you satisfied he's innocent?" Ocean demanded as they neared the two-story house where she had a room.

"I am. Don't know what the judge will say. But for my part, I'd say brag about it, Miss Galliard. You were right. Now to convince the sheriff. After you and I witnessed those two shoving Sleeper's cattle onto Dzik's homestead, I don't think he'll have a choice."

"Oh!"

Ocean's exclamation had Ash reaching for his gun. Until she muttered, "Sorry. I just remembered. When I was looking for Fedor's things, I found paperwork about Mr. Dzik's homestead. And bills of sale for his cattle. I brought the papers with me to show the sheriff. And some money, too." She hesitated. "It didn't seem right to leave those things there, unprotected, where just anyone could walk in and take them." She pulled the packet from inside her coat and handed it to Ash.

When she looked across at the deputy, she saw his surprise, then his grin.

"Seems Peck Peckham and his partner will be a couple of mighty disappointed men," he said. "Which doesn't exactly break my heart. You've done a good night's work, Miss Ocean Galliard. Be proud."

Truth to tell, she was proud. Also, blushing a little under Ash's approval, relieved to have the business over and done. But there was one more thing. Her brows rose. "Peck Peckham? Isn't that the man who accused Mr. Dzik of murder in the first place?"

"One and the same. Accuser. Cattle rustler. And likely murderer. Him and his partner Aaron Fuller."

"Oh. Well then," she said, a wealth of satisfaction in those two little words.

WHEN ASH HAD a second to think about the situation, he wasn't so sure there was anything good about Peckham and his partner being disappointed when they discovered nothing of value in Dzik's cabin. Lord only knows how much mayhem the man might be able to stir up when he discovered himself thwarted. No papers to destroy, no money to steal. Ash huffed to himself. Nobody to shoot. And mostly, nothing to show the world Artem Dzik was anything but what he said he was—thanks to Miss Ocean Galliard's help.

And about the child. Ash didn't think Ocean had considered what the rustlers might've done with the kid if they hadn't gotten there first. He sort of hoped she never did.

He saw her safely into the boarding house and heard the lock click behind her. Riding Ranger and gathering Daisy's reins in hand, he deposited both horses at the livery before walking back to the jail. Too weary to tread even the few blocks to his room over the drug store, he figured to bed down in an open cell tonight. And be there, just in case Peckham and Fuller showed up trying to instigate more trouble.

Checking on Dzik, he found the man and his son wrapped in blankets, both sleeping like the dead. The dog, who lay on top of them, lifted his head when Ash peered in, then dropped down again. Evidently, the tiny pup was as tired as the people.

Ash found himself a blanket, removed his gun and boots, and lay down to catch what sleep he could manage before daylight. Which wasn't enough, he found, when Sheriff Welburn awakened him four hours later at daybreak. The rough hand on his shoulder indicated Early's displeasure.

"Get up," the sheriff said roughly. "You've got some explaining to do."

Ash tried to wave him away, only to find it didn't work. Early shook him again.

"Now," Early said. "Then I got to get over to Seibert's cafe."

Giving in, Ash groaned, got himself upright, and fumbled for his boots even before opening his eyes. "I'm up."

Dzik still slept. So did the boy, but when Ash checked, the dog stood at the door, swishing his fluffy tail and jumping up and down. Ash figured if he'd been human, he'd been crossing his legs. Getting the key, he let the dog out. "C'mon, you."

The sheriff was waiting, seated at his desk and frowning as he examined the contents of the packet of Dzik's belongings Ocean had packed.

Ash let him wait until he'd turned the dog out to piddle and brought him back in. He didn't want to be responsible for the little mutt either peeing on the floor or running off.

Once inside, he found the sheriff still going through the packet Ocean had secured. He looked up and motioned Ash into a chair. "What's all this?" he demanded.

Assuming Early meant the packet since he had his reading spectacles perched on his nose, Ash decided not to bring Ocean's name into it. Enough if the sheriff, and everyone else, thought her only a caretaker to help bring in the kid, and someone who spoke enough Polish to make sense of what the man had said.

"Some of Dzik's business. I figured he might need the money and that the paperwork would be more secure locked up here in the safe."

Early tapped a finger on the uppermost document. "Did you look through it?"

Ash, who'd taken Ocean's word that the papers

were important, shook his head. "Some. Enough to see it's mostly bills of sale for his cattle, homesteading land documents, and immigration stuff. Fortunately, most all of it in English. I didn't count the money."

"Four hundred dollars. A lot for an immigrant. How'd he get all that unless he's been rustling cattle on the side? Most of them are so dead broke they can barely buy food."

Ash looked at him. "Not all of them are."

At this, Early eyed the papers again. "No. Not all." He tapped an official-looking document. "This one looks like it might explain the situation." Tilting his chair back, the wheels under it squeaked.

"Did you see the bill of sale for *two* fine young draft horses in that pile of papers? They were bought before he came to Clovis Creek." Ash prodded at the papers, tapping the uppermost one. "He has thirty-two head of beef cattle and one milk cow, dry now. I counted them. They're all there with clear brands, and he has proof of ownership of all of them. I did a search of the place for running irons. There were none."

"Then dammit, Ash, why'd he kill Roy Sleeper?"

"He didn't."

Welburn's chair jerked forward as he slammed a hand down on the desk, then shook the resulting benumbed fingers. "Didn't? What are you talking about, Ash. We got an eyewitness."

Ash refused to be shaken by the sheriff's irritation. "Do we? You probably ain't gonna like hearing this, Early, but Peckham is an out-n-out liar. In fact, he's most likely the one who killed Roy Sleeper. Either him or his partner, Aaron Fuller."

The sheriff's face was burning red. "How do you

know? My God, Ash, what happened last night that made you change your mind? Was it that girl? Ocean Galliard? Is she in cahoots with Dzik? If that's even his name. Did she put a spell on you?"

By this time, Ash's own irritation had him hot under the collar. It took just about all he had to hold onto his temper. "I think you know me better than that, Sheriff. And Miss Galliard, too." Then he waited. He wasn't gonna get caught up in defending himself against a charge brought on by pure disgruntlement. Everyone in the county knew the sheriff had a short fuse, but most times, he got over his tantrums in short order.

Welburn sat there panting out his agitation, his attention wandering until his eye landed on the dog, waiting patiently for attention. He pointed. "What the hell is that?"

Ash, worrying over the sheriff's color in case he was about to have an apoplectic fit, eyed the direction of Early's pointing finger. "It's a dog."

"I can see it's some sort of dog." Early glared at the small creature whose matted hair had not been improved by the ride to town stuffed in a saddle bag. It stood proud, ears pricked, tail curled, round black eyes staring at the sheriff in a reproving manner. All five or six pounds of him appeared ready to do battle. "Whose dog? Where did you get him, and what's he doing in here?"

"He's the kid's. They seem to be a set, the boy and the dog. I don't think the boy would've survived until we got there if it wasn't for the dog."

Welburn stared at the animal. After a while, his face cleared, and he said, "Huh. It's a handsome little feller. Wonder if he's full-growed." Taking a breath, he scooted his chair back and allowed his high color to fade. "But that's neither here nor there. Tell me about Peckham. Why do you think he killed Sleeper?"

Thankful the sheriff seemed ready and willing to listen now, Ash pulled his own wheeled chair over to Early's desk. With both of them at ease, it didn't take long to recount what he'd heard and seen. He also informed the sheriff it wasn't just him. Miss Galliard had witnessed Peckham and Fuller with the Sleeper cattle as well.

"We'll head out to the Sleeper ranch this morning and bring the pair of them in. See what they got to say. I'll ask Judge Fedderer to hear Dzik's case right away. This afternoon, if possible." Welburn shook his head. "I don't like the idea of a kid in a jail cell."

Ash, rolling his chair back to his own desk, chuckled. "Knew you wouldn't. Ocean...Miss Galliard... talked me into it, but if you'd seen the look on that man's face when we handed the kid over to him, you'd have been glad she did."

"Think so?" At Ash's sober nod, the sheriff lumbered to his feet. "I'm hungry. I expect our prisoners are, too. And I ain't forgotten I promised the little gal I'd clear her if she was late to work this morning. Reckon I'll keep that promise now. You better come with me. Might take the two of us to talk Mrs. Seibert down. You know how she is. Good thing she fancies you. We'll have a bite and bring something back for Dzik and his kid."

"Fancies me?" Ash, appalled and embarrassed by Welburn's laughing comment, knew when his face flooded red.

AT THE CAFÉ, finding all the counter stools filled, Ash and the sheriff seated themselves at the same table they'd occupied the previous night. They found Ocean already on the job, rushing around the dining room with barely enough time to tell them all was well. A minute later, she swept past again with an armload of heavily laden plates, steam still rising from the flapjacks. Seconds after that, she stopped to take their order and have a short word.

As it turned out, she told them, she hadn't needed Sheriff Welburn's intervention with Mrs. Seibert. The woman, doing a stint as the breakfast cook this morning, had been too busy in the kitchen area to even notice anything amiss in the dining room.

"Elsie isn't the most noticing of women unless something strikes her as a personal insult," Ocean whispered.

The sheriff nodded. He had, after all, known the woman for a long time.

It helped that Ocean had beaten her to work and had gotten most of the debris from last night cleaned up before Elsie arrived, but the shadows under Ocean's dark eyes were proof she'd gone short on sleep to do it.

Ash and Early were considerably relieved not to deal with Mrs. Seibert in a mood. Her complaints as to her lot in life sounded over the rattle of the plates she skidded onto the kitchen pass-through for Ocean to serve, then yelling if Ocean was more than a step away from picking up the order.

They'd just finished eating and were swallowing the last of their coffee when Clarence Bullenzer, one of the ranchers nearest the Sleeper place, stopped by their table. Ocean, who had just put the meals packed up for Dzik and his son on the table, yelped when an elbow in her ribs shoved her aside.

Ash, looking up, caught the motion and her pained response. He started to his feet. "Watch—" he began, but the rancher, his attention on the sheriff, cut him off.

"I hear you caught the man who killed Roy Sleeper," Bullenzer said. His scowling face was livid with either anger or excitement. Ash couldn't tell which.

Welburn looked up. "We've got a man in custody," he admitted. "Now you'd best apolo—"

"I say we get a rope and take care of him, right here and now." Bullenzer interrupted yet again, speaking loudly enough for everyone in the restaurant to hear. "Another damn no-account furriner we don't need in these parts. Next thing you know, that could be me layin' there dead with my cattle stole out from under me."

Behind him, murmurs of what sounded like agreement buzzed.

Sheriff Welburn rose to his feet and cast a warning look at Ash, whose hand had settled on his gun.

"There'll be no lynching in my jurisdiction, Bullenzer." Welburn smacked his empty cup into the saucer with a click. "The man we brought in will go before the judge in a day or two. I believe he'll be exonerated as we've got a new, more likely suspect. Leave this to the law."

Bullenzer's mouth twisted. "Exonerated? What the hell does that mean?"

"Means they'll turn the Russkie loose," someone called, not exactly helping matters already tense.

"Like hell you will," Bullenzer roared. His eyes bulged as he lunged forward and grabbed hold of the sheriff. His fist shot out, clipping the sheriff's jaw.

Welburn grunted, the table creaking as it took his off-balance weight.

Faster than a snap of the fingers, Ash's .44 was in his hand. "Stand back."

Wisely, Bullenzer stopped, his clutching fingers releasing Welburn's arm. He glared at Ash.

"Sheriff?" Ash looked at Welburn. "What do you want me to do with this one?"

The sheriff stared at his would-be attacker and, feeling his jaw with cautious fingers, answered slowly. "I'm wondering why he's so all-fired set on promoting a lynching. Makes me wonder if he's covering up for his own actions. Or it could be he's drunk. Run him in for assaulting a peace officer for now, Deputy Jones. We'll hold him in one of the cells until I figure he's learned his lesson." He eyed the gawpers. "That goes for anyone who steps out of line. Hear me? There'll be no lynching in this county. Period." His voice rose. "Got it?"

A few mutters and complaints answered, along with several nods, but mostly silence.

Ash, removing the startled Bullenzer's firearm from its holster, caught a glimpse of Ocean's taut expression.

She'd gone pale, her dark eyes wide. What, he wondered, was she thinking just then?

5

OCEAN STOOD FROZEN, HER HEART POUNDING LIKE the din of an Irish frame drum. Had Ash seen the other man, the one who'd yelled about turning the Russkie loose, with his long-barreled revolver half-drawn? He'd been going to shoot Ash. Only Ash's quick action in disarming Bullenzer stopped him.

What if Deputy Jones had been shot right in front of her. She'd seen the like before. The blood. The stilling of a heartbeat.

She didn't think she could bear it again.

But then the commotion died away. Elsie screeched "Order up" at her from the kitchen to come collect someone's meal. Her feet obeyed, even if her mind did not. Aware of the sheriff soothing the customers who hadn't fled—several had stayed to weigh-in on the conflict—she managed to regain an even keel as she went about her business.

"Don't you let on to anybody about what you and Ash did last night. Or about what you heard. Could be dangerous." Welburn, stepping over to pay, spoke low, smiling at Ocean as he counted out coins for his and Ash's breakfasts. He signed a chit charging the county for the prisoner's—though not Bullenzer's. He might've simply been making conversation. Ocean, however, nodding and forcing herself to smile back, knew it for a warning.

Feelings over Roy Sleeper's murder were running high. And then there was Peck Peckham, a potential murderer running loose. The sheriff meant it best if she remained unknown for her own safety.

"You be careful, too, Sheriff Welburn." She returned the chit to the drawer where the county clerk would settle up at the end of the month. "You and Deputy Jones."

"You bet." He tipped his hat and hurried to catch up with Ash and Bullenzer, who were already halfway to the jail.

Bullenzer kept cursing and trying to break apart the handcuffs. Without, she saw with some satisfaction, the least effect.

Ocean's smile wavered. Why on earth had she allowed herself to become involved with a situation that threatened to get out of hand? Regret washed over her as she chided herself for being drawn into what was rapidly turning ever more violent.

Taking a moment, she watched the sheriff go before turning back to the customers. Several had questions for her. What was Welburn going to do with Bullenzer? One man thought he'd heard the sheriff say something about another suspect in Roy Sleeper's death, one apart from the Russkie. Did she hear who he was talking about? Didn't she think they should go ahead and execute the Russkie right off?

She didn't feel safe with a man like that on the loose, did she?

"I don't think anybody should be executed without a trial," she countered, feeling a bit desperate over what she dared say. "You shouldn't speak of such things. And the..." she hesitated, "...Russkie isn't running loose. If I'm not mistaken, he's penned up in a jail cell."

"Mind your tongue," Elsie snapped, coming out of the kitchen at just the wrong time to overhear. "I won't have a worker in here insulting the customers. You understand me?"

"I didn't insult anyone," Ocean retorted. "I simply stated facts."

"One complaint, and I'll toss you out on your ear without a reference, Miss Hoity Toity, no matter what Mr. Seibert says." Her yellowed teeth—lacking the one to the right of center that had gone missing—showed all too clearly in a triumphant grin. "Maybe you can find work at the Red Hat."

The Red Hat being the local brothel.

Ocean had never felt more like ripping off her apron, rolling it into a ball, and throwing it in Elsie Seibert's ugly face. But she didn't. She needed the job.

Without a word, she turned her back on the woman and went to work, answering someone's call for a coffee refill. An hour later, glancing through the window, she happened to spot Sheriff Welburn and Ash Jones riding down the street headed out of town. A shiver went through her, as though the spirit world had sent a warning. A portent of things to come?

At ten o'clock, as usual, Elsie considered her duty done and left, Ollie having arrived to take over cooking for the noon meals. Sick of the woman's snide comments and squinty-eyed glares, Ocean was even more relieved than normal, as this gave her an hour to have a little rest and a bite to eat before the lunchtime crowd arrived.

She took one of Ollie's hot beef sandwiches—sliced beef between thick slabs of bread and doused with rich brown gravy—to a window table, where she could look outside and see the sun shining. She planned on a walk after eating, which is when it occurred to her that Fedor's little dog might appreciate a walk as well. Not that she needed the exercise, but she did need the air. Most like the dog did, too. Besides, it just wasn't right to pen up a dog and then blame him if he did his business inside. She couldn't see an old duffer like the sheriff's fill-in man attending to a dog's needs.

Letting Ollie know she was leaving the building, though not her destination, she pulled on her coat and headed toward the jail. As soon as she left the main street, she became aware of a noise sort of like the buzzing of distant bees. Nearing the jail, it not only became louder, but the cause apparent. A word here and there became understandable. Understandable in noise level, that is, if not in content.

A half-dozen men had gathered in front of the sheriff's office. A rowdy bunch, they were pushing forward, each one seeming to out-talk the other. Trying, at any rate. One of them had a half-uncoiled rope with a noose dangling free on one end. He stood flipping it against his leg as he talked real loud and rough to, or maybe she meant at, part-time deputy Ned Hazenberger. He stood in the jailhouse doorway with a shotgun in his hands.

Shocked, Ocean stopped as if she'd run into a wall. They intended on hanging Mr. Dzik. They really did.

To his credit, Mr. Hazenberger, a notably tough old bird, wasn't backing up. Not one inch, and he didn't bother to shout when he told them, in no uncertain terms, "Git. Go about your business."

Just as well not to strain his vocal cords, Ocean thought, forcing her feet to carry her forward. They weren't listening to him anyway.

"Get out of the way, Ned. Let us in," the loudest one said. "One way or another, we're taking him. Gonna string him up on that big pine over there. Hell, Welburn don't care. He ain't even around. He left you here so's you could take the blame and he can say it ain't his fault."

"No need for you to get hurt," another added, standing at the back of the pack. He held a shotgun in a sloppy kind of grip. "Step aside and it'll all just be easy."

Easy to hang an innocent man? Ocean's heart thumped so loud she wondered nobody heard as she reached the rear of the bunched-up men.

"We're doing this," the fellow with the rope said. "We outnumber you six to one. And you, like it or not, Hazenberger, are old. Too old to fight us. Step aside right now if you plan on getting any older."

She never knew where it came from, but suddenly, Ocean felt on fire. And strong. So strong. She used her shoulder to knock into the man with the shotgun. Off balance, he lurched aside, and she grabbed the shotgun from his hand.

"Hey," he said, stumbling away.

The shrill whistle she emitted was plenty enough to garner every man's attention. They turned to look.

"Six to two." Her voice didn't shake. Not noticeably, anyway. "And I'm not old. What is with you people? Don't you know what you're doing is not only illegal but wrong? What's more, I do believe Deputy Hazenberger and I have you in a crossfire. It'll be like shooting a deer with a light in its eyes. If it comes to that, which I trust it won't. Will it?" She raised the borrowed shotgun and took aim at the man with the rope.

One of the men—a ranch hand from the Sleeper ranch, if she remembered correctly—lunged toward her as if intent on taking away the gun.

Turns out Ocean wasn't the one who fired the shot that plowed dirt right into the man's face as it struck just in front of him. Hazenberger took the credit.

"Next time, I aim at you," he said.

A silence descended. For a moment. A moment lasting long enough for her to think of something else to say. Something else she hoped might stop them. Logic. Did they even know what that was?

She'd seen them all in the café at some time or another. She could see they were recognizing her now, too, as they figured out why she was familiar. It gave a reason for her to repeat what she knew. But only the parts she wanted them to know. Logic.

Let Elsie hear about this. Ocean didn't care.

"Who put you up to this?" She aimed the question at the man holding the rope. Crenshaw, he was called, if she remembered correctly. One of Bullenzer's cronies, he'd made trouble at the café more than once. So had the one she was pointing the shotgun at. "I know somebody did. Why?"

His face held an ugly twist. "I didn't need nobody to put me up to nothin'. I guess I know what needs done. You talk about wrong? Well, I'm goin' to right a wrong. You'd best go about your business afore you get hurt."

Ocean let her gaze go from face to face of the men before her. "If you know right from wrong, then you also know what you're trying to do is wrong. We have laws. There is a man in custody, and people heard the sheriff say he is going to talk with another suspect. One or the other of them may be guilty. Neither may be guilty. That's for the sheriff and the courts to discover."

Hazenberger, spitting to the side, added an exclamation point to her words.

The man with the rope cursed at her and called her a couple names she was quite sure she'd never heard before, even though, sad to say, a waitress hears a lot of uncouth opinions.

"What are you basing this accusation on, anyway?" she demanded. "Is it because Mr. Dzik was born to speak a different language? If so, think again. I'd wager at least half of you, maybe more, if not born elsewhere, are no more than a generation from a different language."

She eyed several of the men. "You, Mr. Schultz? You, Ari Finn? You, Antoine LeMans? I can speak with any of you in your previous language if necessary. Do you plan on hanging me because of it? Are you actually taking the word of a no-account ranch hand over the word of a hardworking immigrant? Just because he doesn't yet speak much English? Shame on you. Shame, shame, shame. You should go home, get down on your knees and beg for forgiveness. Meanwhile, nobody is going to be lynched here today." That end part came out louder than she'd intended.

Silence. A couple men eyed their leader, angry expressions changing to red-faced and embarrassed. Feet shuffled and backed away.

Though she probably should have let the matter drop right there, Ocean had more she thought needed to be said. Her dark eyes flashed. Now she spoke directly to Crenshaw. "I wonder, sir, why you are so eager to hang this man. What do *you* have to gain? Your actions are making me wonder if you had a hand in Mr. Sleeper's death that you're trying to cover up." He and Bullenzer, two-of-a-kind bullies hellbent on blaming Artem Dzik for a killing. And that voice. She'd heard it earlier, in the café, siding with Bullenzer and making a threat against Deputy Jones when Ash had drawn his gun.

At this, two more of the men backed off from Crenshaw and his rope, distrust suddenly showing on their faces.

"She's right. I'm leaving," one said, another agreed, and both started away.

'Chicken-livered cowards!" Crenshaw bellowed his anger. "Scairt of a woman and an old man. I'll show you!"

Which is when Deputy Hazenberger, unappreciative of the chance to be shown anything, thumped him on his head with the barrel of his shotgun. Crenshaw's eyes rolled up in his head. He collapsed directly onto a pile of horse manure laying in the street without further sound.

Someone snickered.

Not Ocean. Not out loud, anyway.

The one whose shotgun she'd commandeered was the last to leave. "Thank you," he said. "I don't know what come over me, joining up with Crenshaw like I done. I know he's a hothead, always looking for trouble. And a friend of some of the hands from Sleeper's ranch. Glad you stopped me. Stopped us."

Ocean handed him his shotgun. Spent of words and drained of energy, she nodded. He walked away.

Meanwhile, Mr. Hazenberger collapsed onto the low step into the sheriff's office. Sweat ran in rivulets from under his hat's sweatband. He removed the hat, placed it beside him, and stared up at Ocean. Like an afterthought, he cracked open his shotgun and fished a shell from his vest pocket to replace the one he'd shot into the ground.

"Thanks." His throat must've been dry as he choked on a swallow and croaked his words. "For a minute there, I thought I might be a goner. You got nerve, young lady, bulling your way in and breaking up a mob like you done."

Did six men qualify as a mob? One thing for certain, six against one—or even two—made an unfair advantage.

"Luckily for us, Mr. Crenshaw seemed to be the only real determined one."

Hazenberger nodded. He replaced his hat and made it back on his feet with the aid of the post holding up the porch's roof. "He's Bullenzer's pard. Two-of-a-damned-kind." Echoing her own opinion, he huffed out a gust of air and looked at her again. "Mind if you tell me what you're doing here?"

The thought striking her that perhaps the sheriff didn't want even this deputy knowing her part from last night, Ocean prevaricated. "The sheriff mentioned a little dog staying here. I had a few minutes off for lunch and thought to take him for a short walk. I like dogs."

Surprising her, Ned said, "So do I. And that one is a character. You don't have to worry about him." Bending down to the prostrate Crenshaw, he patted—just short of slapped—the man back to consciousness before helping tug him onto his feet.

Crenshaw moaned, the closest he came to protesting when the deputy shoved him into the jail cell with Bullenzer.

Ocean, who'd followed him into the jail, gave a quick sideways glance at Dzik, who stood at the tiny window of his cell. She shook her head the least little bit. Apparently, he understood and had probably even heard most of what had gone on outside just now, as he appeared shaken. He nodded to her. A sign he and Fedor were all right. Or so she trusted.

"I'd better get back to work," she told the deputy. "No time to walk the dog, now. You'll be okay?"

"Yeah. They won't try that again." Hazenberger sniffed. "Not in daylight anyways. Still, I'll be glad when Early and Ash get back." He led the way to the office and plopped down in Welburn's chair. "Crenshaw is right. Frankly, though it pains me to say so, I am too old for this. It's my good luck you showed up when you did. And we're both mighty lucky you managed to persuade those other fellers to back off."

She'd felt brave at the time. Not so much now. Now her belly quivered, and her head felt light enough to float right off her body. Thinking it over, Ocean couldn't believe that had been her facing up to those men. Holding a shotgun on one of them. Threatening him, calling him out. It must have been Elsie Seibert's fault. She'd made Ocean so darn mad, she'd still been fired up during the conflict.

The café had a couple men already perched on stools at the counter when she got back. Tying on her apron, Ocean forced a smile onto her face and took their orders for the lunch special, Ollie having outdone himself with chicken and dumplings.

THE SLEEPER HOLDINGS lay just up out of flood reach of the Dairy River. Ash didn't know if the stream got its name because one of the old-timers in the country had had a milk cow, or if it was due to the peculiar whitish color of the water as it tumbled and twisted for a mile or so through a gorge under a stony bluff.

Not that he cared all that much. Right now, his attention centered on a set of weather-beaten ranch buildings sitting a quarter-mile off the main road. His eyes narrowed, focusing on the smoke rising from the house's stone chimney. That and the yard to the side of the house.

"Roy Sleeper wasn't married, was he?" He glanced over at Early to see if the sheriff had noticed the same thing he had.

"Nope. Confirmed bachelor." Welburn grinned. "As I remember, he always said he had no use for women and wouldn't have one in his house unless it was his sister. And he didn't have a sister. Considered women untrustworthy. Personally, I always figured he was more than half-scared of them. That, and maybe liked men a little more than is proper."

Ash's lips compressed. "That's what I thought."

"Why?"

"The house looks occupied to me. If he isn't married, which I take to mean he hasn't got a family, who's living in the house?"

"Huh?" Welburn, who'd been slouching, sat up straight and pulled his horse to a halt while he took a closer look.

"If I'm not mistaken," and Ash knew he wasn't, "that's a woman's dress hanging on a clothesline there in the side-yard."

Welburn squinted. "You ain't mistaken, Ash. You got eyes like a hawk." His whole face took on a settled expression. Drawing his .45, he made a show of checking the loads before holstering it again. "Guess we'd best go see what's what. When I was out here after Sleeper was shot, the place was empty. A few of his men had already moved on, and the rest were living in the bunkhouse."

"Including Peckham and Fuller?"

"Yeah. But I also know left a will. His lawyer has written to the heir, a nephew, or maybe a cousin, I disremember which. Although last I heard, he hadn't gotten a reply as yet."

"Give it time. Only been two weeks since Sleeper was killed."

"Which means the place oughta be empty until the nephew shows up. Unless he, whoever he is, says different." Clucking to Buck, the sheriff cut across the pasture and headed straight for the house.

Ash followed. Eyes like a hawk, eh? Which he supposed meant he'd better keep them peeled for anything amiss. From what he'd seen and heard last night, he had no doubt Peckham would not be amiable to a quiet arrest.

"Stay behind me," Welburn said as they drew up outside the house. "Watch my back."

"Yep," Ash said.

Although they didn't exactly sneak up onto the porch, Ash figured they could've clomped, spurs jingling, if they'd so desired. That was on account of the front door standing open and sounds of loud talk, raucous laughter, and clinking glasses all wafting to them, along with the odor of cigar smoke, spilled liquor, and something burning on the stove.

Some of the laughter came from a woman, or maybe two.

Ash stopped at the doorway, where he had a good sightline into the house's interior but could keep an eye on the outside as well. The sheriff went on in. He didn't bother knocking. Not that Peckham noticed one way or another. Welburn, with Ash behind him, had plenty of time to study the room's layout and its occupants.

Peckham and his *friends* didn't appear to have worried about housekeeping for some time. Somebody had ground out more than one cigar or cigarette on the floor. Scorch marks scarred the surface.

It seemed evident every receptacle on the place capable of holding liquid had been pressed into service, then abandoned wherever it had been emptied. Same with dirty plates and pots and pans. Some of the smoke in the room came from a skillet with flames leaping upward, still on the stove at the far end of the room. Soot was turning the ceiling black.

For some reason, the women both found the sight hilarious. So did Peckham's partner, Aaron Fuller, who sprawled on a couch with one of the women on top of him.

Peckham, himself, seemed not as amused. "Don't you floozies burn my house down," he shouted. "You hear me? Somebody put a lid on that frying pan."

One of the women, a blonde still wearing her dress —more or less—finally pulled herself from his lap and stood. Swaying, she caught sight of the sheriff and affected a shrill scream. "Who are you?"

Welburn ignored her.

Gradually, the din died as the others realized the woman stood still as a cornered rat with her mouth hanging open, not the loveliest sight Ash had ever seen.

Peckham was the last to turn around. "Well, well. If it ain't the sheriff. What're you doing here?"

The woman, collapsing back down onto Peckham's lap, fixed her gaze on the star decorating Welburn's chest. She acquired what she may have thought to be an inviting smile. "You're the sheriff? Have you come to join the party? Peck has come into some money and is throwing a fine shindig."

"Shut your mouth, woman." Peckham's hissed warning did its best to drown out what she was saying. A little late, as it happened.

It was pretty clear, however, in Ash's opinion. *Come into some money, eh?* And he knew right where it came from.

6

For a shindig, Ash observed, the party guests were on the sparse side. The idea made him a tad antsy.

"Where's the rest of the Sleeper crew?" he demanded from behind the sheriff, the thought striking him that Peckham wasn't above murdering a few ranch hands, too. The ones that hadn't abandoned the ranch right away, but the ones who'd stayed to do the job Roy Sleeper had hired them for, if only until the heir showed up.

At his question, Fuller removed his gun hand from where he'd been using it to fondle the floozie on his lap. He shoved her hard enough she landed on her butt on the filthy floor.

On the stove, the pan continued to burn.

"Get that pan," Sheriff Welburn barked at the woman with Peckham. As she jumped to obey, Peckham reached for the six-gun hanging on the back of the chair he—and she—had been occupying.

Welburn put a stop to that, snatching the holstered

gun out of reach and handing the rig back to Ash. Ash thumped it down outside on the porch, well out of reach.

"I wouldn't," he said, glancing at Fuller, who'd been going for his gun.

Unmindful of the good advice, Fuller didn't stop until a bullet from Ash's .44 winged across the top of his hand. Staring down at the blood, he screeched worse than the woman he'd dumped on her arse.

"Try not to be stupid," Welburn said to him. "Use some sense. Drop the gun on the floor and kick it over to the deputy.

With the preliminary actions accomplished, Early went back to Ash's question, nodding toward his deputy while directing the question to Peckham in a hard voice. "You heard the man. Sleeper's crew. Where are they?"

"How the hell should I know? I told them they wasn't getting paid, so's I expect they left."

As long as he hadn't bushwhacked them, Ash figured they would've been smart to do so.

"We'll take a look in the bunkhouse before we leave," the sheriff told him. "Make sure we ain't missing any bodies."

"Bodies?" the woman on the floor said. She looked nervously at Fuller. Her face, previously reddened from the fall, turned a few shades whiter. "You mean they might be dead?"

"Might." Welburn nodded. "Didn't say are."

"If they're dead," Peckham blustered, but not like he cared, "I didn't do it. Look at the Russkie feller. He kilt Roy. I reckon he ain't above killing them, too."

"If he had," Welburn said, "it's too bad he didn't start with you."

Peckham, taking umbrage even as the sheriff grinned at him, started up from the chair.

"Sit down." Welburn reached over and gave him a push.

Peckham sat.

Ash, under the impression Early wasn't exactly tending to business as he ought, him being the law of the county and all, cleared his throat.

Welburn frowned at him as if to hint Ash was spoiling his fun.

"What are you even doing here?" Peckham demanded. "You got that Russkie for killing Roy. You got no business coming here."

The sheriff shook his head. "You're a fool, Peckham." A glance at Aaron Fuller included him in that category. "Both of you. And you're both under arrest. Maybe these women, too."

Shrieks abounded. The one wearing only a loose shift said something about her dress hanging on the line outside and that she needed to get it. Sidling past Ash, she darted toward the side-yard. He let her go, hoping she'd keep on running.

Meanwhile, Peckham continued to bluster. "Arrest? What for?"

"Peck?" Fuller didn't seem to be liking the direction this had taken.

Welburn did another of those sad head shakes. "Got a lengthy list that just got longer. Deputy Jones? You want to start? Mind you, whatever Ash says goes for the both of you boys, seeing as how you're pards."

"Huh?" Peckham grunted. "Pards?"

Ash spared a few seconds to settle a hard gaze on the two men, ignoring the woman over by the stove banging on a lid that didn't quite fit the flaming fry pan. She made enough racket for a cattle drive. Fuller shifted uneasily, his good hand clamping down on the other where Ash's bullet had peeled away the skin and was bleeding profusely.

"How about squatting in another man's house?" Ash started and the sheriff nodded in agreement. "As welling as trashing the interior."

"Don't know who did that," Peckham said self-right-eously. "But Roy would want me to stay and keep it up."

Ash mentally described the care of the house on the opposite end of kept up. "Then there's the matter of cattle rustling," he continued and paused for Peckham's quick denial to die down.

"And?" The sheriff urged.

Ash nodded. "And the murder of Roy Sleeper."

Fuller flinched. "Peck? You said—"

"Shut your mouth," Peckham said, which Fuller did. Peckham sat up, maybe not as drunk as he'd been a minute ago. "Murder? Hell, no. I told you. I seen that Russkie over yonder ride in and gun Sleeper down. Right here in the yard. And I hear he's got Lazy ZZ cattle over on his place."

Welburn made a "tsk, tsk" sound. "So you said about the murder when it happened. And if there's Lazy ZZ cattle there, they got put there after Dzik's arrest. Thing is, Peckham, I've found out circumstances was a little different from what you told me. Here's another little secret. Got two witnesses who heard you talking about both the rustling and the killing. You and Fuller. A confession, of sorts."

Ash would've preferred that remained unspoken—at least until the pair were safely in a jail cell.

The whites—admittedly a bit bloodshot at the moment—of Peckham's eyes showed wild. "We never..." he started, then stopped. "Witnesses? Who? They's lying, whoever they are."

Welburn shook his head. "Nope. Don't think so. Got other evidence, as well. You're not very smart, Peck Peckham. Nor much of a planner."

And Ash was surprised at the sheriff running his mouth like he was doing. Time, he figured, to cut the chitchat short. "Get up," he told Peckham, reaching into his back pocket for the set of handcuffs he carried there. That's when Peckham's lady friend must've decided she owed her host a free ticket out of his dilemma. Or maybe she just didn't like lawmen. Whichever, when she plucked a 12-gauge shotgun from behind the stove and pointed it at the sheriff, the situation got a trifle complicated.

In plain fact, Ash wasn't quite sure how it all went down, but when she fired off the first round, a scatter of shots reached both him and Early. Luck for her—and Peckham—not entirely for him or Early. Most of the buckshot missed, and while Ash wasn't exactly incapacitated, he wasn't unscathed, either. In plain fact, his belly felt like it'd been made into a sieve. Not lethal. He knew that. Just bloody and painful. As for Welburn, his gun arm ended with his fingers dangling in a bloody mess. The whore fired off a second round at random, dropped the gun, and ran out the back door quick as you could say Grover Cleveland.

Meanwhile, Peckham jumped up and dashed out

the front right from under Ash and Welburn's nose. Knocked Ash down on the way out, too, which Ash didn't figure he could've done if he hadn't been put about by the buckshot peppering his belly.

That's when Ash realized the other woman, the one without the dress but now wearing the one from the clothesline, had led three saddled horses up to stand beside Ranger and Buck and was trying to shoo the lawmen's horses away. She also had the holstered pistol he'd tossed outside the door buckled around her waist.

She'd been real fine at readying their escape, unfortunately helped by Welburn taking all that time to brag about catching them. She'd been sneaky enough that neither he nor Early had heard a thing. Probably, he figured later, when he'd had a chance to think, why the ones in the house had been making so much noise.

In fact, the getaway might've been part of an escape plan. It stood to reason the two whores may have had practice at such goings on. Peckham too.

Slow in picking himself up, his belly smarting like a whole hive of yellow jackets had attacked him, Ash had his revolver in hand as he got to the door. The two women had already mounted. One held Peckham's horse, the same one he'd been riding the previous night, for the outlaw to climb aboard. Which he did, leaping astride like a wild Indian and leaving the stirrups to flap in the breeze, urging the horse to greater effort as it broke into a startled run.

He shot after them. Looked as if he might even have hit Peckham, but if so, it wasn't enough to take him down. The three of them were onto the main road in a matter of seconds, soon disappearing over the hill and out of sight.

A low sound from behind him made Ash turn around. The sheriff, still on his feet, was dead white as he stared down at his hand and the blood dripping from his fingertips. At least he still had fingers, although it looked as if he might have a broken hand, too.

Ash said something. He didn't know what. Probably something best not to repeat.

"I'm shot," Early said, as if Ash couldn't see for himself. "Bleeding like a stuck hog. It hurts."

Leaking plenty himself and also hurting, Ash forced himself to speak. To think. "Got a clean kerchief? Wrap your hand. Quick. Wrap it tight." He didn't know what to do for his belly. Let it bleed, he guessed.

Welburn fumbled, calling on Ash to help in knotting the kerchief around his hand. Ash bound the kerchief tight until Early cried out and sank down almost into a stupor.

It took a small quiver, a sense of movement, to draw Ash's attention to Fuller, who lay flat out on the floor behind the couch. Blood was spreading in a puddle beneath him. Lots of it.

"What the..." Ash stumbled over to the man and dropped to his knees beside him. Close up, he could see Fuller was dying. The second shotgun blast had taken him in the chest and nearly cut him in half.

"Why'd he tell her to shoot me?" Fuller whispered. "We...I..."

"Because you knew he killed Sleeper," Ash said.

"I told him I wouldn't talk." Fuller's whisper grew fainter."I wouldn't have." But then he ran out of breath —and life.

All in all, Ash and Welburn, when he decided he might not be following Fuller's example after all, at least not right away, agreed this had not been their most successful day as lawmen.

"Well, damn." Welburn, having stumbled over to stare down at the body, growled his chagrin. "Here's a situation that didn't exactly follow the plan."

"Theirs or ours?"

"Either," Welburn said.

But at least, when Ash stopped over at the bunkhouse before they left the Sleeper ranch, there'd been no dead bodies inside.

In Ash's opinion, the whole botheration had been a failure. For everyone.

What's more, sympathy and accolades did not greet them on their return to town. Only news of the attempted lynching, one more unwelcome problem to address.

———

THE SAME MESSENGER boy from last night ran into Seibert's Café with news. If anything, he appeared more wound up today than he had then.

"Sheriff is riding in," he announced. "He's been shot, has blood all over him, and he's got a body slung over a horse."

"Shot? Body?" Ocean's squeak echoed the question asked by several others. She stopped, frozen in her tracks with both hands full of plates filled with the chicken and dumpling special, completely unmindful that the plates were hot and burning.

A deafening thrumming inside her head kept her from hearing what all was said next. Hearing it clearly anyway. Some of the news faded out entirely; some came in extra loud, like what the boy was saying when someone asked about the body: "Yes, sir. Deader than a doornail." He was excited as could be at this new turn of events.

Ash Jones. He must be saying Ash Jones is dead since he and the sheriff had started out together this morning. Ocean felt dead herself.

More questions hammered at the bearer of bad news. The boy's voice came to her only vaguely as he answered. "No, sir. He's wounded, but he's leading the horses."

A piercing whistle drew her attention. The portly mayor, his rear end overflowing the chair, sat waving his arms and acting as if he was starving to death. "Over here, miss. What's the matter with you? Got roots growing out the bottom of your shoes? I've got important business elsewhere." He and a fellow diner—diners if she ever got their food served—laughed heartily at his wit.

"Sorry," she mumbled and thumped the plates down. Didn't the mayor even care what had happened to the sheriff and the deputy? Or was that his important business?

"Hey!" the mayor said as gravy splashed his vest.

Ocean hardly heard him. She couldn't breathe. Whirling, she dashed through the kitchen where Ollie was slapping a couple rare steaks onto plates and ran on out the back. A half-barrel—upside down so it had an enclosed bottom—served as a seat. Usually, Ollie sat there to have a nip of whiskey and a smoke between filling orders. For now, Ocean claimed the seat, huddling while shaky breaths went in and out, and a few tears spilled from her eyes. Minutes passed.

Ash Jones, dead. She had...did have...*feelings* for him. She admitted it, though he hadn't ever noticed her until she'd spouted off in Polish. And now?

Now nothing, she thought regretfully.

The tabby cat who patrolled the area to keep rats away sidled up and brushed against her ankles with a soft purr. Reminded, Ocean picked her up and fished a bit of chicken from the piece of paper she'd wrapped it in, feeding it to the hungry cat. Somehow, the simple act made her feel better. Vaguely aware of a cheer coming from inside the café, she forced the tears to stop, drying her lashes and cheeks with the bottom of her skirt. From the kitchen, Ollie bellowed her name.

"Missy," he yelled. "Got customers lining up to pay. Get in here."

With a last catch of her breath, she put the cat down and went to serve the plates Ollie had ready and take folks' money. Hardly caring of what went on around her, the noon rush swelled then ebbed. Time dragged. Finally, the waitress on the second shift arrived, looking fresh as a newly plucked flower. Ocean, sure she resembled something left to dry in the sun, couldn't wait to get off her feet.

Ollie was waiting to get off shift, as well. "We got one more chore." He pulled off his stained apron, wadded it into a ball, and tossed it in a basket destined for the Chinese laundry down by the river. Ocean's apron followed, which left her skirt relatively unmarked.

"What?"

Eyeing Ocean's woebegone face, he handed her a

heavy basket and picked up another for himself. "Got orders to take dinner over to the jail. Reckon the prisoners went hungry at noon due to the ruckus with the sheriff coming in wounded."

The jail. Where she'd be forced to face not only today's tragedy, but the incident with Bullenzer. She didn't know how she could do it.

Ollie didn't mention Ash, though he'd teased her more than once about him. Ocean's lips clamped together, the better to hold onto her calm. Upon which Ollie's woolly eyebrows wriggled. "What's got you all upset, little miss? I heard something about what happened at the jail this morning. No reason for you to be mopin' around. You been like your dog died ever since you got to work this morning."

Dog died? Moping? Well, how would he know how she felt? She sincerely hoped he wouldn't!

UNLIKE AT THIS morning's disturbance, the sheriff's office was quiet. The front door stood open, letting air and light penetrate into the jail section. The moment Ocean walked in, she could hear men talking quietly in the back where the cells were. Once, she thought she heard a groan. Then Fedor began prattling to his father inside the cell. He was asking about his dog, and for a moment, fear touched her that something had happened to the little creature. But no. There he came, running toward her, no doubt drawn by the scent of food, and acting like he was the boss of the place.

She knelt down to pet him and lay out the scraps she'd brought especially for him.

"Ho," Ollie called out to whoever was in the back. "Got your dinner from the café here. Where do you want it."

Footsteps sounded from the back as someone hurried toward them.

7

Ocean heard Deputy Hazenberger's footsteps headed toward them as she watched Fedor's dog devour the scraps she'd brought for him.

The little dog paused eating long enough to bark at the deputy as he appeared in the doorway. Hazenberger motioned Ollie and Ocean forward. "About time you got here," he grumbled. "Got some hungry folks in back acting like they ain't et in a week." Eyeing the dog who wolfed down his chicken and gravy, then daintily licked the last smidgeon from his snoot, the deputy broke into a grin. "Guess we know who got in line first."

To Ocean's puzzlement, Hazenberger was holding his gnarled hands away from his body and flapping them as if to create a breeze.

"Well, bring the grub on back," he said. "Maybe a couple of them folks will shut their traps then." His voice lowered. "That there youngster is a whole lot less demanding than some grown men. Beginning to think I shoulda shot Crenshaw when I had the chance."

Evidently, Fedor and his dog had made a friend.

Sad as she was, Ocean felt a little better, but still, why didn't he speak of Ash? Or the wounded sheriff?

Then he did.

Hazenberger, with his hands still at that unnatural angle, nodded toward a small table sitting by the door. "Set the baskets there. I got to get back in the spare cell. Doc has Early and Ash in there. He's just finishing up cauterizing Early's bleeders right now, and I'm his helper. Sheriff's hand is shot to hell, but Doc says he'll heal up fine. Ollie, if you can hand Bullenzer and Crenshaw their food, I'd appreciate it. Don't let them grab onto you. Best if you can slide the plates through the slot at the bottom of the door. Miss Ocean, maybe you can see to the foreigner feller and his kid." He turned back to the spare cell. "Key is on the hook. Help yourself if you feel safe enough."

Ollie waited until the deputy turned away before whispering—or saying in what he may have believed to be a whisper—to Ocean. "Why's Ned waving his hands around like that? He got something wrong with him?"

Ned whirled back. "Hell, no. I'm fine as a fig. I told you. I'm helping the doc. He says I'm sanitary and not to touch anything except what he says to touch."

Ollie stared at him. "You're sanitary? What for?"

The deputy studied his hands, then shrugged. "Damned if I know." He disappeared into the third jail cell. Inside it, someone, the sheriff, Ocean supposed, emitted a low groan.

Turning away, Ocean hurried to take Artem Dzik and his son their dinner. Fedor greeted her with a little smile and seemed relieved when his dog followed her into the cell. After three tries, the dog managed to jump onto the bunk where the two sat. The boy hugged the dog to the point his father remonstrated and told him not to squeeze the *pies* so tightly.

"Dog," Fedor said, having learned the word from Ocean the night before.

Normal, she thought. Just like anybody anywhere. Why did so many Americans act as if people from other countries were any different than themselves? They'd all come from somewhere once upon a time. It didn't make sense.

Sighing, she packed up the empty dishes, restoring the café's implements to the basket. Ollie did the same, growing more and more impatient to get on with his after-work libation. Finally, he stomped away, declaring she could return both baskets to the café without his help.

The cook had barely escaped out the door when voices rose from inside the third cell.

"Dad-blame it, Ned," a man said, his tone decidedly exasperated, "I told you not to touch anything. Step back. You'll have to be doused with alcohol all over again." Ocean figured that must be the doctor.

"Sorry." Hazenberger sounded put out. "My fingers don't fit in such a bitty hole anyways. You need a better assistant, Doc."

"That's no lie." The doctor sounded as if his attention was focused elsewhere. "I need four hands. He's bleeding too much. My fingers don't fit, either. We need someone who—"

"Got an idea." Ned's grizzled head poked around the cell door frame. "You. Miss Ocean. Get in here. Doc needs you to dig some buckshot out of this poor feller's belly."

Poor feller's belly? Whose belly? She thought it was

the sheriff's hand that required doctoring. Then the import of Ned's demand struck, and Ocean's dark eyes widened. "Me?" she squeaked. "I'm not a nurse."

No. And she had no intention of becoming one.

"Don't matter," Ned stated. "I ain't either, but Doc pressed me into service. He says anybody can do it."

She shook her head. "I don't like blood."

"Eh, blood. It's not so bad as long as it's not yours," the deputy said. "You wasn't a deputy, either, but you acted like one today. Guess you can act like a nurse too, if you want to save this man's life."

She hadn't thought the sheriff in danger of losing his life. His hand must be very bad, and apparently, his belly as well.

"I'm unsanitary," she said, using his words as an excuse, but Ned shook his head. "No problem. I'll douse you with some alcohol. You'll be fine."

"Wait a minute, Hazenberger," the doctor said from inside, his voice muffled. "Who is that you're talking to?"

"Miss Ocean from the café."

"Ah. Just the one." The doctor raised his voice. "Please, Miss Galliard, I need your help. My patient needs your help."

Ocean, a sinking feeling weighing her down, allowed her dragging footsteps to take her into the cell. Could she do any less?

The cell, except for a lantern hanging over a table, was dim. Ocean caught a glimpse of a man lying immobile in one of the two bunks. Ash's body, she supposed, but she couldn't bring herself to look. As for the man on the table, she couldn't really see him, what with the doctor's thick torso blocking the sight. The most she could see was blood-stained cloths lying everywhere, including the floor, and vivid red drops rolling off the side of the table. Her stomach roiled.

"Get a move on, if you please." The doctor's impatience manifested in a muted roar. "Miss, kindly roll your sleeves above your elbows. Ned, pour alcohol over this woman's hands and arms. And since you're already contaminated, how about cleaning up some of this mess underfoot. Meanwhile, let's all be careful not to slip in the blood."

"Yessir." Ned glanced at Ocean. "That's how I got unsanitaried. I slipped."

She couldn't even raise a smile at his modified use of the unfamiliar word. The alcohol still stinging her hands, the acrid scent stinging her nose, it wasn't until she stepped up to the table on the side opposite the doctor that Ocean got a look at the patient.

Ash! He lay very still. Unnaturally still.

For several seconds she faltered, then, voice trembling, she blinked up at the doctor. "Is he alive?"

God knows he sprawled slack as the dead. And was pale enough to be a corpse.

"I certainly wouldn't be trying to operate on a dead man. He's unconscious, is all. I gave him ether. Removing this shot would be extremely painful, otherwise." The doctor drew a piece of lead from around Ash's belly button with his forceps and dropped it, clanging, into a basin. "Here now, listen to me carefully. This is what I want you to do."

She hardly heard him—and yet, she did.

The doctor, or maybe Ned, had cut away a mangled shirt. Buckshot had made a gory mess of the area around Ash's waist above his belt, though not gone in deeply enough to be lethal. In some places, where Doc had managed to pick out the shot and stitch the probe holes, the bleeding had eased. But there were still two, larger and deeper, he hadn't been able to tend. His forefinger was inside one, fishing in the wound, trying to find the shot. Unsuccessfully, as it happened.

Ocean, gorge rising, swallowed hard.

Doc grunted something unintelligible, a curse most likely, as blood surged from the wound.

Ocean had the impression he might've said something worse if she'd been a man. But all that was fleeting, something to put out of her mind. Right now, she stood trembling, wishing she could just leave like Ollie had managed to do. But then the man groaned.

"Ash!" His name escaped before she could quell it.

The doctor flicked her a surprised glance. "You know the deputy?"

She could barely speak. "He's a customer at the café." The doctor didn't need to know any more than that. "I heard...I thought the boy said Deputy Jones was dead." She half turned. "The sheriff? Is he dead?"

"No. Both men were shot up some, neither is dead. Yet. Jones might still be if you don't pay attention and do exactly as I say." Upon which, he indicated gauze swabs to mop up blood and a tray of evil-looking instruments. "Bring those closer. I'll show you what needs doing."

Properly chastened, Ocean breathed deep and slow in an attempt to calm her racing heart. Let the doctor, let Ned, even let Ash, should he awaken, all think the sight of blood upset her. And it did, but not for the reason they might think. She'd done something similar to this before, back in Denver when she'd still been with her father. Twice. She'd done it twice, actually. The last time, the time she fled, leaving her father and all of his unlawful offenses behind, she also left her cousin Nico lying on a table much like this. He'd had two bullet holes in his chest, and she'd been the one probing for the lead. Too late, as it happened. He bled out and died under her hands.

What if Ash did the same? She didn't think she could bear it.

"Hurry now, you can do it. I'll guide you," the doctor said, and breathing deeply, she nodded. Lips tight, she concentrated, probing with a finger until she felt the lead, then used forceps to extract it. The doctor hovered, standing ready to close the wound, but then she spied a tiny piece of Ash's shirt caught at the edge. Waving the doctor back, she carefully extracted the bit of cloth.

The doctor watched her, surprise on his face.

At some point, although Ash lay still, she felt his muscles quivering with pain and knew he'd awakened. She put everything but the job out of her mind until she finished. Her father had taught her to never leave a job unfinished.

When she stepped back, she saw Ash's eyes were open. The look he bestowed on her was aware and wary. Well, could she blame him?

Ocean stepped back. "I'm sorry to hurt you," she said, blinking back moisture welling in her eyes. Not tears. Absolutely not.

"Mmm." Ash emitted a sound, something like a groan, and said in a whisper, "Ocean? How'd you—"

"Yes," the doctor said. "I think he's asking how you

learned to do that? A rather professional job, if I do say so."

She stared at him, deliberately misunderstanding. "I...I...surely cloth does not belong in a wound."

Ned puffed out his chest, quick to her defense. "She's a fast learner."

"Where?" Ash said vaguely and closed his eyes. From the look on Dr. McPherson's face, he heard something beyond one mild word. A word echoing his own question.

"Well," Doc said. "However you came by the knack, Miss Galliard, it's a job well done."

Ocean heard something, too. Suspicion.

THE WHIFF of ether Doctor McPherson used to knock Ash out didn't last long enough to get him through the ordeal of having somebody poke around in his belly. Ash figured to complain to the doc—as soon as he was able to speak more than a few words. But just because he didn't feel up to talking, didn't mean he'd lost his grasp of things. For instance, the realization that instead of the doc, it was Ocean Galliard extracting the lead pellets from Peckham's whore's shotgun.

He'd opened one eye at some point and discovered her dark eyes so intent on the job at hand she didn't even realize he was awake. Or that her face was set like stone, rock hard and expressionless. He'd mention it to her, later. Or maybe not. Depended on if he lived—which he was determined to do.

Why did it strike him that she hadn't needed the doc's instructions?

Since the ether hadn't agreed with him, he suffered a bout of sickness. He lost track of her while McPherson bandaged him up, and when he'd been transferred from the table to one of the cell bunks, she'd disappeared. Sheriff Welburn, in the opposite bunk, had recovered his voice and querulously demanded Ned explain what had been going on while he'd been away getting shot. He didn't like Ned's stammered reply, something about a lynch mob, and didn't care who knew it.

Ash was relieved when Mrs. Welburn came to collect the sheriff and take him home. As for himself, he felt—or told Ned he felt—better by evening and walked himself over to his two- room living quarters located above the drug store. By morning—his middle wrapped in several protective layers of gauze beneath a shirt, an old one since his spare had been ruined already—he settled in behind his desk hoping nobody noticed how slowly he moved and how often he grimaced.

Ned, awakened from his nap in the cot the sheriff had occupied yesterday, proved only too happy to expand on his report regarding the lynch mob who'd tried to take Artem Dzik from the jail. His feet propped on a chunk of firewood, Ned tilted the sheriff's chair back and puffed comfortably on a long-stemmed pipe.

"You should've seen little Miss Ocean, Ash. She was fierce. Who'd ever a guessed it seeing the way she serves at Seibert's. And puts up with Elsie. I always thought she was meek as milk."

Ash considered how she'd hung back, only admitting to speaking Polish when Dzik had grown frantic over his son. She was good at hiding her abilities, he'd discovered. Odd. And why should she?

Nodding at Ash, Ned went on with the story. "I knew Miss Ocean didn't want to mix it up with the mob at the jail, but when she saw what was happening, she did it anyways. When Crenshaw bragged about having me outnumbered six to one, she yanked a shotgun outta Caleb Brown's hand slick as a frog can catch a fly and told the rowdies that the odds had changed to six to two. Said we, her and me, had 'em in a crossfire. She held down on Crenshaw until he had to say uncle. He didn't much like it, either, a woman getting the best of him. I figure he's still madder than a rat in a cage." Ned laughed, then grew sober. "I hope what she done don't come back on her. Crenshaw, he's apt to do her wrong if he can."

Just what Ash had been thinking.

"And to think she just showed up to walk that there little mutt of the kid's," Ned added thoughtfully. "She's a kind lady."

A DAY LATER, Ash received a summons to appear in Judge Orrin Fedderer's court on Monday. He wasn't the only one to receive such a letter.

8

OCEAN SPOTTED THE ENVELOPE SHOVED UNDER HER room door first thing when she awakened. Her innards gave a sort of lurch at the sight, a reminder of how her father used to poke a note beneath the door as a summons when they stayed at a hotel and he didn't want anyone to see they were in communication. It appeared the landlady, Mrs. Alice Mercer, had adopted the same means.

"It's safest for you," Dad had always said, "if nobody knows we're related."

She didn't imagine the landlady cared about safety. Just her own convenience.

Ocean figured he, however, was right. For instance, when she had to bail him out of jail, she always used the made-up name they'd agreed upon in advance and a good disguise. Usually, one that made her look even younger than she was in a kind of sympathy ruse. As far as she knew, except at the jail, the authorities had never put them together as father and daughter. Not as a grown woman, anyway.

But this, as she discovered as she retrieved the envelope from the floor, was a different kind of summons. The letterhead stating it came from the county courthouse and the office of Judge Orrin Fedderer proved even more daunting than a fatherly note. It demanded her presence in court on Monday morning. In court and not one word of further information. The mere thought proved more terrifying than meeting up with the outlaw Peck Peckham. Or worse, having to face for a second time, the "Mad as a rat in a cage" Crenshaw, as Ned had called him.

But first, she had to confront Elsie Seibert and arrange for the time off from her job. She doubted Butch would be a problem, but Elsie? Ugh.

Ocean's eyes were barely open, and she was already worried. Maybe she should simply leave the town of Clovis Creek, Washington, and never look back. Just disappear into some other town, some other low-paying job. If, that is, she even had the wherewithal to afford a stage ticket, let alone one on a train, which would've been her preference. She hadn't totaled her tip money for a while, hoping to be surprised. Surprised in a pleasant way, at any rate.

Still pondering any options and wondering if she actually had any, Ocean gathered her weekly laundry and hauled it downstairs to the back porch where a washtub and scrub board, sitting atop a couple rickety sawhorses on the sagging floor, awaited. The chore might have been soothing, except minutes later, Mrs. Mercer appeared. Spreading her arms from door jamb to door jamb, Alice eyed her like a feral cat eyes a bug, then pounced.

"A word, Miss Galliard." Alice—Mrs. Mercer, to

her boarders—spoke coolly. Tall, gaunt, with graying brown hair and spectacles over faded green eyes making her appear older than her years, Alice stood blocking the doorway as if to hold Ocean prisoner.

Ocean's hands, already red from the hot water and sudsy from harsh lye soap, stilled. She looked up. "Yes, ma'am?"

Mrs. Mercer folded her hands over a concave belly. "I assume you got your letter this morning?"

"Yes, ma'am," Ocean said, so prim and proper. "Thank you for bringing it to my attention."

The landlady waited as if expecting Ocean to supply her with the letter's contents. Waited in vain. After a few uncomfortable moments, she asked, "I noticed Judge Fedderer's name on the envelope. Are you in trouble? I won't tolerate anyone in my house who is in trouble with the court."

Ocean straightened. "I'm not in trouble." Not that she knew of, anyway, and if she were, she'd hardly tell the landlady. Not that she knew why her presence had been demanded in court. The letter hadn't said. Was she a witness? Was this about Mr. Dzik and his child? Or about Peckham? Or perhaps Crenshaw stirring up a lynch mob and the way she'd disarmed him?

"Then why were you sent a letter?"

"I don't know. I suppose I'll find out on Monday. The judge has asked for my presence in court then." There was no way for the woman to guess the anger flooding Ocean's veins. Nosy old biddy.

"Don't try pulling the wool over my eyes, Miss Galliard. You must know." Mrs. Mercer's voice rose. "And I insist you tell me. My reputation depends on my clean house, the quality of my food, and the decency of the people under my roof. I won't have a criminal in my house."

"Are you accusing me of being a criminal?" Ocean shot back. Personally, she wouldn't brag too much about the food, Ollie's restaurant chow being much better. And she knew for a fact two of the gentlemen on the top floor ran an illegal gambling game almost every Saturday night after the landlady went to bed. They served liquor up there, too. Meanwhile, the woman slept like a two-day-old corpse, only to arise the next day as cold, unfriendly, and sanctimonious as ever. Everybody in town knew about the poker games except the one person who should have. And that included the parson, who'd been known to sneak up the back stairs for a hand or two.

But, she conceded, the house was clean, due to the hired girl's efforts.

She took a short breath, staring down at the soap-suds in the tub. "Or of being indecent?" she said at last, only a slight narrowing of her eyes indicating her rage. She knew the sign was showing because she felt a quiver in the lower lids. Nico had said once it was her tell, though a hard one to spot.

Perhaps Mrs. Mercer saw something to make her realize she'd gone too far. Or could be she'd seen the coldness creeping over her previously mild, polite boarder. A boarder who paid on time every week.

"No," the woman said after a pause that went on a little too long. "But I need to know if this is going to affect my boarding house."

Ocean shrugged. "I can't imagine why. Unless it has something to do with you and the boarding house. Might it?" That was the trick. Always throw the problem back onto the questioner. Could she make it any plainer? Evidently not, as Mrs. Mercer persisted for another good five minutes in denying any wrongdoing on her part. Ocean almost laughed. Not, in this case, anything to give her a feeling of triumph.

IN THE AFTERNOON, when she left to work the late shift, she found the key to her room and carefully locked the door behind her. Mrs. Mercer no doubt had a master key and the ability to get in to pry if she insisted, but the other boarders would not. Either way, she'd know if anyone had. The silver metallic thread she'd used at the top of the door casing would be broken if the door opened but would be basically invisible to anyone doing so.

Anyway, she had nothing incriminating to hide. Why would she? She hadn't done anything wrong.

EVEN ELSIE SEIBERT turned out to be easier to deal with than Ocean had feared. She sniffed her rather bulbous nose and agreed to allow the hired help a day off for whatever business the judge deemed necessary. Not but what she could resist a mild—for her—warning. "Just don't come crying to me when your paycheck won't cover your rent," she said. "A lesson about sticking your nose in where it don't belong and seeing where it gets you."

Ollie, busy stirring up a pot of goulash from a recipe Ocean had given him, winked at her as soon as Elsie was out of sight. "Don't you fret. The sheriff already fixed you up."

"Sheriff Welburn? Fixed me up how? For what?" She didn't bother hiding her surprise or her puzzlement as she tied on her apron and fluffed the bow in the back.

"Yeah, Sheriff Welburn. Only sheriff we got. Him and the judge had their noon meal in here. Sheriff had to have soft stuff like soup and mashed spuds that he could eat with a spoon since he couldn't handle a knife. Said he'd be back tonight for the goulash after I told him the meat was tender enough to eat with a fork. No cutting. Fingers on his right hand is out of commission for a spell."

As Ocean already knew. She gave him a look, the message being for him to get on with it.

"Anyways, they was sitting over here by the kitchen, and I heard them talking about the hearing on Monday. Judge said something about a going rate."

"A hearing? Is that why the judge asked for me?"

Ollie sighed impatiently. "Yeah. The hearing for Dzik."

"Oh." How was she to know a hearing had been scheduled? The summons hadn't said. She thought a moment. "The going rate for what?"

"Don't know what going rate exactly, but it sounded like money to me. Guess you'll find out Monday."

"They're going to turn Mr. Dzik loose?"

"Think so."

A relief. "Well, good. A little boy shouldn't be kept in a jail cell."

Ollie held the spoon to his lips and tasted the goulash. "Whoa. Feller's are going to like this batch. It's hot enough to singe your hair."

Ocean glanced at his bald pate. "If you had any." The rest of her shift went well after this bit of back and forth.

———

At the boarding house that night, she found the silver thread broken. Snapped between the door and the jamb, proof of Mrs. Mercer's inquisitiveness. Well, she believed Mrs. Mercer was the guilty party. Who else could it be? Ocean, not amused, didn't quite know what to do with the information. Had the woman done this before? There'd been a time or two she'd noticed things not sitting quite right, like the silver-backed brush and hand mirror on her commode. Elegant items one might not necessarily expect to find amongst a lowly waitress' belongings.

The set was a family heirloom Ocean's father had given to her on her sixteenth birthday. It had belonged to her Polish great-grandmother, lovingly preserved for several generations. If she wasn't mistaken, her father used the items more than once over the years as surety for loans in pawnshops. But he always redeemed them, which made her happy. When the set had come into her possession, the brush still had a few strands of blonde hair caught in the boar hair bristles.

She'd laughed. Whoever she took after in previous generations of her family, it must not have been the Polish side. Not with her dark mane and even darker eyes.

Mrs. Mercer—or whatever person had invaded her privacy—had been more careless in her search this time. For one thing, the silver dressing table set had been placed in reverse order to the way Ocean always... always...arranged the pieces. For another, the freshly washed laundry in her drawer had been straightened and refolded, not along the same lines.

Evidence, she supposed, of the spite Mrs. Mercer had always seemed to feel toward her. She didn't know why. Ocean resolved to look for a different boarding house, even if its reputation was not so pristine. After all, the poker games were proof that clean reputations did not always represent the truth.

On Sunday, Ash, though still feeling a bit on the puny side due to the doctor's—and Ocean's—rough and ready treatment, quit sitting behind a desk and resumed his full deputy duties. That included a walk around town, which left him more tired than he wanted to admit.

Early Welburn, who'd seemed the worse off of the two lawmen at the time, was recovering faster, probably thanks to Ash's quick action in binding his fingers. At any rate, after a morning spent lazing at his desk, a trip to the telegraph office to send out warnings to other towns about Peck Peckham and his two female cohorts got him moving.

Ash had been thinking. Every mealtime, they ended up at Seibert's café, toting food to the jail to feed the prisoners, then making another trip to return the empty dishes.

"Got an idea, Early," he said.

The sheriff looked up from twiddling his sore fingers in an attempt to regain the fluidity of movement the swelling hampered. "What kind of idea?"

"How about taking Dzik and his kid along to the café when we go. That'll save us a trip."

Early didn't disagree—exactly. "Kind of counting chickens before they're hatched, ain't we?"

Ash had a convincing argument. "Maybe. But if the man is going to live here, make a living, and raise his son here, folks will need to accept him, even if he doesn't speak such good English. Get them used to seeing him with us, calm them down, and we'll have less trouble all around. We don't want another set-to with the likes of Crenshaw and Bullenzer."

"Can't argue that." The sheriff scowled at him. "As long as the Polack minds his manners. And as long as Judge Fedderer turns Dzik loose."

"Well, he ought," Ash said. "Dzik hasn't done anything wrong."

"That you know of."

"That I know of. That isn't all. Dzik doesn't even know about the hearing in the morning. Might be a good idea to have Ocean...Miss Galliard...explain to him about it ahead of time. Let him know she'll be there to help him out. And give him time to put his thoughts in order."

IT DIDN'T TAKE LONG to bring Welburn around to his way of thinking.

Minutes later, with the little white dog trailing determinedly behind them, they headed over to Seibert's café. The little boy, excited to be out of the dark cell, swung from his father's hand, laughing in the sunlight. Once, he grabbed hold of Ash's hand and swung between the two men. Dzik sent Ash a dubious look, but, to his own surprise, Ash allowed the boy to cling and swing.

Sheriff Welburn, viewing Ash's red face with a barely hidden grin, stopped at the café door and pushed it open.

"Miss Galliard?" Artem Dzik's expression grew eager when he realized where they were.

Ash nodded, a twinge prickling as he noted the eagerness Dzik showed in saying Ocean's name. It didn't help when the busy place grew silent as folks saw who stood at the door. And he didn't like that Ocean stopped in her race to the kitchen, an uncomfortable expression crossing her face.

Just as quickly, it was gone.

The dog entered first and, to Ash's amusement, made a beeline toward Ocean. He sat in front of her and uttered an imperious "ruff."

Ocean gazed down at the dog, cast a wary glance around the room, and spoke firmly. "You'll have to wait your turn."

It was the right thing to say. Customers laughed. Even those who'd looked at first as if they'd protest the dog's presence. As for Ash, he had an idea the dog's patrician appearance had something to do with it. Sparkling white, smoothly brushed—it wasn't like Dzik and the kid had much else to do—and cute as an exotic bug as opposed to some scraggly mutt.

It didn't hurt when the little boy, well-behaved and smiling shyly at Ocean, gleaned the group some acceptance, as well. The stage was set for the next day.

9

A BUZZ OF LOW-VOICED TALK SURROUNDED OCEAN as she slipped into the courtroom. She was early, but so were a good many others who'd made sure to have a good seat at the proceedings. She recognized some from outlying holdings, ranchers, farmers, and even some of the loggers. They had a large contingent of immigrant workers. She supposed they were doubly curious as to how a non-English-speaking man would be treated in this American court.

Like a shadow, she stepped to the side of the doorway and sat in the last row of carefully aligned benches. At first, no one took notice of her. Which, she had to admit, was how she preferred it.

It wasn't until Sheriff Welburn and Ash walked past her, sandwiching Artem Dzik between them, that the place grew silent. They hadn't handcuffed Dzik, she noticed. A show of confidence in his innocence. They'd also made sure he had a clean shirt to wear, had a chance to trim his beard, and appeared ordinary and respectable.

The trio reached the front of the courtroom, where they sat on the witness bench. Ash and the sheriff conferred together, with Ash looking around and seeming a little anxious. Until she caught his eye. Relief on his face, he made a little jerk of his head.

At that, Ocean, wondering who'd been put in charge of Fedor and the dog, instantly forgot about them.

Heart sinking, she knew what the gesture meant. He wanted her to come forward and sit beside him in the front row. She'd have to do it, too, if she didn't want to make a scene and have the situation get blown out of proportion.

And, of course, to be handy to do the job she'd been given. At least the sheriff had explained that much to her, and she'd informed Dzik.

Grimacing, she stepped into the aisle to obey the summons and almost got plowed over by a man smelling strongly of the cow manure on his boots.

"Outa the way," the man gritted, muttering something about women staying in the kitchen where they belonged as he shoved his way forward.

Seeing the rough treatment, Ash started from his seat, but gathering her balance and aplomb, Ocean shook her head. More cautious now, she darted through a barricade of elbows and shoulders to the front, stopped once by Horace Freeman, the newspaper owner/editor/writer, saying, "Miss Galliard? Why are you here? This is a rough crowd."

But she only smiled vaguely at him and continued on without speaking. Unfortunately, even that short delay left her and a man she recognized as a customer at the café meeting at the only remaining seat in the front row. The man took the seat just as she started to sit, his triumph leaving her standing. Which, stranding her like a gopher out of its hole, left her with a face glowing hot.

"Scat," the man said. "You don't belong here."

Frankly, Ocean's temper had begun to fray.

Welburn looked up. "Nah, it's you who don't belong in the front row. Move it, Quackenbush. That seat is reserved for the lady."

Ash's narrow-eyed stare stopped any protest the rancher might have had.

Ocean had never felt so small. Not even the last time she'd been in the courtroom with her father on the day he'd been sent to prison to serve a three-year term. Which was, she realized with something of a start, just about to come to an end.

Hurriedly, she sat down, then popped right back up when Ned Hazenberger came in, shouting over the noisy room. "Everybody rise. Court is in session, Judge Orrin Fedderer presiding."

Ash urged Dzik to his feet.

Ned had a commanding voice. Silence fell as a smallish man with stooped shoulders wearing a black robe strode in and sat behind the imposing desk at the front. He picked up the gavel waiting there and pounded on a wooden round.

"You heard the man, court is in session." He stared out over the crowd with blue eyes bright enough to penetrate the smoke-filled room. "That means shut up and don't interfere. Get outta line, and I'll have Deputy Hazenberger toss you out. Got it?"

Beside her, Ash choked on a chuckle, although his

face remained perfectly serious. She guessed it was an oft-repeated threat. Or maybe more than just a threat as complete silence prevailed.

The judge nodded satisfaction. "All right. First on the docket is consideration of the charge against Mr. Artem Dzik for the murder of Roy Sleeper. Stand up, Mr. Dzik. How do you plead?"

Dzik, upon hearing his name—mangled only a little —looked up. His face had gone pale, and he looked worried. Very worried. And bewildered.

Quickly, Ocean leaned across Ash and whispered to Dzik, giving him the correct words.

Dzik popped to his feet. "Not guilty," he said, his English barely audible in the large room.

Upon which, the judge held up his hand to stop proceedings. "Sheriff, come up here. I want to talk to you."

Welburn, himself appearing ill at ease, tromped forward to stand before the judge's desk. They conferred in low voices, whereupon Early turned and beckoned for Ash. He also went forward.

"It'll be all right," Ocean said in Polish. Dzik, staring straight ahead, nodded.

The short conference done, Judge Fedderer explained the delay to the courtroom. "Mr. Dzik doesn't speak English too well. Fortunately, we have someone to translate back and forth from what I'm told is Polish to English for us. Consequently, I'll have Mr. Dzik be seated next to my desk where everyone can see him, and our translator will stand behind him. I don't want anybody here questioning the accuracy and fairness of my decision after hearing the events."

By this time, Ned had brought in a chair and placed it beside the desk. Ash escorted Dzik to the chair and Ocean to a place behind him. Her knees shook, her skirt visibly in motion. Every one of the eyes on her felt like an individual weight.

She couldn't help it. Her shoulders slumped.

Ash touched her hand. "Easy," he murmured and went to take his seat again. Ocean wished she could call him back.

The testimony seemed to go on and on. Sometimes it seemed to her that she lost track of who was speaking what in which language. Feeling a trifle dizzy, at one point, she grabbed hold of the chair's back. At the time, Ash was seated there, speaking of how when he and the sheriff learned they'd inadvertently left Dzik's small child at the homestead alone, he—he mentioned only himself—had ridden out to recover the boy. He'd not only discovered Peck Peckham driving Sleeper cattle onto to Dzik's homestead in a blatant attempt to throw the cattle rustling charge onto the foreign man, but overheard Peckham speaking freely to Aaron Fuller, his partner, about the crime.

Ash faltered once, when her cold fingers inadvertently touched the back of his neck.

Sheriff Welburn finished the testimony, telling how upon learning this, he and Deputy Jones went out to the Lazy ZZ ranch the next day, where they found Roy Sleeper's regular hands gone and only Peckham, Fuller, and two whores illegally in possession of Sleeper's house. He said how the fight occurred. How Peckham's woman murdered Fuller and how the others escaped after himself and Ash were wounded.

All that pretty much ended the doings. Judge Fedderer went into his back room to spend several minutes pondering, as he called it. Upon which, he came back in and said Dzik was cleared of all charges and was free to go.

Ocean dutifully translated everything, almost weak with relief. The courtroom erupted with noise. Some applauded the decision, others were against it, their questions turning ugly. At least her part was over. The dissent landed on the sheriff and Ash's shoulders.

Her relief faded when Judge Fedderer called her into the back room. Hesitantly, every nerve in her body tingling, she followed him and perched on the edge of the chair he indicated. Did he realize she, also, was a witness to Peckham's guilt? Had the judge discovered she was her father's child? She supposed his name might be known to people in law even here in the west.

The judge steepled his fingers and studied her over them. Ocean forced herself to sit quietly, as if his regard didn't disturb her. But it did.

At last, he spoke. "Deputy Jones tells me you speak several languages. Fluently, by your own account," he said.

She drew a breath. "I do."

"Which ones?" His brow creased. He seemed surprised she hadn't nattered on about her talents of her own accord.

Did she have to answer? According to his stern regard, she did.

"Polish, German, French. Greek. Some Russian." She just wasn't mentioning those she was less fluent in. Like Finnish. Or Swedish. They both were difficult languages to master, and she hadn't known their native speakers long enough for easy conversation.

He stared at her. "No Chinese?"

Relief surged. "No, sir."

"Too bad. I have a trial coming up over in Spokane next month. A man accused of murder. He speaks only Pidgin English. Not good for his defense."

Ocean, careful to keep her expression clear, nodded. "No. It isn't. But you might be surprised how many Chinese do speak decent English. I'm sure there's someone who can speak for him within the tong."

"Tong?" he asked, almost carefully.

A test? "I'm sure you're familiar with the Chinese tongs. I expect Spokane has a large enough population to support one or two."

"Hmm. I'm just surprised a young woman such as yourself is familiar with the term."

Ocean shrugged. "I don't live in a cave."

"No. But you do live in a backwater. I doubt many women in this town would know a tong from a fork prong."

She stood and forced a smile onto her lips, deciding no answer was the best answer. "I'm sorry I can't help you, sir."

He didn't move. "Sit down, please, Miss Galliard. I'm not finished. Frankly, I didn't think there was much hope you'd be able to help with the Chinese. But French. That's a language you're fluent in, yes?"

She sat and said slowly, "Yes."

"And German."

A nod, more hesitant this time, sufficed.

Judge Fedderer sighed. "See, I've got a problem. A case pending between two adversaries who not only don't speak each other's language, but don't have much English either. This shouldn't be the court's problem. Each man ought to be liable for making himself understood, whether they pay someone or they know someone who does this for free."

Ah. They were talking money now? Ollie had said something about her not having to worry about her missed day of work. Her eyebrows arched.

"Normally, the state would pay two translators, one for each, but the county coffers are running over budget. That means I need someone who can work both sides. From where I stand, that means you."

"Me?" Oh, but Ocean had questions. Lots of questions. For instance, was it even legal for her to translate for two different sides at the same time? Wouldn't the losing side contest her translations? What if her sympathies lie with one or the other?

"I'm thinking you would translate exactly. In fact, I'd be depending on you to translate exactly."

"But how would you know."

His beady-eyed examination landed on her again. "I'm known as a pretty decent judge of character. I think I'd know."

Ocean shivered. She didn't doubt him.

"This shouldn't take more than a day or maybe two of your time. I'll arrange the trial to take place here in Clovis Creek and set a date for your day off at the café. Please, Miss Galliard. What have you got to lose?" He smiled then and named a figure that would pay her rent for a month.

How could she say no, she wondered, even as her nerves tingled? Would he even let her?

So she said yes.

When the judge finally excused her, the front of the courtroom was empty. Ocean walked out, the heels of her shoes sounding loud on the plank floor. At least her pocketbook contained a dollar in payment for today's work. She hadn't expected so much, especially as the hearing—events not having qualified as any kind of trial —had only lasted an hour or so.

It hadn't been so terribly hard, in retrospect. Speaking with the judge afterward had been much harder.

And their deal meant she'd have to spend some time with him again. She imagined he would want to know about her. About how she came to speak so many languages. Why she'd come and stayed in Clovis Creek. He'd already hinted that he thought it odd. Who, he would demand, was her family?

"Nobody," she'd say. "They're dead." But they weren't. Not all of them. Or not the last she knew.

Now Dzik had been officially cleared of Roy Sleeper's murder and was free to go, Ash discovered the man had relaxed enough to find more of the English he'd slowly been learning. In fact, when Ash offered to accompany him, his boy, and the dog to Dzik's homestead, he seemed to catch on real quick.

"Miss Galliard," he said, showing Ash the things— money and paperwork Ocean had packed up from his homestead and brought to him as a precaution, "she says she not trust peoples. Maybe one steals. You come see. These she keeps safe." He gazed down at Fedor and his cache of personal items with undisguised relief. "Didn't steal son."

The thing is, Ash didn't trust people not to steal, either. And in this case, stealing might've been the least of it if they hadn't come in time. After overhearing Peckham and Fuller talk about searching for money on the night he and Ocean rescued Fedor, he figured Dzik would be lucky if they hadn't burned his cabin to the ground while they were at it. If so, there would be yet another thing on the list of charges against the outlaw and his two prostitute accomplices.

They rode side by side, more or less, the Polack's big plowhorse taking one stride to Ranger's two. Even so, Ranger was the faster. Conversation came in small bunches, using simple words, even though Ash came to understand Dzik was an educated man. The Pole was in America because his father had been on the losing side in a land dispute between Prussian and Russian forces. In the end, the family's estate had been confiscated by the Russians. Dzik's father had urged him to go to America. Vigorously urged. He'd financed the enterprise, selling jewels and other family treasures to make sure his son had funds. Artem's young wife had already been dead by then, and although Fedor's grandparents had objected, he'd insisted on bringing the child, then an infant, with him. He'd been proven wise when word came last year that both his and his wife's parents had been murdered, caught in a crossfire between factions.

Ash shook his head, dismayed by the story, and even more glad for the slip of a girl who'd helped this man. And, he admitted, kept him and the sheriff from making the blunder of charging the wrong man with murder. All due to being able to speak his language and her innate wisdom in saving both the man's child and his possessions.

The sun was high when they reached the meadow where Dzik's cattle were pastured. They were nearing the cabin when DzikArtem hauled on his horse's reins. He pointed. "Not mine," he said, frowning at a cow and calf standing off by themselves.

Ash pulled up. "Not yours?"

"Him." Dzik urged the horse toward the wayward pair. "Not mine." He peered more closely at the cow. "See? ZZ's."

Surprised by the man knowing his cattle by sight, Ash had to admit this had been something of a test. And Dzik had passed. He saw at a glance these were two of the animals Peckham had brought during the night he and Ocean rescued Fedor. Glancing around, he spotted the other pair some small distance away.

He nodded. "Sleeper's. Not yours."

Dzik nodded. "You take them away."

"I will."

They continued on to the cabin. Even at first glance, Dzik's reaction proved interesting. His nostrils flared. He slid to the ground and held out his arms for his son, setting him down. Fedor started to run into the cabin through the open front door—until Artem roared, "Nie."

The boy stopped, face puckering as if he thought he'd done something wrong.

Instantly, Dzik's frown disappeared, and he spoke in a softer voice. Fedor's expression cleared, and he nodded and stepped back. Dzik put a leash on the dog and gave the boy orders to hold on to it.

"Door open?" Dzik stared disapprovingly at Ash. It was a question.

Ash shook his head. "No. Miss Galliard made certain to close it. Appears as though you had visitors after we left. They left Sleeper's cattle here and ransacked your cabin."

Dzik's mouth tightened under his large mustache. He muttered something, and if Ash had had a guess, he'd have said he was finding thieves and outlaws no different here than they were in his own country, if only on a smaller scale.

Nodding at Dzik, he stepped on through the doorway first, not much surprised by destruction that seemed committed for the pure hell of it. Even the stove pipe had been pulled away from the ceiling. Scorch marks on the floor showed where, despite Ocean's care to extinguish the fire, there'd been a coal or two hot enough to mar, though not light a bigger fire.

The bed Fedor and the dog had hidden under had been torn apart. The contents of the apple box cupboards tossed down and strewn about. Everything that could possibly have concealed valuables was torn asunder.

Ash gazed around, shaking his head in disgust. As for Dzik, he tossed aside a chair with a broken leg and started speaking. Ash figured it was better that he didn't understand the words, but he sure enough had a good idea what the rant meant.

"I'll help you clear things up," he said. "Get your stove safe and ready to make a fire. Splint the chair leg. Rebuild the bed. Re-hang your cupboards." He didn't know if DzikArtem understood a word he said just then.

Dzik's breath wheezed in and out. "He would have killed my son."

And Ash, staring into the man's fury, slowly nodded. "I think so. He's a bad man. A man who likes killing. But we'll get him. Don't you worry."

But he didn't figure his little speech reassured Dzik. He wasn't sure himself.

10

Ocean knew the only reason she kept her job at Seibert's Café in the first place was due to Sheriff Welburn's intervention when he requested her special services withArtem Dzik. Then afterward, to Judge Fedderer's demands for her talents. Butch had been quite easily convinced, or so she heard. Elsie, not so much. Not really a surprise.

"The court requires her expertise next Tuesday with a case concerning a French-speaking party and one speaking German." Judge Fedderer, his face stern and very judge-like, held an important conversation with Butch and Elsie only two days after Dzik's release. This, after paying for his dinner in Seibert's when his more usual eatery was Dobby's Hotel.

Also, oddly enough, the meeting took place in public with plenty of witnesses, including Ollie, who reported back to Ocean as soon as he had a minute. He had the conversation down almost word for word.

"In order for justice to be served, someone has to translate our new immigrant's languages for everyone to understand," the judge had said. "This county is lucky to have someone like Miss Galliard living here who can speak for these people. Several of them, at any rate. We need to make sure we keep her available when necessary. I trust you will cooperate and allow the lady time off to serve the state?"

He'd made what sounded a lot like a demand into a question.

The change that came over Elsie provided laughs—or maybe snickers—to everyone who saw Ocean's worst enemy suddenly preening and saying with a certain coyness, "Why, of course, Judge Fedderer. We're real proud to help you out. It's our civic duty."

"A bare-face lie," Horace Freeman, the newspaperman, whispered to the man on the stool beside him as, ears pricked, they eyed the trio. "Though you'd think by hearing her she's the one the judge asked to translate."

The man next to him nodded. "Yeah. When everybody knows the ignorant old cow has been working the girl to death and trying to get Butch to fire her."

But to Ocean, none of the situation made her laugh. Or even much appreciate Ollie saying, "You're making friends in powerful places, Missy. Looks like I'd better watch my step."

If anyone had better watch their step, Ocean thought as she swished away with an armload of hot plates, it was her.

ON TUESDAY, in an unsuccessful attempt to make herself invisible, Ocean dressed in a drab brown skirt over a single petticoat, a tan shirtwaist so plain it resembled a man's dress shirt instead of a lady's garment, a short jacket with tight sleeves she found horribly uncomfortable, and a straw boater—although full spring, let alone summer, had yet to arrive.

In truth, the less-than-pretty outfit did not suit her coloring, but if she thought it made her invisible, she was mistaken. Ash took one look and scowled when he saw her. She saw the scowl, but didn't realize why—at first. Not until he touched a fold of the skirt and said, "Brown," in a certain tone of voice.

Judge Fedderer, on the other hand, seemed to think her choice of garb appropriate and nodded approvingly as she entered the courthouse. He made certain to seat her beside the sheriff before he went into the back room to don his black robe.

The sheriff and Ash were not required to be in attendance since this was a simple hearing for a civil case. Even so, they were on the lookout for trouble. Both litigants had spoken of violence, and the sheriff and his deputy had needed to pay them visits on more than one occasion.

Unlike the hearing for Artem Dzik, here, the two main actors were seated on opposite sides of the room, each at a small table. Looking around, Ocean saw a steady stream of mostly men, although there were a few women as well, filing in to sit on one side or the other. The noise level rose with the staccato rattle of French spoken to the left, and the guttural harshness of German to the right.

Listening closely, her nervousness grew. Her hands, resting in her lap, clenched tightly enough her knuckles showed white.

Ash noticed. He leaned over to whisper close to her

ear. "What are they saying? Is there going to be trouble?"

"It's confusing," she whispered back. Her dark eyes flicked toward the French side, where a wiry older man was making no bones about his displeasure over the sanctimonious Dutchmen, who seemed to think their religion guaranteed their cause was the only right—or righteous—one.

Meanwhile, the blond-haired German fellow—or Dutch, Ocean wasn't quite certain as his accent puzzled her—preened himself while looking down at the Frenchman, which pretty much agreed with what the French fellow had said.

"Are these the people you told me about?" she asked. "The people with the still arguing with those who don't hold with liquor?"

"That's them." He sounded grim.

She listened to the German side a moment longer, then said fervently, "I wish I hadn't gotten mixed up with this argument. Ten to one, when the fists fly, some of them are going to blame me."

Ash's lips may have twitched over her fists-flying comment, but he didn't deny its validity either.

Ned, whom Ocean had by now discovered was the court bailiff, keeper of order, and general dogsbody, stood up and announced that court was in session. A sigh went through the courtroom.

Judge Fedderer made his appearance and beckoned to her. Compelled to step forward, knowing everyone's eyes were on her, Ocean not only had second or third thoughts on this endeavor, but kept right on counting objections. The number one? That the translator always got blamed by the losing side. She'd seen it before. Only, she wasn't going to mention to Judge Fedderer where the information came from. Nor to the sheriff or Ash.

Though certainly no more than a few seconds passed as she crossed the floor to stand behind the witness box, the walk seemed to take eons.

As soon as she was in position, Ned called for the Frenchman, Edouard Ledoux, to step forward. The wiry fellow smiled, his expression confident, as he followed Ocean's instructions as she repeated everything in French and German. His bonafides accepted, he seated himself in the witness chair and looked to the judge expectantly.

"This is a hearing," Judge Fedderer said loudly. "Not a trial. We're here to determine if the complaint warrants going to trial. That's all. I'll decide based on the testimony presented today. Are we clear? My decision is final."

Ocean put the little speech into German and French.

For the edification of the onlookers, between the judge, Ocean, and Ledoux, the situation from the litigant's side got presented first.

"Vogel demands we shut down our still. According to him, his women can smell the fumes, and it makes them drunk." Ledoux laughed just a little at the absurdity of it all. He snorted. His mouth turned down in an expression of scorn. "Ridiculous! He accuses me of using two-year-old rancid wheat. I do not. I only use the freshest and best to make my alcohol. He thinks the still is illegal. It is not. He tells lies that I sell whiskey to the Indians." His sharp nose pointing to the German, he glared directly at Vogel. "I never sell whiskey to Indians. Nor to children. I do not make whiskey, only alcohol. I make it for antiseptic use."

Ocean, already exhausted from repeating every word into both German and English, almost lost her place when Günter Vogel, representing the counter-litigants, interrupted harshly, disputing Ledoux's explanation. He was not polite. Even the judge could not restrain his outburst.

Ocean, taken aback, stared at Vogel.

"Say it," he snarled at her. "Stupid woman. Say it. I will know if you lie. Do not try." Without stopping at that, he added more disparaging remarks. Finished, he glanced toward a man sitting in the second row, and she saw him nod. So. He had a ringer and probably understood well enough himself.

A wave of heat coursed over her, especially as she became aware of Judge Fedderer pounding his gavel on a birch round set on his desk for the purpose and demanding silence from an overly enthusiastic courtroom.

When it finally came, he bent toward her, quietly asking, "What was that all about?"

"He, Herr Vogel, is detestable and rude. He called me stupid and a liar, among other things," she said. "And don't believe it when he says he doesn't understand English. He does."

"Ah." Judge Fedderer's lips twitched. "I suspected. Take extra care with your translations, Miss Galliard. We want to hear every word and know it's accurate."

"*He* already lied when he swore he didn't speak English and required a translator."

"I'm aware. Go ahead now, and repeat what he said.

All of it." The judge sat back in his chair, his face expressionless.

The part where Vogel called her a stupid woman, let alone an ignorant American who not only didn't know her place but was no lady of quality, raised a murmur loud enough for the judge to pummel his birch round again.

There were several in the crowd she recognized as customers at the café. At least, she admitted to herself, it was gratifying to discover some of them didn't like the way he sneered at her.

Eventually, although Mr. Ledoux took his time defending against Vogel's accusations, he had to step from the witness chair and allow the German to take his place.

Herr Vogel, hot on the hunt from the first word, proved relentless in proving his case. He demanded two hard-faced middle-aged women come forward to attest to the headaches and blurry eyesight they'd suffered from smelling the fumes from Ledoux's distillery. They swore they smelled rancid wheat. He swore he'd seen an Indian haul a barrel of whiskey off to the reservation. And he acted positively triumphant when he announced, "It is illegal to make whiskey. Throw him in prison, where he belongs. Confiscate his premises. I, Günter Vogel, will buy the property and burn this devil's work to the ground."

Ocean's eyes were wide as she translated this last part. She knew some people from Vogel's community were difficult to deal with, but this seemed extraordinary. The man must be a maniac.

To his credit, Judge Fedderer's expression didn't change as he called Ledoux's closest neighbor to the stand. A farmer who had several milk cows, his farm was located between the two litigants. Obvious to everyone in the courtroom, Vogel, his eyes glittering his anger, jostled the man as he came forward.

A warning to sway the farmer's testimony? Ocean wondered.

The farmer, his jaw set, grunted and raised his hand to be sworn in.

Judge Fedderer steepled his hands in front of him as he formed his first question. "Tell me, Mr. Pence, from which direction do the prevailing winds blow in your neck of the woods?"

The man frowned. "Same direction as they do everywhere else around here. Come out of the southwest and blow northeasterly. Most of the time. If the wind does come out the north, it means we got a storm brewing."

The judge nodded right along with most everyone else in the room. "Are you much troubled by odors—fumes—blowing in from the Ledoux distillery?"

"Nope. If there are fumes, they blow the other way. Truth to tell, I ain't never been troubled by anything stinkin' from Ledoux's place. Now, Günter's farm, that's another story. I get stunk out by his pig manure when the wind comes up strong. My wife about has a conniption fit. Says we should complain." He eyed Vogel. "Hogs!" he added in clear disgust.

A spate of laughter rose. Judge Fedderer banged his gavel. "That will be all, Mr. Pence. Thank you. You may step down."

Ocean, who'd gotten through the translation without trouble, sighed a little. But there was more.

"Anybody else got anything to say about fumes from

the distillery?" the judge asked the room at large. No one spoke. "We'll move on. Anybody know anything about the Indians hauling away a barrel of whiskey?" He paused thoughtfully. "A barrel seems a mighty amount. Potable whiskey is worth a lot of money. More than most Indians got handy."

A man in the middle of the room stood up. "I live north of Ledoux. The road to the reservation passes my place. My son got crippled up a few weeks ago with a busted leg. He spends most of his time looking out the window. If he'd seen an Indian with a barrel of whiskey, he'd a said something."

A woman stood. Her voice shaking at the prospect of speaking up in a courtroom in front of a crowd of men, she had a question. "How would Mr. Vogel know about it anyway? His place is in the wrong direction for him to see anything. The tribe avoids going by his farm, you see. They don't like the hogs, and he—Mr. Vogel— always shouts insults at them. Once, he even shot at one of their dogs. I was passing and seen him do it."

"Thank you, ma'am. A good point." Since no one disagreed with her, although Vogel jumped up, Judge Fedderer moved on before the German could protest. "Now, as to the last object of disagreement, the distillery itself. Mr. Vogel contends it is illegal for the still to be operating. Mr. Ledoux says he makes only medicinal alcohol, which in certain instances is not against the law. Mr. Vogel says it's drinking whiskey. Is there anyone here who can attest to this, one way or another?"

Ocean's job got easier as utter silence prevailed. She bit back a grin. If anyone bought booze from Ledoux, they weren't about to say so in this courtroom.

Judge Fedderer tapped his teeth with a forefinger. "I will have to shut your distillery down and investigate, Mr. Ledoux."

Without waiting for Ocean's translation, Vogel grinned at Ledoux as if he'd scored a great victory.

The judge was still speaking. "Those certain instances I spoke about, Mr. Ledoux, I'm sorry to say..."

Ledoux, not appearing sorry at all, reached into his jacket's inner pocket and drew out an envelope. He proffered it to the judge. "Here is license to operate distillery. See. Is legal. I win."

And he laughed in Vogel's astonished and angry face.

The courtroom spectators broke into huzzahs and a smattering of applause. Vogel shouted vigorous response.

Ocean, wincing quite a lot, carried on with the translation until the judge allowed her to stop. While she wasn't displeased Günter Vogel had gotten his case thrown out, she had no desire to congratulate the Frenchman, either. Why on earth had this even come to court, wasting everyone's time, when all he would've had to do was show the license to distill medicinal alcohol? Even though Ocean figured that in the end, the alcohol would find its merry way into men's, and perhaps a few women's, stomachs.

But what bothered her the most was the way Vogel's squinty blue eyes settled on her just before he left the room, glowering as if he considered her to blame. His tongue flicked out like the forked tongue of a poisonous snake, and he mouthed some words at her. She wasn't sure what. One was "You," and he added something else. A threat.

Ocean's blood ran cold. She shuddered, the thought chasing through her mind that she'd rather deal with Peck Peckham than this man.

Or no. She wanted nothing—nothing at all—to do with either.

Ash was waiting for her outside the courthouse, leaning against one of the pillars that held up the portico over the building's front entrance. Most of the crowd had cleared by this time, although she heard the farmer, Mr. Pence, telling someone how Günter had whipped his carriage horse as he retreated from the fiasco his claim had turned into.

"He's a mean man," he said solemnly, and the other man was agreeing.

"Sore loser," he responded.

Ash nodded toward the two and went down the steps alongside her. "Mr. Pence is right, you know. Vogel is mean, and a sore loser. He won't take this well. Does he eat in Seibert's?"

"He has, once or twice." Ocean forced a smile. "He complained about the prices." But remembering, her smile faded. "Did you see him glaring at me? He acted as if Judge Fedderer's verdict was my fault."

"I saw. Can you avoid him?" Ash asked, and going by his stern expression, Ocean thought maybe he hadn't much liked it.

Well, she hadn't either. "As long as he doesn't come into the café." A problem that kept her jumping at shadows as she walked home to the boarding house alone that night after work. Once, she even cried out when the yellow tomcat dashed across the street in front of her.

But in truth, as far as she knew, Vogel didn't come

into town in the following week. At home, licking his imaginary wounds, or so the scuttlebutt and accompanying laughter went.

Even Peck Peckham, also having disappeared, took a hind seat.

As for Ocean, well, she wasn't laughing.

11

BETWEEN THE TWO OF THEM, SHERIFF WELBURN and Ash kept a close eye on Ocean over the next few days, on the lookout for any steps Vogel might take against her.

"Kind of wish I hadn't told the judge about Miss Galliard speaking Polish, let alone those other languages," Early told Ash one day after he overheard another German farmer saying he didn't think a woman able to speak the truth. That he was certain she made most everything up and put her own words in the men's mouths. 'Is not right,' he'd said.

Ash, scowling, growled something unpleasant.

"Yup," Early said. "That's what I thought."

Upon hearing the story, Judge Fedderer agreed with their precautions, but it didn't stop him from approaching her at the end of the week with yet another pending case and, with some clever coercing, once again hired her translation services. "A Greek this time," he said to Ash when they met in the street, "one with the proclivity of shooting anyone who gets in fights and tears up his saloon. Especially if it means he'll have to buy a new mirror for behind the bar."

Ash laughed a little. Until he heard the rest of Judge Fedderer's plans.

"The trial will be in Colville," he said. "That'll take Miss Galliard out of town for this one. Since it's nothing to do with Vogel, he'll have time to get over spewing his venom regarding her. And don't worry. The defendant didn't kill anybody. It was just a flesh wound."

Ash hoped the judge was right.

They'd take the Monday afternoon stage over to Colville, Judge Fedderer announced, stay the night at a hotel and hopefully, get their business done in time for the return stage on Wednesday. If not, there'd be another night in the hotel. He didn't figure the proceeding would take longer than that. "I'll probably just fine the Greek. Make it costly enough for him to see he's better off buying a new mirror than paying a fine. The lesson might last a few months until the next time. But he'll have had his day in court. That's all he wants."

Ash, thinking it over, had a protest. Ocean taking the stage made him uneasy. He couldn't exactly say why. It just did. "I've heard about him. The Greek. He must speak English if he runs a saloon. Why would he need anybody to speak for him?"

The judge shrugged. "He speaks some. Maybe he thinks he doesn't speak English well enough to defend himself in court." He grinned a little. "I figure news of Miss Galliard has gotten around. Could be he wants the prestige of haven't a pretty young lady do his talking. He may think it'll bring him sympathy."

Ash didn't find anything amusing about the situation. "Don't forget Vogel has been going around making threats. I don't trust him. And Peckham, he's still on the loose, too. You and her both might make it onto their lists of folks to retaliate against."

Sheriff Welburn had an opinion about that. "Peckham ain't smart enough to write out a list."

"I wouldn't bank on that," Ash said. "I know he's dangerous, with or without a list."

Judge Fedderer waved aside their concerns. "Be assured I'll carry my gun on the road." He leaned toward Ash and added quietly, "I'm handy enough with it. You won't need to worry about Miss Galliard's safety."

Ash frowned. As if that was supposed to reassure him. What did the judge even mean when he said *handy enough?*

EARLY MONDAY MORNING, Ash happened to be standing outside Dobby's Hotel when he spotted a certain Mr. Allmann, one of Vogel's fellow churchmen and near neighbors, hauling eggs and butter fresh from his dairy into the building. On the off chance the man had heard anything new about what Vogel had been saying, he sauntered over to Allmann and began a conversation.

"Vogel was powerful het up at the judge's decision when Judge Fedderer denied his scheme to get hold of Ledoux's still," he started off when he doubled down on the conversation. "We, the sheriff and I, hope he's cooled off. The decision was fair."

Allmann nodded. "I know it vas. He did not come to meeting yesterday. His wife tells everyone he is sick.

I know he is not. But she says he is still angry, too. At the judge. At the woman who speaks for Ledoux. At the sheriff and all other peoples."

Ash figured those "all other peoples" included him.

"But then," Allmann added thoughtfully, "the fraú, she look guilty and hurries away like she should not tell anyone of this. He don't like her talking out of turn. Some think him crazy angry still." He spat into the street. "Günther has temper. Bad temper." He made a motion with his hands as if they exploded apart. Ash got the picture.

The meeting Allmann referred to, as Ash figured out after a while, was the weekly prayer meeting of the religious group both the men belonged to. A bit of a cult, from what he could tell, although this man seemed normal enough.

"Crazy angry, you say?" He eyed the farmer. "Do you think he might take steps against Ledoux? Or Judge Fedderer?" He hesitated. "Or even the translator?"

"Huh. Maybe. Better if judge stays away." The farmer shook his head. "Better for Ledoux and the voman."

Ash had to agree.

———

DISTURBED BY ALLMANN'S WORDS, he saddled Ranger and took a ride out that way right after their talk, just to see what he could see from a knoll overlooking the hog farm. Which wasn't anything out of the ordinary. For instance, the two-story house set a couple hundred yards off the road was kept tidy. To the side of the house, he saw a large garden spot with the soil turned within the last day or so, and sheets and shirts hanging from a clothesline. A quick look was all he could tolerate as the stench rising around the hog pens soon drove him away. As for Ranger, the horse kept snorting his displeasure halfway back to town. How did those folks abide living amongst an odor so rank?

But, normal and quiet as Vogel's farm had appeared, he worried right up until Ocean, almost running, arrived at the stage station right at one o'clock Monday afternoon with a small carpetbag in hand. She hurried because the stage was waiting for her out front at the passenger loading area, and she already had them five minutes behind time. The driver hustled her into the stage where Judge Fedderer had taken his seat, so Ash didn't have time for a last word with her. Only a wave of acknowledgment.

No sign of Vogel.

Ash gave a small sigh of relief as he stood in the dust of the departing stage. But he wouldn't be comfortable until Ocean returned. He confessed to an uneasy feeling that refused to go away.

———

THE STAGE SWAYED, bouncing when it fell into a rut deep enough to shake Ocean down to her bones. As it did all too frequently. Or maybe she shouldn't say bounce, she thought, since every drop to the bottom jarred her back until she felt like crying out. At this rate, she figured by the time they reached Colville, it would've rattled the teeth right out of her mouth and turned her skin black and blue. How did some of these other passengers, all older people, stand it? When she arrived in Clovis Creek last fall, the road hadn't been this bad.

She became aware of Judge Fedderer leaning toward her and saying something she hadn't heard. "Pardon me?" she said.

"The winter weather damages the roads with the melting snowpack," Judge Fedderer said. "With the drier weather, the county will be scraping these ruts down. Maybe even by the time we return to Clovis Creek."

She gave him a look. "Too bad this trial couldn't have been delayed until after they finished."

He'd claimed a seat across from her by the window. A strap hung down, and he'd latched onto it, holding himself from the beating passengers in the middle seats received. She'd had to shuffle around him when she entered the stage and took a center seat, only to be squeezed between a large man who reeked of cheap cigars, and a boy who looked and smelled like he'd missed his weekly bath by a month.

Ocean settled her skirt, hoping the odor wouldn't transfer onto her clothing as they rubbed shoulders and hips in time with the coach's sway. The man on the boy's other side simply stared out the window.

The judge didn't appear to notice the complaint locked inside her comment. He merely nodded and closed his eyes against the afternoon sun shining in through the window opening. She settled down to be miserable during the five-hour journey.

Across the aisle, the woman sitting next to the judge was staring fixedly at her. Though terribly outmoded, the bonnet she wore concealed most of her face. All

Ocean could see was a thin-lipped mouth and the gleam of narrow, almost colorless eyes.

She tried a smile, thinking a little conversation with another woman might help pass the time, but the woman sniffed and looked away. The man next to her pulled out a fat book—a bible, Ocean thought—and began reading. She couldn't imagine how he kept from becoming nauseous with the print most certainly jumping around. At least that woman wasn't crowded with four people in the seat.

Sighing, Ocean resigned herself to an uncomfortable journey and began speaking internally to herself in Greek, rolling the language over her tongue as if tasting a fine wine. It had been several years since she actually carried on a conversation in Greek. Practicing the nuances of another language seemed a good idea.

Hours passed, and despite herself, since she'd never been this way before, Ocean nodded off. When she awakened, the terrain had changed. Mountains still thick with snow appeared in the distance.

Patting into place a lock of dark hair jostled into falling over her right eye, she glanced over at the judge. "Still lots of snow in the high mountains," she said when he noticed her looking at him.

"Almost there." He pointedly ignored her comment regarding snow.

AT THEIR DESTINATION, she was stiff and sore enough to stumble on the steps. But not as badly as the judge, who actually groaned. And not as badly as her corpulent seatmate, who managed to bump into her.

Although Judge Fedderer had hired her to translate during this trial, he'd been adamant they not be seen hobnobbing. Folks might question his impartiality and her veracity in the translation if they were seen to confer—or so he said. Therefore, after checking into a room no larger than the hall bathroom at her boarding house, Ocean trailed down to the hotel dining room by herself to be seated at a small, a very small, table. Her knees barely had enough room to tuck out of the way beneath it. She felt quite lonely and out of place ordering a meal. But then she laughed to herself. Tried to, anyway. How silly. She worked in a restaurant. Nothing here was different enough to intimidate her. Nobody here knew her. Why should they? Why should she even care.

But then, seated at a table for six placed right in the middle of the room, she spotted Judge Fedderer. He was accompanied by a woman wearing a lovely forest green taffeta gown and a matching swirl of netting and feathers in her blonde hair. She was near him in age, as were the two other couples. Seated around a table spread with a snowy linen tablecloth, they were laughing at some tale one of them had told and sipping in a most genteel fashion from crystal glasses filled with a deep, dark red wine.

Ocean felt like fainting when she realized she'd seen one of the men before. It had been quite a long time ago in Chicago. She didn't remember his name. Hadn't known it, in fact. But she remembered her papá had called him Mr. Mark #22. The number had designated her father's twenty-second important grift. Papá had taken Mr. Mark for quite a large sum of money with one of his schemes, and Mark #22 hadn't been pleased when the perfidy was discovered.

Although she'd been starving only moments before, she quite suddenly lost her appetite. But then anger surged, heating the blood in her veins to the point she felt perspiration on her forehead. What was Mr. Mark #22 doing here, in a little western town like Colville? Why hadn't he stayed in Chicago, where a man with his interests belonged? Whatever his interests might be. Hadn't she come west specifically to escape people like him? Investors, they called themselves, always on the lookout for a profitable deal. Usually to the detriment of some naive innocent. People like Mr. Mark and her father, the pair of them, were not much different in their *business* dealings, in her opinion. Either of them would take your money in a heartbeat, their only difference being the size of the con.

As for Judge Fedderer, she'd thought him a small-town official, not so very urbane. What next? she asked herself. Would Deputy Ash Jones turn out to be the president's step-son or something? And why had she even thought of him? Stupid.

Studying a menu the waiter had handed her when she hadn't even realized he was there, she took care to keep her head down and turned away.

Surely Mr. Mark wouldn't recognize her. She was a grown woman now. Mark #22 happened a long time ago, when she'd just been a girl.

"Ma'am?" she heard the waiter asking.

Drawn from the thoughts ricocheting through her head, she glanced down. "Chicken and dumplings and a salad," she said. It was the first thing on the dinner menu. And the least expensive.

Also, as it turned out, not nearly as tasty as Ollie's. Leaving half of it, she made her escape from the dining room. No one seemed to notice.

———

THE NEXT MORNING when Ocean arose from the lumpy bed—one that made the thin mattress provided at her rooming house seem almost comfortable—she found an envelope shoved under her door. This must be a favored communication form of Judge Fedderer's, she decided wryly. And she didn't like it. Annoyed, she tore the paper open with the tip of her finger. The note, short and to the point, gave succinct directions to the courthouse and told her to be there ready to work at nine o'clock.

The hotel, though far from modern, bragged of a bathroom on each of the two floors that contained rooms. Taking due advantage—and thankful she'd arisen before most other patrons were awake—Ocean made her way downstairs in plenty of time to linger through breakfast in the nearly empty dining room. Having reclaimed her place at last night's tiny table, when she glanced around, she was surprised to discover the thin woman from the stage seated near the dining room door. The woman perched on her chair like a brown sparrow, ready to take flight.

A waitress stopped at the woman's table then, at what Ocean took for a sharp command, almost fled.

Under different circumstances, it could've been funny. The woman certainly didn't appear to be making friends. She was drinking what looked like tea, but had nothing in front of her to eat. Something about her expression made Ocean wonder if the prices were too dear for her pocketbook. She certainly didn't seem to be enjoying herself, and her gaze as it settled on Ocean was as cold and steely as it had been on the stage. And every bit as penetrating.

Ocean had the uneasy feeling the woman was keeping a close watch out for someone, and that someone was named Ocean Galliard. Why? Wracking her memory, she didn't think she'd ever seen the woman before yesterday. She'd certainly had no dealings with her, and that must mean the woman was acting for someone else. Who?

What little appetite she'd had disappeared. Worse, even though she'd been running drills in Greek through her mind, she worried whether she was up to the task ahead.

Ash Jones had watched the stagecoach bearing Ocean and Judge Fedderer leave Clovis Creek in a whirl of acrid dust abrasive enough to start him coughing. "Folks ought to demand the town-fathers put down a load of gravel," he muttered to the man standing next to him.

"Or the stage company. Send the bill to them." Olson, also coughing, worked in the hardware store next door. He'd just helped pile a coil of chain in the vehicle's baggage area to be shipped to Colville. "I hear the road is bad all the way to Colville. Hope the stage doesn't loose a wheel going through the pass." He coughed again. "Might be enough to cause the judge to speak to somebody about some grading. He's got clout, doesn't he?"

Ash didn't know if Judge Fedderer had clout or not, though the possibility of a lost wheel plagued him all night. Not so strangely, he forgot about the road when he got to the sheriff's office the next morning. Vogel's neighbor, Allmann, already occupied a chair across from Welburn. They were waiting for him.

"Mr. Allmann's got a story you might find interesting," the sheriff said to Ash, motioning him toward the other chair. "First, how about you tell him what you noticed at the Vogel place yesterday."

"Huh. Mostly the stench." Ash, needing coffee to clear his head, fetched a couple dippers of water from the pail on a stand by the door into the jail and used it to start a pot. Sitting, he told Allman about his ride to Vogel's farm. "Not much going on. I didn't see anybody."

Allmann nodded. "You vas maybe there at the wrong time," he said. "After I see you last morning, I take a barrel of sour milk over to Vogel. He buys it to slop his hogs. I seen something then. I seen someone."

Ash's ears pricked right up at the mystery Allmann implied. "Yeah? Who did you see?"

The farmer sat taller. "I see Peck Peckham. Him and Günther, they vas standing behind the voodshed, vhere nobody can see them from the road. But me, coming in the back vay, I see them. And I see Marta Vogel there, too. All talking."

Early and Ash exchanged an uncertain look. It seemed unlikely, a hog farmer and a ranch hand cattle thief and murderer, chatting away like friends.

After a moment, Early said, "Are you sure it was

Peckham? Were they arguing or did they seem friend-ly?" Fair questions.

Allman waved his hands. "Didn't nobody start shooting. And I am sure. I seen Peckham before, lots of times. He used to come tell us to keep our cows from mixing with Sleeper's." He snorted. "Problem is not my fence. Is his. Peckham is lazy and Sleeper, he does not care anymore. I got Jerseys. Do not want them mixed with beeves."

Welburn and Ash shared a glance.

Frowning, Ash asked, "This Marta Vogel—who is she? Why would she be there?"

"I do not know why she is meeting them. I only am saying what I see. As for Marta Vogel, she is Günther's sister. She is not married. Not ever." After a moment, he added. "Is not a nice woman. Her eyes, they are sharp like ice picks. Poke holes in you." He made a gesture like stabbing someone.

Ash sucked in a breath. He'd seen a woman just like that only minutes ago. "This Marta Vogel, is she tall and scrawny? Hair in a tight bun going gray, and wearing a funny cap over it? Don't look like she smiles much?"

Allmann nodded. "Sounds same."

"Does she travel by stage often?"

"Never heard of it." The dairyman shrugged. "Far as I know, she don't go anywhere. Not even to meeting much. Only comes outside to work and glare at people who pass Vogel's farm gate."

A cardinal sin, Ash surmised as he and Early exchanged another look. Why would this woman be getting on the same stage as the judge and Ocean? Especially right after having a confab with Peck Peckham, who'd been reported to have skedaddled the territory?

Only one reason occurred to him. Vogel had a grudge, and Judge Fedderer had been on that stage. And Ocean. And Peckham wouldn't balk at murder for hire when he heard Judge Fedderer cleared Dzik.

Allman left then, saying it was coming on time to milk his cows. The sheriff and Ash thanked him a couple times for the information, although Welburn stared after him as he strode toward the small buckboard he was driving.

"Vogel may not know it," Welburn said gravely, "but he's made an enemy of his neighbor. Not smart with the trouble he's stirred up. Allmann probably figures he's next in Vogel's sights."

"Right after Ocean and the judge," Ash said. "But Vogel and Peckham? That's a pair to reckon with."

Welburn snorted. "Best not forget this Marta person either, from the sound of things." He took a deep breath. "What would you say, deputy, to taking a ride over toward Colville first thing in the morning? I understand the state of the road is something terrible. Maybe you can persuade the feller in charge of county roads into grading the ruts out before they get any worse."

Ash stared at him. "Me? Is that my job?"

Early tapped his desk. Another thought seemed to occur to him. "Or if you'd chance to meet the stage and the driver says he's a little worried about a hold-up, you can just ride with them the rest of the way back."

"Sure thing, Sheriff."

The sheriff gave a little hitch of his shoulders. "I can depend on you to do what needs done to keep order in this county. Whether we're talking about roads or outlaws."

"You bet." Yeah, even when it required a gun in his hand, Ash reflected, which may have been Early's intention. He'd left the way open for whatever Ash found.

"That's what I figured." Welburn nodded.

12

MADE AWARE OF THE GRIM-FACED WOMAN'S STEADY regard by a certain tingling in her bones, Ocean finished her breakfast—what she was able to eat—and rose to make her escape to the courthouse. No sooner had she stood up than the woman gathered her own legs under her and also rose.

Funny how old habits returned, familiar as combing her hair, Ocean thought. The careful watching from the corners of her eyes, the stopping to stomp a foot as though a stone had somehow lodged inside her shoe. All meant to create the opportunity to look behind her. She spotted the woman trailing several yards back. The woman stopped when she did. Started walking again when she did.

Yes. She was being followed and not very professionally. Why? And all the way from Clovis Creek? It didn't make sense. This wasn't the kind of woman Papá's enemies would send after her. They'd all be considerably more circumspect, and all would be handsome, though not so stunning as to draw special attention. The premise held whether for male or female.

No. They'd be more like the man Judge Fedderer had been speaking with at dinner last night.

Besides, if Papá's enemies had tracked her to Clovis Creek, they'd know she hadn't once been in contact with her father during all the time he'd spent in Joliet prison. She'd covered her tracks well. Even Papá didn't know where she'd gone—at least as far as she knew.

However, it occurred—and not for the first time—that he was due for release sometime this month, which might have some bearing on the reason the woman watched her so closely. There'd been a lot of money the authorities had never found. Perhaps someone believed she had it.

Well, she didn't.

Ocean shuddered at the mere thought. Thoughts so overwhelming she arrived at the Colville courthouse almost before she realized. Mounting the steps, she pulled open the door and entered, taking one more look behind her. Yes. The woman was still there, holding back until Ocean went inside.

Letting the door slam behind her, she worked her way through the lobby and hall until she reached the assigned courtroom at the back of the building. There she found a large, dark-paneled space with little sunlight to brighten it. Appropriate, most probably. From there, she wended between backless benches to the front where the sheriff, recognizable by the star pinned to his vest, sat beside a man wearing a neat suit and an ultra-stiff collar. The man she assumed was her client slouched beside them. The client looked Greek, going by his dark hair, olive complexion, and flashing eyes almost as dark as her own. Flamboyant, too, with a red, green, and black plaid suit and a flowing tie. Appropriate for the owner of a saloon, she imagined, if too loud for her taste.

The sheriff glanced up at her as she stopped beside him. "Miss Galliard?"

"Yes."

The other two men eyed her appreciatively.

He motioned to the neatly dressed man. "This here is Aaron Helman. He's taken on the chore of defending the Greek. This other feller is the Greek, Dimitris Galanos." The sheriff made short work of the introductions. "I'm Sheriff Burnside, in case you didn't guess."

He'd have been disappointed if she'd said she hadn't known his name ahead of time, so, nodding cordially to everyone, she pretended she had.

"*Yassas, kyria*," Galanos said, leering just a little and speaking in Greek. His dialect stemmed from around Athens. "Are you going to be honest in repeating what I say?"

Ocean replied in kind. "I'm always honest. I do request you keep your comments clean."

He laughed, which made the sheriff, the attorney, and everyone standing nearby stare. Galanos had a boisterous laugh. It made them seem like friends. She frowned, uneasy with the thought.

Helman dragged a chair over from the table across from them and motioned her into it. "You'll sit with us until you're called to the stand with the defendant, Miss Galliard," he explained, puffed up a little to show off his importance. "Once the trial starts, you're to repeat anything Mr. Galanos says, as well as everything the other side says. Be sure to keep your voice down. It's not for you to become excited and upset. You're here only to speak his words and repeat the other's words to him. Do not add anything of your own."

She gave him a stern look. "Yes. I am aware of the procedure." Did he think she was an utter fool? Surely he knew she'd done this before, with her efforts proving satisfactory.

He had the sense to clamp his own mouth shut. By then, a man who performed the same duties as Ned Hazenberger back in Clovis Creek entered the room and announced Judge Fedderer's arrival. They all stood as he entered and took his seat behind an oak stand, then everyone sat. He pounded the gavel as a signal to begin.

Ocean took the opportunity to cast a glance around the room behind them. The woman from the stage, her cold gaze fixed on Ocean, was still there. She sat primly on a bench somewhere in the middle of the crowd, elbows askew to keep anyone from crowding.

The prosecution went first. While the attorney laid out the events leading up to Galanos' arrest, the Greek studied her in an admiring kind of way. Unable to help herself, she rolled her eyes. He smirked.

Watching him, Ocean felt certain he understood the proceedings very well and, unworried by it, had decided to enjoy flirting with her. A game he'd have to play without her cooperation. Ocean smiled, but shaking her head, she lost no time in translating the prosecutor's opening remarks. Galanos didn't turn a hair. Once, he winked at her.

Her lips compressed into a firm line, a sign so he'd know she meant only business. He pouted after that— for all of thirty seconds, right up until a man approached from a side door and whispered in the judge's ear. Judge Fedderer straightened, glanced at Galanos, then beckoned the sheriff and the two attorneys forward for a discussion.

Galanos' demeanor changed in an instant. He didn't like this. "What is going on?" he asked, as if Ocean should know.

She shrugged. "You know as well as I do," she said in English. Whispers filled the courtroom. Apparently, none of the bystanders knew either.

A bang of the gavel shut them all up as the others returned to their seats. The judge cleared his throat to make an announcement.

"Jeremy Moore, Mr. Galanos' victim, has died. The doctor states an infection in his wound is what killed him." Judge Fedderer's voice carried well in the room. "The charge against Mr. Galanos has changed from assault to murder. We'll take a recess to determine how to proceed due to these changes. Court will reconvene when I've decided." He turned to Ocean. "Tell him."

Ocean gasped. She had to confess it took a moment for her to find her voice. Repeating the judge's words to Galanos, she knew that, at first, Galanos didn't understand. He shook his head. Then the significance sank in, and he did.

"*Óxi*! No!" He leapt to his feet, his denials growing louder as he realized the game had soured, the stakes grown higher. Slower to move, she rose and stood beside him, wary of his wild speech. From his expression, he hadn't expected this to happen. He shouted curses, even as his attorney tugged the hem of his gaudy suit jacket in an attempt to control him. The sheriff grabbed one of his arms and twisted it behind Galanos' back, struggling to fix handcuffs on him. Unsuccessfully, as it happened.

The uproar in the room behind them almost drowned him out as his denials grew. "Not me. I did not kill him. I wounded only. That was weeks ago. This is different. Not my fault if he took no care." Galanos shouted the words, and this time, she thought that he really had lost his English, for he spoke only Greek. Then, worse, he said, "He deserves this death. His fault. His. Not mine."

Ocean, dutiful to the terms of her employment, repeated his words. All of them. Only later, after it was all over, did she realize perhaps she would've been better off to veer just a little off course. No one would ever have known. Except Galanos, of course, and upon his further reflection, he probably would've demanded not just a veer but a total course correction. Not for her sake, but for his own.

Then everything changed. Someone in the crowd with a voice even louder than the prisoner's shouted words Ocean had hoped never to hear again. "Get a rope," he was saying. "Jeremy Moore did not deserve to die. He was a good guy."

"Yeah," someone else roared. "He just got a little drunk."

"A little rowdy." Agreement, lost in a chorus of voices.

"Having a little fun."

"What's another of Galanos' fancy mirrors? He probably uses them for target practice himself." This brought forth laughter, but it wasn't kind. The noise grew more insistent.

Ocean looked over at Galanos, who'd fallen silent.

"Do you understand them?" she asked in English. She didn't forget to use Greek. It was a simple test.

He grunted. His face froze in a rictus grin. "I understand."

She'd been certain he did. The lark was over. As for the sheriff, he'd given up on cuffing his prisoner. In fact, to Ocean's astonishment, instead of putting down the riot, he was standing back, his expression curiously blank. He hadn't made a move to quiet the fracas. Mr. Helman, the attorney, she saw as she turned toward where he'd stood at the judge's platform, had disappeared. So had Judge Fedderer, whisked away by the bailiff, she supposed, at the first sign of trouble. She wished they'd taken her with them.

The first fellow to suggest hanging—Ocean saw him now—stood on a bench waving his fists and bellowing about the rope. "Who's got a rope? Anybody?" Others were backing him up. Unlike the other day in Clovis Creek, no hardy deputy or foolhardy girl protested. Dimitris Galanos didn't appear to be a popular man in Colville. Maybe the residents hadn't liked his smirk. She hadn't liked his smirk.

One part of her noticed that people had been running out of the courtroom, although the steely-eyed woman, instead of escaping the mayhem, retained her seat, smiling as if enjoying some bizarre kind of entertainment. A half-dozen or so men crowded forward in a surge that brought them closer to where she and Galanos stood. The next time she looked for the sheriff, exactly like the attorney and the judge, he'd disappeared.

To get help? She thought not.

Just then, a fellow wearing the traditional red plaid

shirt, short pants, and heavy boots of a logger burst through the crowd. He leapt in front of them, carrying a rope over his shoulder.

"Got it. C'mon, boys." It was a cry of triumph, and the ringleader standing on the bench jumped down to lead his followers on.

Ocean stood stock still, as if a rigid posture would form a defense around her. And for seconds, it held. Right up until Galanos flung an arm around her neck and clasped her to him.

She couldn't help herself. She screamed.

"Shut up," Galanos shouted in her ear. He pressed hard on her throat, shutting off her wind and dragging her backward in the direction the judge and the sheriff had taken in their escape.

The mob, surprised by the action, hesitated.

"C'mon," the logger yelped. "He ain't armed. Let's take him."

"I'll kill her," Galanos shouted desperately. "I will strangle her."

The logger shrugged. "String him up. Payback for him killing Moore."

Somebody laughed. "Pay him back for watering drinks and cheatin' at cards."

A deeper voice said, "Bet his safe is filled with the money he stole from us."

"We should look."

"*Should* look, hell. We *will* look."

"Yeah!" A whole chorus echoed this opinion, and soon a chant arose saying, "Hang him. Hang him high." And again, "Hang him. Hang him high." And again and again as they surrounded Galanos.

And her. They had no thought for her, struggling to breathe.

All they needed, Ocean's thought skittered through her mind, was to set their chant to music. Meanwhile, she grew weaker, gasping for air as Galanos, choking her into compliance, used her as a shield against the crowd. Her hearing seemed to be failing as all she could hear was his steady stream of Greek curses.

Where is the sheriff? The question resounded in her head. *Why isn't he here? Why isn't he helping me? Where is Judge Fedderer?* She thought she knew the answer to all the wheres, whys, and whats. Plain and simple, they were all cowards. Her mind's eye drifted to Ash, as if the vision of him might help her.

Then, quite suddenly, Galanos' grip fell away. She fell, too. Dropped to the floor, gasping for air, when first one, then more kicks, shoved her aside. Pain soared in her hip. In her belly. With a renewed roar of sound, two men took Galanos from behind.

He fought. Hard.

Ocean, managing to scoot into a corner formed by the dais where the judge had sat, watched in horror as the men pulled him down. Someone yanked his flowing tie from around his neck and tied his hands with it. Pummeled, his nose bled, his lips bled, a gash opened below his eye. He sagged like a collapsed corn dolly when the logger punched him in his belly. Not once, but several times. Men roared their appreciation. Some laughed. The women fled—mostly.

Then they dragged him out of the room, and for a couple seconds, she thought to rise and flee, as well. And later, when things calmed, she'd confront Judge Fedderer and the sheriff. She'd tell them exactly what she thought of men who'd leave her to be made into yet another victim.

She'd grabbed onto the railing around the dais to help herself up when yet another rough hand grabbed her arm. An arm already bruised in the tussle. She gave a pained cry.

The man looming over her appeared unmoved. "Get up," he growled. "You're coming with us. You're gonna tell us his last words."

"No." She tried to pull away. "I'm done. I don't care what he says."

"We do."

She struck out at him, intending to flee, until he slapped her hard enough to run the side of her face into the railing. More blood flowed. Her's this time.

Willy-nilly, he dragged her along, through the now-empty room and outside into the street. The noise of the crowd echoed between buildings. Ocean, peering ahead, caught sight of Galanos as the mob dragged him toward an old giant fir. The intended hanging tree, she supposed. His struggles looked weaker now.

And there, standing at the edge of the crowd, the steely-eyed woman stood alone. She had her eye on Ocean, and she was smiling.

By the time Ocean and her *escort*—she put the word in quotes—caught up and he had pushed their way to the front, the logger's rope had been formed into a noose and looped around Galanos' neck. His olive complexion had gone ashen, and now, probably for the final time, he'd lost his English. But he was talking. Fast.

"What's he saying?" The leader of the rabble looked at her, his expression eager. "Tell him to give us the combination to his safe."

She stared at him. Shook her head.

Her escort jerked her back and forth a few times. Jerked her hard. "Tell him." Her neck popped, making her go dizzy.

Ocean, reeling, turned to look him in the eye. "I don't work for you. My job was for the judge. You'd best let me go."

His arm drew back.

Oddly enough, it was the logger who stopped him. "Better off if you help, ma'am. Don't want you gettin' hurt. Some of these fellers are gettin' kind of rowdy." A master of understatement.

"I've already been hurt," she snapped, her fury and fear growing.

"I can hurt you worse," the escort threatened.

The logger scowled at him. "We'll pay you," he said. "So now you're workin' for us."

Some of the mob agreed, others did not.

Without warning, Galanos began screaming as a big, dark-bearded fellow came up to him and poked the blade of a pocket knife in his thigh. Then he withdrew it and poked again, this time right below the Greek's eye. Blood flowed.

"Stop it," Ocean yelled. "Stop it. This is wrong. You know this is wrong."

They laughed. Laughed.

"Talk for him, for us," the bearded one said. "Or I will do it more." He edged the blade's tip into Galanos' belly.

Did she have a choice? Ocean wondered. Bad enough to hang, but torture? Would it be her fault? Or would she be next?

She talked, repeating his curses, his excuses, his

pleas for life. At one point, his bladder released, turning his pants dark. And at last, she repeated the combination to his safe for them. Several in the crowd took off running. To the Greek's saloon, she supposed, where he kept the safe. Hurrying then, no doubt reluctant to be left out of the pay-off, the logger and the loud-mouthed instigator yanked Galanos' feet out from under him.

They left Ocean standing alone with a still twitching corpse. She wept.

13

By late that morning, Ash had begun to show signs of worry. He paced the jailhouse floor incessantly when he wasn't cleaning his .44 or just sitting with his fingers tapping the top of his desk.

Sheriff Welburn did his best to keep his deputy occupied. Early's nerves, having reached their limit of tolerance, had sent Ash on several extra circuits of the town just to get him out of the office. It's all he could think to do. But here Ash was, back again much too soon.

"Most likely, the trial will be over today. Judge Fedderer didn't think it would last long." The sheriff took out his pocket watch and glared down at it. "Might be done with the trial already. First thing in the morning, you can ride on out and see what's happening," he reminded the deputy. Ash had been pestering the daylights out of him to start out today.

"Won't do any good since there's no stage today." He sighed. "You can't expect them until tomorrow at the earliest."

"I know." Ash's uneasy feeling had been gaining strength. For some reason, he'd been extra antsy all day. He worried something had gone wrong. He couldn't forget that evil-eyed old biddy who'd gotten on the stage to Colville with Ocean. So, whenever he wasn't tromping around town looking for troublemakers, he paced.

"Quit your dangnabbed flibbertigibbeting around," the sheriff finally snapped. "Keep it up and you'll wear a hole in the floor. Go home. Pack some extra duds or something. Curry Ranger and Daisy. I can handle it here."

Ash made his plans, thinking he'd meet the stage about halfway. He'd turn around and escort Ocean and the judge back to Clovis Creek if they were on it. If they weren't, he'd continue on to Colville and see them home when they were ready.

Somehow, he got through the night.

THE MORNING PROVED FINE. Daybreak found him on the road, sunshine in a cloudless blue sky warming him. He appreciated the clean air and scent of pine once he escaped the pall of smoke that lingered over the town. Rutger's sawmill was burning scrap, a regular irritant. On the road, a hawk wheeled overhead while smaller birds hid in the brush and twittered in fear. Once, a coyote slunk across the road in front of him, causing Ranger to shake his head.

Ash laughed. He might not like the reason for the ride, but he prized the opportunity to be on the trail. It had been a while since he escaped the beck-and-call aspect of his deputy job. Ranger, a reliable animal not given to flighty starts, left him free with plenty of time to think. About being a deputy, for one thing. About his chances of being killed one of these days, for another. The almost healed wounds still itching his belly served to remind him death could come at any time. But mostly, his thoughts drifted to Ocean and the mystery she presented.

For instance, how had she come to be in this no-account little Washington town? She made her living waiting tables in a café where the boss disliked her, yet Ash figured her for an educated woman. Most surely, only someone with great learning could speak so many languages. He'd always admired anyone who could maybe speak two, like some of the cow hands who knew a little Spanish if they'd been down in Texas or California. But four or five or...who knew how many?

Why wasn't she using her talents in some big city where she'd be well-paid for her expertise instead of the pittance Judge Fedderer intended on paying her?

Although, he remembered, she hadn't wanted anyone to know she spoke any at all. Only an innate sense of fair play had made her speak up for Artem Dzik and his son.

Ash continued to puzzle over Ocean Galliard's reluctance as he rode. A couple hours later, the landscape began to rise. They were passing through an area where the trees grew thicker, and huge boulders overhung the road where deep ruts made even Ranger step cautiously to keep from stumbling. He figured the stage to have shaken the passenger's innards to jelly in this section. How the driver managed to traverse this trail three times a week was beyond him.

He almost looked forward to a fiery talk with Bert Schuyler of the road department while he was at the county seat. Bert did like to argue. But not now. If he had his druthers, he'd meet the stage and escort Ocean and the judge home all fine and dandy.

Speaking of fire, he pulled up when the scent of a campfire reached him. Ranger, almost as good as a dog when it came to being aware of his surroundings, pricked his ears off to the right. Ash looked where his horse indicated, spotting a cloud of light gray smoke wafting through the trees.

The idea of someone camping that far into the woods struck him as odd. This wasn't hunting season. Nor was it a particularly scenic area, with a lake or stream to serve as recreation. Got cold at night, too, which meant a campfire necessary. Any traveler caught overnight here would normally have moved on by this time of day, though one might've carelessly left his fire burning.

It behooved him to investigate. Carefully.

Back in the old days, this area had been notorious for robbers who preyed on unsuspecting lone travelers. When Welburn took over a sheriff's responsibilities, between him and Ash, they'd pretty much cleaned them out of this end of the county. Men like Peck Peckham had found cattle rustling easier and more lucrative.

Dismounting where he could tie Ranger out of sight, Ash set off on foot, following his nose. Soon the curiously muffled sound of a woman singing a ditty, one well-known in the saloons and brothels, put the birds to shame. That is, it shamed them into flight.

He came upon a horse picketed nearby. A nice

sorrel with a familiar brand on its hip. The horse belonged to the Lazy ZZ. Just beyond the horse, the singer was sitting on a flat rock with her head tilted downward as she swished a brush through her hair. A brassy brown cascade hung over her face in a veil, hiding her from Ash—and Ash from her.

Easing through a few low huckleberry bushes and clumps of bear grass with hardly a ripple, he stepped into a small cleared circle. Ash cleared his throat. "Ahem."

She went on singing and brushing.

He tried again, louder this time. "Ahem! Ma'am."

She froze, but only momentarily. Long enough to take him by surprise when, fast as any gunslinger, she spun around, flipping back her hair at the same time as she snatched up the small revolver that must've been right there on the rock beside her.

She even fired off a shot before Ash got out of the way. A near miss, the bullet thunked into a tree bare inches from his shoulder. What really irked him was that he recognized her as the same damn woman who'd peppered him with buckshot.

Peckham's whore. What was she doing out here in the woods by herself?

Or was she by herself?

Not that he had time to delve into the question at the moment. The pistol's recoil had sent the barrel upward, giving him time to take a flying leap at her. A stretch, but good enough to knock her off the rock.

She—they—hit the ground like a load of sand, causing her to lose her hold on the gun. It flew off somewhere out of reach. But now the problem, aside from the scratching, biting, knee to the groin, and plain old punching the harridan was doing, she also screamed like a Celtic banshee. If she kept it up, he figured to be deafened.

"What's the matter with you? Shut up!" he panted, thrusting her as far away as he could without losing his grip. Hard doing, the way she fought him. He rolled, she rolled. Shoving her back to arm's length, it became apparent they'd gotten closer to the campfire during the struggle than intended. Too close, as her long, unbound hair—and she had a lot of it—started sizzling and shriveling.

He clapped her alongside the head where the sizzling was worst. "Your hair's on fire, you stupid woman. Hold still."

It got her attention. This time her screams changed in timbre, from belligerent to panic. "My hair," she screeched. "Ow. Ow. Son of a bitch." A string of stronger curses blued the air, a sign she belatedly felt the heat. She left off hitting him, sat up, and began slapping at her head instead. She stopped, shook her hands, then slapped some more. "Is it out? Is it out?"

His nose wrinkled in distaste. The hair stunk, but he couldn't help saying, "Woman, you could use a bath." Regaining his feet, he backed away, "Yeah, it's out. What are you doing out here by yourself?"

Ash didn't miss the shifty way she looked around. He figured she was looking for her gun. "None of your business," she said.

"That's where you're mistaken. See, there's a warrant out for you. You, your female friend, and Peck Peckham. Where is he, anyway? You waiting for him to show up here, by any chance? Maybe you've got a meeting planned?"

Her eyes, a kind of frosty pea green, widened. "Me? Why would I be waiting for them, whoever it was you said? And a warrant? Mister, I don't know what you're talking about. You don't know me."

Ash couldn't help chuckling. She was transparent as glass, making it easy to tell he'd guessed right about a meeting. "Oh, I know you all right. Hard to forget somebody who shot you in the gut."

"It wasn't me." She blinked. "I mean, really? Somebody shot you in the gut?"

He just looked at her. Did she truly think he'd failed to recognize her? Even so, he almost wished he hadn't come looking for the source of the smoke. Now, he had to arrest her and take her back to Clovis Creek when he'd rather be looking out for Ocean Galliard and the judge.

"What's your name?" he demanded. Information good to know and make the arrest official.

Evidently, she'd already forgotten his complaint about her needing a bath. She sidled toward him and smiled coyly. Been more effective, he thought, if she'd brushed her teeth lately. Or ever.

"My name is Belle," she purred. "What's your's, handsome? Would you like to diddle, get your mind off what you think I might've done?"

He declined to dignify that question with an answer.

"You know who I am and what you did. You're under arrest. Get your things together, Belle. I'm taking you back to Clovis Creek, where Sheriff Welburn is just itching to have a talk with you. Got a fine jail cell waiting for you there."

"Jail cell?" The screech was back. "You can't do that."

"Sure I can." He nodded around. "Pack up your stuff and throw a saddle on the horse you got tied to that stunted tree yonder." He studied it a moment. "One of Sleeper's, I see. His heir might wonder where the critter got to. He's apt to complain about horse thieves."

"Sleeper's?" she said like she was innocent. "That's my horse. He was given to me."

"Yeah? Who by?"

She clamped her mouth. "Roy."

She was lying. Roy Sleeper, as Ash well knew, hadn't been the kind of man to consort with women like her, let alone give her a horse. Aside from his getting a bit long in the tooth for her services. But she did have to be here for some reason. "Is Peckham coming back for you?" he demanded. "Or did he dump you out here in the middle of nowhere to get rid of you?"

"I dunno what you're talking about." She'd started over to where her little revolver had landed, doing her best to appear as if she was following his orders.

Well, he guessed she was. Sort of. Stepping past her, he picked the gun up from where it had dropped into the middle of a pile of pine needles and shoved it into the waistband of his britches.

He'd get Belle back to Clovis Creek as quickly as possible, then have Early come back with him. He'd ask Early to wait here, out of sight—to see if Peckham showed himself—while he'd ride shotgun with the stage. If the sheriff hadn't seen any sign of Peckham by then, they'd ride back together while making sure Judge Fedderer and Ocean were safe. Afterward, knowing Peckham was near, they could begin a search for him.

But for now, as badly as he regretted turning back to Clovis Creek, he had to take care of Belle. The delay made him wish the smoke and the singing had gone unseen and unheard.

AFTER THE HANGING, Ocean sidled down the street toward the hotel, staying close to the buildings in hopes it made her harder to see. At least the mob's attention seemed fixed elsewhere. Down the street, at Galanos' saloon, the mob still roared their excitement, the sound coming in waves. Hard telling if they'd opened the safe yet, or if they had, what they'd found, but it seemed likely they'd broken open his supply of booze and were helping themselves. Liberally.

It hurt her to walk. Or even to breathe. Her hip bore a deep bruise, her stomach ached, one shoulder hurt to the point she could barely raise her arm above her waist. She thought she might have a cracked rib. A cut along her cheekbone was still oozing blood from being rammed into the dais' railing. An errant thought arose. Would she have a scar to remember this nightmare by? Did a scar matter? How much better if she ever managed to forget.

Finally, she managed to limp into the shelter of the hotel lobby. Over where a floor-to-ceiling stone fireplace filled most of the room's eastern corner, she spotted Judge Fedderer, Galanos' errant attorney, and Sheriff Burnside. Two other men sat with them. One of the others, going by the badge he wore, was a deputy. The other was the man she'd seen Judge Fedderer with last night at dinner. The one she'd recognized from

Chicago. They were huddled around a table in the darkest part of the room, relaxing, drinking coffee while a riot and a lynching went ignored outside. A brandy bottle stood open before them.

She heard somebody chuckle, as if at a joke, and the rest joined in.

Fury rose in a burning rush.

If she'd been able, she would've stomped over to their table. As it was, she hobbled, almost as quietly as a ghost. Stopping at Judge Fedderer's side, she stood face to face with Sheriff Burnside, the first to look up and see her. Burnside's mouth snapped shut. He stared at her as blood rose in a red tide to paint his face.

"You," she said. Her voice hardly rose above a whisper, her throat so tight she had to force out the word. The rest came easier once she got started. "What kind of man are you? A sheriff, sworn to uphold the law? No. A coward, running away at the first sign of trouble."

Their collective indrawn breath sucked most of the air out of the room.

"See here—" he started.

"Shut up," she gritted. "I'm not done with you."

Beside her, Judge Fedderer stirred. "Miss Galliard, I must ask you to refrain from wild speech. What just happened—"

She cut him off, too. "You. You're no better." Her gaze shifted to the attorney, Mr. Helman, dismissed him with a curl of her lip, and went back to the judge. "You ran like scared little bunny rabbits, all of you. Sneaked out the back exit and left me to fend for myself without a word. Such fine gentlemen and upstanding citizens." The need to draw breath stopped her for only a moment. "Are you aware that Galanos is dead? No trial.

No defense. Not one single effort to stop a mob from taking him." She glared at the sheriff again and glanced at the deputy to make sure to include him. "They tortured him first, you know. They didn't kill him until he gave up the combination to his safe so they could take the money they're sure is in it. Confiscate it, someone said. Hah! Then they put him up on a block with the noose around his neck and kicked away the block. The fall didn't break his neck though. It wasn't high enough. He strangled."

She paused, but they had nothing to say. The man from Chicago shifted in his chair as if uncomfortable. He was frowning.

"He pissed his pants. You should've been there to see. All of you. You should have been there. Maybe you would've enjoyed the sight as much as the mob did." Ocean couldn't stop herself from talking, her horror from flooding out. "Maybe you would've laughed to see what they did to him, like you were laughing just now. The mob, they wouldn't let me go since they needed me to translate. I thought they were going to hang me, too, afterward. But no. They just knocked me down and trampled me. It must have been quite an amusing show to see. A real comedy. Oh, yes. You should've been there."

Judge Fedderer rose to his feet. He reached out to her, but she brushed him away as if he were a fly on vomit.

He swallowed. "Hush now, Miss Galliard. I'm sorry. I admit it. We should have taken you with us. I actually thought you were following us out. I'm sorry. We're sorry."

Her gaze traveled around the table. The men sat

like statues, mouths shut tight. "That's it, Mr. Fedderer? You're sorry?" Still, she waited. No one else spoke. She made a funny sound halfway between a snort and a disillusioned chuckle and spoke one word none of them understood, which she declined to translate.

"No, you're not," she said, studying them one by one. "You're not sorry at all. Each and every one of you. You're glad I was the victim instead of you."

Her shoulders straight, she stalked away—as much as her badly bruised hip allowed her to stalk. At the stairway, she stopped, the height seeming insurmountable in view of her injuries. Then, almost sobbing, she grabbed hold of the rail and began pulling herself up.

Ocean had never felt more alone. Not even when— her father in prison, her cousin dead, and the rest of the family already scattered and in hiding—she took the train west. The more remote, the safer she'd be. Papá's victims were bound to want revenge. On her, if they couldn't reach him. Or so she'd thought. She hid in plain sight, moving on from town to town, never staying long in any one. She'd made herself small to escape notice. But not sneaky. People notice sneaky.

And it had worked for three whole years. Until Sheriff Welburn, Ash Jones, and Artem Dzik entered Seibert's café that night and everything changed.

Apparently, there was no real safety anywhere.

In her room, Ocean lay on the bed, hoping to ease her aches. It didn't work. Neither did closing her eyes in hopes of blotting away the scenes imprinted there. Her strained and abused muscles tightened, the pain growing steadily worse. In the hall outside her room, she heard a woman saying to someone farther along that she was done with her bath if he needed the room.

"No," he replied. "I'll wait until evening."

A bath. It sounded just the thing to ease her soreness. Forcing herself onto her feet again proved no easy task. She gathered up towels, soap, and clean clothing—thank goodness she'd brought a change. At first, she hadn't planned to. But now there were rips in her third-best dress, along with blood and filth from squirming on the ground while that man kicked her. She couldn't bear them on her body a single minute more. Or no longer than it took to get to the bathing room.

To her delight, Ocean discovered the hotel had hot running water, an amenity she hadn't enjoyed for months. Her boarding house had nothing so progressive, utilizing a galvanized tin tub for bathing. The same one all the boarders used for laundry. She'd had to fill—and then empty—the tub herself after folding herself in half to fit inside. The men took themselves to the barbershop to bathe in the community baths once a week or so. The women had no other choice than the wash tub.

Here, she lay back full length and let the hot water wash over her. If only it would wash away the visions of Galanos strangling at the end of a rope. They kept reappearing and she couldn't make it stop.

Finally, a heavy thump on the door and a "get a move on in there" roused her from the horror. Her fretting over speaking Greek after so long a time last night seemed silly now.

But she sat there anyway as a sudden realization poured over her. What had she done? She'd accused the sheriff, his deputy, the attorney, and—God help her—the judge of cowardice and dereliction of duty, that's what. True, but oh, so awfully unwise. She'd let her rage bury her good sense. These were powerful, well-known, and respected men. She was a nobody. Worse, though not accused of a crime herself, she was the daughter of a criminal. Who would listen to her if her past became known?

These were men who could deny, and they would be the ones believed.

It was time to move on. Another town, another state, another job. Another hidden life.

And Ash Jones. She'd be leaving him behind, too. Would it matter to him? Did it matter to her?

She thought it did.

Heavy in heart, Ocean rose from the tub and pulled the drain plug. It took only minutes to dry and don her clothing.

Heavy-hearted or not, frightened for her life or not, she refused to stay in her room any longer. She planned on the most expensive meal on the menu charged to the county. They owed her that much, and she was going to take it. She'd demand her pay, too. And while she'd have to go back to Clovis Creek to collect her few possessions, afterward, she'd go. Maybe west, toward the coast. Or maybe east, toward Montana. Even south, to California. Maybe instead of a small town, she'd see what Los Angeles had to offer. Find some place where she knew no one and no one knew or noticed her. Hide in plain sight. And never again let on to anyone about her ill-fated abilities as a translator.

In the night, she dreamed of Ash. And awakened with tears clinging to her lashes.

14

"What are you doing back so soon? It's hardly gone ten o'clock." Sheriff Welburn looked up from the paperwork he was laboring over and peered across his desk. According to a stain in his mustache, he'd been chewing on the end of his pencil. Then he took another look and shot to his feet. "Well, lookee there! You've caught the woman who shot you. Shot us. How'd you manage that, Ash? Where'd you find her?"

Ash, who'd had about all his ears could tolerate of the woman's caterwauling over the last couple hours, blew out a relieved breath at making it back to Clovis Creek alive. Huh. With her alive.

"This is her, all right," he said, neglecting to elaborate, "and now I'm turning her over to you."

Since Belle had taken up a mile-a-minute speech with which she may, mistakenly, figured to draw the sheriff's sympathy, Welburn's glee was already turning to dismay. By the end of the first minute, his mouth hung open, and his eyes bugged like a grasshopper's. "She always talk this much?"

Ash shrugged. "Pretty much all the way from just this side of the pass. I got an idea on how you can get away from it if you think Ned can put up with her chatter." He paused a second. "And her stink. She smells like she's been sleeping with polecats."

The sheriff's nose twitched. He nodded. "What's your idea?"

"Mount up and ride with me, Early. Right now. I found her camped out where the woods thicken and that big outcropping of boulders overhangs the road. Just about where those two traveling whiskey salesmen were held up last year. I figure she was waiting for Peckham to join her." He frowned. "I'm guessing they plan to hold up the stage."

The increase in loud denials coming from Belle's mouth proved to convince them both that his guess was good. They turned to stare at her.

Early glanced out the window to judge the time. "Tomorrow, about this time."

"Best opportunity we've had to catch him."

"And Judge Fedderer and Miss Galliard are likely to be on it." The sheriff's eyes narrowed.

"Yes."

"I'll see if Ned can hold down the fort while we're gone. He's probably getting..." Early, who had returned to staring at Belle with a puzzled frown, changed what he had started to say. "Uh, Ash, what's the matter with this woman's hair? It looks kind of...frazzled. Burnt?"

Another story Ash had to tell before they could all move on.

Ned Hazenberger, when contacted about keeping an eye on the town and the prisoner while they were gone, admitted he'd heard all his wife had to say ten times over in the last couple weeks. "I learned how to shut out that kind of noise after a while. This'un won't bother me none."

"Sounds to me like going a little deaf is a piece of luck, Ned," Welburn said. "Yours and mine. But Ash and me, we got a lead on Peck Peckham's whereabouts, and we got to take advantage."

"Sure," Ned said. "Him and his pals have caused enough trouble around here. You go ahead and get him, sheriff. I can take care of this town just fine."

Ash and the sheriff headed out on the trail an hour later. Their idea was to be on hand when Peckham got to the campsite, which could be at any time between now and when the stage was due in the afternoon.

Ash didn't like the timing. Welburn didn't either, which was why they pushed their horses hard. Neither admitted as much, but both were considerably excited.

***

WHEN THE NIGHT finally turned into morning, Ocean was glad of it. The town had settled down quickly after the hanging and subsequent mob demolition of Galanos' saloon, maybe in an embarrassed reaction to events that got out of hand. Not that she knew what people were saying. Ocean had kept to her hotel room for the most part, never venturing beyond the dining room to take her evening meal.

Perhaps that was why she was taken aback when it came time to board the stage for the return to Clovis Creek. Waiting at the station, she spied the woman who'd kept her pinned under an iron gaze when they left home two days earlier. The woman who'd watched the trial and smiled.

Only two days? It felt like weeks.

The driver, keeping to schedule, opened the coach door for them to load. Ocean led the way, making slow work of the two high steps due to the pain lingering in her hip. The woman mounted the steps into the stage-coach practically on her heels, crowding close behind Ocean, near enough to feel hot breath on her neck.

Near enough, in fact, to snag the shoe right off Ocean's heel. The tug had been deliberate, she knew. A try to trip her. And after all that had happened, she'd had enough of acting Miss Retiring Nice Lady. Turning to the woman and seeing a smirk as though daring her to say something, she complied.

"Back off." She sounded like a lioness snarling.

"Move along," the woman said right back, obviously undeterred by the snarl. "You're taking too much time and holding me up."

"I don't care," Ocean snapped and, spreading her arms so the woman couldn't get past, proceeded to take a great deal longer than necessary.

In the act of boarding, the woman had somehow crowded Judge Fedderer into taking a place behind her. He gaped at Ocean to the point she expected a repri-mand. To her surprise, he nodded slightly and took her part.

"My dear Madam," he said, though the steely-eyed woman was no such thing, "we have plenty of time. There's no need to push and shove or to be rude. The stage won't leave without us." Something—regret?—in his tone indicated there was one passenger, if left behind, would leave his feelings intact.

Perhaps the woman had gotten on his nerves with her infernal constant staring. Unless, Ocean couldn't help thinking, *she* was the one he'd prefer to leave in the dust.

There were only four people in the coach for the trip to Clovis Creek. Three women and the judge. Judge Fedderer sat across from Ocean, taking the place deliberately as if to guard her from the pugnacious woman. The third woman, besides Ocean and her nemesis, already looked travel-worn. She wore an old-fashioned veiled hat over blonde hair, and a flowered shawl over a workaday dress of plain blue chambray. Shyly, she took her place, sitting as far from Ocean as possible. Her nemesis sat across from the shy one. They were able to spread out.

Ocean, for one, was happy not to be crowded this trip. She still hurt too much to contend with the jostling of a full-capacity load. She hadn't seen Judge Fedderer since the evening before, when she'd gone to the dining room and ordered the most expensive thing on the menu. Then, she was able to eat only about a third. He'd paid her bill without a single angry word. She refused to feel guilty. Or repentant. It wasn't her fault the job had petered out—if that's what one would call an impromptu hanging.

But she was uncomfortable under the judge's studious observation. "You don't look well, Miss Galliard. Are you in much pain from your injuries?"

Beside him, evil lady—or Nemesis, as Ocean had taken to calling her—perked up.

"I'm fine," Ocean said. She wouldn't admit any weakness, no matter what, even though her hip and ribs still ached dreadfully. Worse, she knew black shadows lay beneath her eyes, and her cheekbone bore an unsightly scab from where the railing had scraped down to the bloody parts. All in all, this had been a rough couple of days.

At least sitting next to a window allowed her to see out. She'd never been to Colville before. There'd been no point. Setting her mind to enjoying the scenery, the first hour or so passed quickly. Starting into the second hour, not so much. The horse's hooves roiled dust into clouds that found a way into the body of the coach. Grit burned her eyes and got in her mouth. The judge mentioned to them all that although smoother, the dust would be even worse when the county finally graded the ruts into submission.

"So we may count ourselves lucky," he said.

Ocean, unable to decide which would be worse, was surprised when the nemesis spoke. "I suppose they have paved roads where you come from," she said to him. "Chicago, isn't it?"

"No," he said coolly, "Joliet." He didn't answer the part about paving.

Joliet. Where Papá is in prison. Ocean remembered the man the judge had dined with, the one she recognized as one of her father's best cons. Could there be a connection? As if to hide, she huddled deeper into her seat. That position is what allowed her to spot a rider spurring his horse down a steep incline toward them. He seemed determined to head off the stage in a narrow part of the road. Shockingly, he was waving a gun above his head and shouting.

Then she heard a shot as he fired at the sky.

"*A holdup!*" She cried out the warning.

Two shots sounded, then more as he scattered a

shot into the woods, another over the stage team's heads and one into the body of the coach. No matter. She saw him holster the empty gun and draw another, presumably loaded. So. They were being robbed by a gun-happy outlaw.

Judge Fedderer, in watching the robber, didn't leave himself enough time to reach the revolver he'd bragged about having handy. The male robber shot right through the coach window, taking the judge out first thing. He collapsed in a heap, crumbling against the leather seat. Blood blossomed in a wide stain across his dark coat. The noise—Ocean guessed it was the noise—of the gunshot set the shy female passenger to screaming and carrying on. Her noise proved a strong distraction.

The outlaw, judging by this little exhibition, was a darn good shot, Ocean thought ruefully. Something Judge Fedderer must not have taken into consideration.

She heard the stage driver protesting loudly from his seat outside. The stage rolled to a stop, so apparently, he was still intact. But he had not taken any action to stop the highwayman. She wondered about that.

The robber dismounted and, strutting like a cock pheasant, approached the coach and flipped open the door. "Howdy," he said. "This here is a holdup. But I 'spect you figured that out already."

As for Ocean, she took the seconds between the robber exhorting everyone to put their valuables in a little bag he passed around, and all of them obeying, to observe the passengers' varying reactions.

The judge, breathing with suppressed pained gasps, looked to have suffered a serious wound. "This is a bad idea," he told the thief, his voice barely audible but still commanding.

"For you," the thief said, "not for me," and chuckled. He wore a dirty neckerchief over the lower half of his face, but from the way his eyes crinkled, she knew he was smiling.

"No. For you," Judge Fedderer said. "If not now, later. Count on it." Defiant to the end, the judge's reaction surprised Ocean. He hardly seemed the same man who'd callously abandoned both a prisoner and a translator to the mob. Still, she thought him unwise to rile the outlaw. For her and the other two women's benefit, if not his own.

As for Nemesis, she turned white and set to making a funny "mmmm" sound. One might've thought she had taken the bullet instead of the judge.

The little velvet bag contained very little when it came to her. A few silver dollars, the judge's gold pocket watch and fob the outlaw snatched from his vest, and an incongruously jeweled necklace nemesis woman wore hidden under her clothing. How had the outlaw even known—or guessed—she had it?

But come to find out, although he took what he could, the thief had another object in mind.

Her.

But the shy woman puzzled her most, right up until Ocean caught the exchange of meaningful looks between her and the thief. That was when the woman produced a gun from under her skirt, pointed it directly at Ocean, and said, "You. Get out of the coach."

And when Ocean was slow to obey, she swung herself out and prodded her into submission with the barrel of the gun without missing a beat. Nothing shy about her now.

They hadn't even troubled to pass the bag to her. Nemesis still moaned. The judge lay quiet on the seat. His eyes were closed. Ocean didn't know if he was dead or alive.

"What do you want with me?" she gathered her courage and demanded. "I haven't done anything to you."

"Like hell." With an angry motion, the outlaw whipped the kerchief off his face. "It's your fault I'm on the run. Now you owe me. It's your turn to pay up."

"Me? Owe you? I don't even know who you are." Although she had a very good guess.

"Huh. If it hadn't been for you understanding Dzik's lingo, that Russkie would've been hung, and nobody would've questioned whether he killed Sleeper."

"Until the next time you pull a stunt like that," she retorted. "Which men like you always do."

He shook his head. By now, he'd remounted and, from somewhere, gathered the reins to a couple spare horses. One for the *shy* woman and, as it turned out, one for Ocean. His demands weren't spur of the moment, she realized. The abduction had been planned.

"Git on." He gestured at the horse.

She shook her head and watched the woman swing her skirts awkwardly into the old saddle, gracing the other's back. The man she knew must be Peck Peckham grinned down at her and pointed his gun into the coach at the judge.

"Do it, woman. Or I finish off the judge. Or shoot the woman." He paused, "Or you."

Ocean's dark eyes flashed. No choice occurred but to clamber into yet another worn saddle. It looked as if the outlaw had ransacked a trash pile.

Peckham cocked his pistol. "I stole that horse just for you this very morning. She's nice and fresh." Glancing around for his woman accomplice, he found her already aiming at the judge.

"Hurry up. Let's go," she said.

Grinning, Peckham shoved his gun in the holster and, leading Ocean's animal, spurred his horse into a lope straight up the steep hillside. Then, once they reached the top, horses' iron-shod hooves clattering over the stony ground, they rode straight down the other side.

Ocean, mad enough to chew horseshoes, could do nothing but cling to a high saddle horn sure to punch her in the gut if she leaned too far forward and hope not to fall off. Her ribs and hip, already hurting at every touch, set up a steady, pulsing ache. She almost wished Peckham would just shoot her. It's what he had in mind anyway, wasn't it?

They rode north, toward Canada.

15

Ash surveyed Belle's abandoned campsite with a jaundiced eye.

Earlier, when he'd hauled her off to Clovis Creek, he'd allowed her to take along what she'd called her luggage. In other words, a pillowcase carrying a dress, probably stolen from some clothesline, and some knickers. She'd been wearing trousers when he found her. But they'd left behind the few rudimentary cooking items, like a battered pot she'd used for everything from boiling coffee to warming tins of beans. There'd been an enameled plate, a couple spoons, a ragged towel, and a grubby blanket.

Now they were gone. The rope where she'd picketed her horse dangled from a low tree branch. The bark had been ripped from the tree as if someone jerked the rope free in a fit of temper. The only thing remaining was a scattering of wood chunks turned to charcoal.

He started to curse before cutting himself short.

Grimacing, Early watched him. "Somebody else got

here first. Probably Peckham. We missed him." He added a couple cuss words to Ash's.

There were footprints visible where a horse had emptied its bladder, and a man on foot had walked through the wet. Ash pointed.

Welburn looked. "That a notch in his boot heel?"

"Yeah. It's Peckham's all right." Ash didn't figure he'd forget Peckham running out of the house and himself sending a bullet after him. Boot-heel, he thought in disgust. The way Peckham had limped off to mount the horse that woman brought around, he'd thought the shot had been a little more useful. Except, they hadn't found any blood.

Not that they'd looked real hard, since Early and himself were leaking enough fluid on their own at the time.

"Huh," he said sharply as another memory of that day occurred to him. "I wonder where the other woman is now. The one that helped Peckham and Belle escape. Remember, Early? We keep ignoring her."

Welburn snapped his fingers, a habit he'd formed after the shooting. "Right. She dang near burned the place down. I almost forgot her. Kind of busy dodging the other two, as I recall."

Ash squinted into the sky, judging the time by the position of the sun. "I got a feeling we'd best not forget her. Turned out she had more to do with their getaway than Peckham did. Smarter, too, so's she didn't call attention to herself. I doubt she just rode off by her lonesome after she rescued them." He paused a moment, thinking. "Makes me wonder if she might be on today's stage along with Judge Fedderer and Ocean."

The sheriff, in the act of uncorking his canteen,

gaped at Ash. "On the stage?" Then a second or two later, "Could be you're right. Dammit! We should've thought." He took his drink, recorked the canteen, and hung it from his saddle. "Stage ought to be nearing the pass about now. We'd best get down to the road to meet it before Peckham does."

Seemed to Ash that more likely they were a day late and a dollar short. His thoughts turned sour. They'd dallied around—arranging this, ordering that—and gotten a late start. Had they actually figured Peckham would wait until everything was set to their satisfaction? Stupid! Some kind of lawmen he and Early were. They both deserved to be fired.

They had no idea when Peckham had cleaned out this campsite and gone to meet the stage. That's assuming it was Peckham and not some wandering down-and-outer. Might've been as soon as the stage cleared Colville for all they knew. That's *if* he'd even gone to meet the stage. On the other hand, maybe he hadn't at all. Maybe all this with Belle was a simple distraction. In which case...

He didn't believe it.

The two of them didn't talk much as they spurred their horses into a lope. Urgency rode with them. A justifiable urgency as minutes before they hit the main road, they came upon a horse running loose. It sported a collar with trailing lines still attached.

"Recognize the nag?" he asked Early.

"Yup. He's from one of Patterson's teams." The sheriff sounded grim. Well used to seeing the animals hauling the stage, there was no mistaking this one as he bore the stage company's brand on his hip. Leather straps dangled along his withers, showing the traces had been deliberately cut, not a victim of worn equipment.

Silent, Ash put a rope on the horse, noticing the the dried sweat.

"An accident?" Early asked, but not as if he believed it.

"No."

Leading the horse, they continued down the road, going at a lope. A couple miles farther on, they spotted the stage. It sat in the middle of the road like a pumpkin cut from the vine. No horses were hitched to it, although Ash saw two of the team had been caught and tied in the shade. Looking closely, he spied a man and a woman sitting on the trunk of a fallen tree. A space of three feet or more separated them. Judge Fedderer? Ash wondered. Judge Fedderer and Ocean? But he knew it wasn't her. This woman had considerably more bulk than Ocean's slim figure. Moreover, going by what looked like a white mobcap covering her hair, he thought it the same bitter-appearing woman who'd taken the stage with Judge Fedderer and Ocean three days earlier. That's if his eyes weren't fooling him, and he knew they weren't. But where was Ocean?

That was the first thing he asked, his throat tight enough to choke a crow. "Where's Ocean? Miss Galliard?"

Judge Fedderer's answer came slowly. He squinted into the sun and stared up at Ash and Early like a blind man. "He took her. Peckham took her."

Ash's guts seemed to twist into a hard knot. Had anyone even defended her? He figured not.

That's when the Vogel woman spoke up, as harsh and bitter as ever. "The whore helped him. We should've known she was up to no good. I could tell just by looking."

A flush of anger nearly consumed Ash. "The whore?" he said, real soft, and all the more dangerous because of it.

Hastily, Fedderer intervened. "We had another passenger on board this morning, Jones. Turns out she was helping Peckham."

"A blonde woman?"

The judge nodded. "Yes, as a matter of fact. A shy, retiring young woman. But with a hard face," he added as if just realizing the fact.

Early sighed. "Me and Deputy Jones wondered if she'd turn up." He paused without explaining further. "You've been bleeding, judge. How bad are you hurt? And where's the driver? Peckham shoot him, too?"

"A flesh wound, I'll be fine," Judge Fedderer said, although he twitched as if in pain, and his eyes looked a little glazed. "Miss Vogel here got me patched up. As for the driver, he's off looking for the other two horses. One of which," he added, "I see you've found for him."

"The driver is a coward," grim Marta Vogel snarled. "He should've shot that man dead when he had the chance."

Ash agreed, although he didn't say so. For that matter, why hadn't Fedderer? Something to take up later, he determined. Getting after Peckham to free Ocean is what concerned him now. "Which way did Peckham take her?"

"Pardon me?"

"Miss Galliard. Ocean. Which way did Peckham take her?"

Miss Vogel shrugged as if it didn't matter.

Judge Fedderer said he didn't know, but then Ash noticed the way his gaze went straight to the top of the hill rising behind them as if seeing them disappear over the crest. A lot of bare ground and huge boulders there, looming over the road where they stood. It was the only almost treeless stretch for miles. Ash had been told those outcroppings were left behind by gigantic ice masses moving through the area thousands of years ago. He didn't know if he believed it or not, but what he did know was that the terrain would make Ocean harder to track. Because no matter what the judge said now, Ash figured he knew where to start looking.

Meanwhile, the sheriff had another question.

"How'd the Greek's trial turn out?" Welburn asked.

And the judge, still looking off in the distance, the words pulled slowly from him, answered.

The reply set Ash to fuming and made Welburn, aware of his deputy's rage, clasp his arm in an iron grip and shake his head.

"Won't do you no good," he warned, his voice low. "And it sure won't keep Ocean alive."

"She's hurt, Early. Hurt, and Judge Fedderer played possum without lifting a finger to help her." Ash didn't bother to hide his fury.

THE AFTERNOON WORE ON. Twice, after first mounting, then plunging down that steep, barren hill to reach flatter, less rocky ground where more trees grew, at Peckham's growing agitation, they stopped. First, because Peckham decided he had to relieve himself, immediately, after all the excitement. The second time because the woman said she had to go.

"Take this one with you," Peckham said, indicating Ocean. "I don't want to stop again. Not until we get to the shack."

"All right, all right." The woman—Ocean had heard Peckham call her Jillie—slid lithely from the horse and motioned Ocean to do the same.

How it hurt, even easing into each movement. However, according to Jillie's impatient, "Hurry up. I'm about to pee in my good drawers," she moved like an old granny.

Ocean didn't care a thing about Jillie's drawers. But, confession time, she not only needed the break, but she felt like an arthritic old granny.

Jillie led them off behind a double-trunked fir tree with low-hanging branches. "This'll do," she said.

"Here?" Ocean looked around.

"Here. Squat. Anyways, you ain't got nothing Peck hasn't seen before."

"No doubt," Ocean agreed.

At least they seemed to be out of Peckham's line of sight.

Ocean would've laughed if she hadn't been so scared. Laughed at the sight of the woman struggling to keep a heavy revolver pointed at her, lift her skirt, and pull down her drawers all at the same time. This would've been the perfect opportunity to run, she figured, if it hadn't for Peckham sitting his horse not thirty yards away keeping his eyes and ears open. All Jillie had to do, even if Ocean wrested the gun from her and ran for her life, is was make one warning squeak.

The trees were still fairly sparse on the steepening

hills, the forest having fallen victim to fire sometime in the recent past, most probably last fall. The underbrush had yet to regrow. No place to hide that she could see, but still too easy to get lost. Worse, she didn't think she was able to actually run. Even lowering herself to do her business had brought pained gasps at the effort.

Later, she resolved, fighting her rising panic. There'd be a time later, when she felt stronger. When more hiding places presented themselves. When someone came looking for her.

If anyone did.

Meanwhile, they rode farther and farther away from the road. She was afraid she was losing all sense of direction. How far were they from Clovis Creek? How far from wherever Peckham was leading them?

Maybe it didn't matter, because Peckham, as he crested another of those everlasting hills, let out a bellow loud enough it startled the horses. "Son of a..." He stopped, gaping at the hillside ahead of them. "This weren't here two years ago."

"You was in jail two years ago," Jillie said, but almost as an afterthought as she was staring, too. Her face set. "What do we do now, Peck? Go back?"

"Go back? Hell no. We go on."

"Over that?" Jillie sounded appalled. "The horses won't make it, and I ain't going on foot."

Peckham eyed the expanse and finally shook his head. "No. We go around."

Ocean gazed at the broad stretch of tumbled rocks, uprooted bushes, and fallen timber barring their way. To the left, a deep canyon opened in the earth. She heard water running at the bottom.

IN THE END, they did go back, but only to where they were able to cut around the rock fall. Peckham grumped about the delay. Jillie grumped about her plug of a horse that kept stumbling on loose stones and yanking her hither and yon. Ocean applauded the time it took to backtrack in hopes Sheriff Welburn or Ash might hear about the robbery and shooting and come after her.

They would, wouldn't they? A persistent little voice kept asking that question.

But meanwhile, her horse stumbled along as well, wrenching her hips and ribs and rubbing her thighs raw. Unable to stay sitting upright, although she'd been taught to ride alert and erect, she sagged in the saddle. Her teacher, as she remembered, had clearly never expected Ocean to face circumstances like these.

Eventually, they passed beyond the rough section. Underway again, the blonde woman sang as they rode. Ocean's nerves reached a point when Jillie's voice began to grate worse than chalk screeching across a slate. As for Peckham, for a while, he applauded Jill's efforts—until he didn't.

"Enough, woman," he said like a dog growling. "You sang that same song six times already. Let's have a little peace and quiet. Let the birds do the singing for a while."

Ocean was surprised he had that much sensitivity.

"I'll sing if I want," Jillie retorted. "Folks say I sing good enough to be on the stage."

"Yeah?" Peckham snorted. "The stage to where?"

Ocean, whose sympathies lay with Peckham in this case, stifled an unexpected surge of amusement at his deliberate play on words. Credit where credit was due. But if the woman's singing irritated, the subsequent quarrel the two fell into afterward raised the hair on her nape. Back and forth they went, Peckham now gulping from his flask, his eyes reddened, his words loud and slurred.

Jillie had her own smaller flask, and while she didn't hit it as hard as Peckham, she grew careless. Ocean didn't believe the woman's heart was really in tune with Peckham snatching her from the coach and carrying her along with them. She had the sense Jillie would've been happier if he'd just plain shot Ocean dead, same as he had shot the judge. Although Judge Fedderer might not *be* dead. He'd still been moving last she saw.

"You ain't using good sense, Peck," Jillie whined. From Peckham's flinch, he didn't care for her opinion. But the woman seemed oblivious. "Why don't we just make her dead now? Throw a few rocks over her—Lord knows there's plenty around—and nobody'll ever find her body. What're you gonna do with her anyways? I don't wanna see anything too nasty. I'm a lady, ya know. That's why Belle shot that sheriff and the deputy. She don't mind blood."

But she wouldn't mind if someone else did the deed, Ocean thought.

"Well, I wish Belle was here and you was there—wherever she is—just as much as you do," Peckham groused. "You bitch and moan around worse than my old granny's ghost. I'm tired of listening to you."

At this, for some reason, Jillie went pale, although it didn't take long for her to recover. "What you gonna do with her?" she asked again two minutes later, meaning Ocean. "I don't wanna take care of her no more."

Ocean could barely breathe. A plain question.

"If you know what's good for you, you'll do what I say." Peckham, sending a deep scowl her way, then told Jillie to keep Ocean between them. Which meant Jillie would be riding in the dust—if there'd been dust—and she didn't like being last. Twice, Ocean lagged behind, until Peckham looked back and, drunk or not, yelled at the blonde to tend to her business.

Then she yelled back about this all being stupid. That if Peck had a brain, they all would've been in British Columbia by now, Belle included, free as the breeze.

"Yeah, and free of you, too," Jillie added when she thought he couldn't hear.

And Ocean agreed he probably couldn't as he had no reaction. On the other hand, maybe he was just ignoring the woman, especially when she said, louder this time, "But no. Not you, Mister Smarter Than the Law. Now Belle is gone, probably in jail, all because you was careless enough to get caught rustling and had to go and kill that old rancher. Which didn't turn out like you expected, did it? That sheriff and his deputy, they weren't as dumb as you made them out."

"Shut up," he snarled, turning in his saddle to glare at her. He'd obviously heard her this time. His hand crept to the six-shooter in a low-slung holster and rested there. Then, slowly, it moved away. "Just shut up."

Jillie had seen, too, and wisely closed her mouth on any more jibes. For the moment, at least. Ocean sensed turmoil behind the woman's darting eyes. Eyes that always came back to stare at Ocean. Seeing pure evil in the stare, her heart pounded.

The swigs Jillie took from her flask grew more

frequent. The reins in her hand went slack, her horse stretching his neck to snatch at the grass growing in clumps alongside the trail. Ocean stuck with Jill's pace. They lagged farther and farther behind Peckham, who, busy with his own flask, paid the women no mind.

It was the longest two hours of Ocean's life.

Just before dark, they came upon an old cabin set with its back almost touching a rocky cliff. The cabin, in rough shape with two window openings but no windows, an abandoned stove but no stovepipe, and a single doorway but no door, allowed a plain view into the interior. It had probably been built by some enthusiastic miner back when folks thought there was gold to be found in this neck of the woods. Needless to say, it hadn't panned out with any gold rush. Ocean had heard customers at the café talk about it, dating from twenty or more years in the past. As it turned out, a little gold was still found in the creeks running through the area, but never enough for commercial mining.

"Home again," Peckham said as if the place was a mansion. He pulled his horse to a stop and dismounted. "Well? C'mon, woman. Get a fire going. I'm hungry."

A ring of stones surrounded the remains of a campfire. A metal rack of some sort made a level cooking area where an unwashed skillet and a smoke-blackened coffee pot sat.

Jillie muttered under her breath. Something along the lines of, "This ain't what you been promising me, you lying batwing."

Ocean had never heard of calling someone a batwing.

Louder, for Peckham's benefit—and maybe to impress their captive—Jillie said, "I ain't a maid. You want a poke, I'm your girl. You want a fire, build it your own self." She took her time getting off the horse, looking around as if she expected a lackey to appear and help her.

"I'm taking care of the horses," Peckham said. "Lazy bitch."

This time, the quarrel lasted all of ten minutes. Long enough for Ocean to gather her wits and examine the area around the cabin. She thought Peckham didn't plan on killing her tonight. In plain fact, now that he had her, he appeared not to know what to do with her. Kill her now? Later? Have his girlfriend do the dirty work? Or did he have some other horrid plan?

If he depended on Jillie's cooperation, events might have to wait until they'd both sobered up. Which meant Ocean needed to get away tonight. She supposed one or the other of them would be charged with keeping an eye on her, but with the amount of white lightening each had consumed during their flight over the mountain, she had doubts either would be able to stay awake and alert. She'd go then. Saddle up the nag she'd been riding for a good part of the day and skedaddle as quickly as those four legs could carry her.

If she could find the way down the mountain.

"Well, don't just stand there. What are you, an ijit?" Jillie's hand slammed across her face. Struck hard enough, she almost fell down herself when Ocean staggered back from under the blow.

She'd been studying their back trail, taking note of the line they'd taken through the woods. It would be hard to see in the dark.

Jillie drew her arm back for another go, but Ocean skipped away in time to avoid the blow. Didn't avoid the pain in her hip though. She pushed past the blonde woman and found a stump to sit on. Peckham, she saw, had gathered all three horses' bridle reins and was leading them off to the side where a small corral was built around a spot free of trees. He wasn't paying her or Jillie any mind.

Not that she was to have any peace with him gone.

Jillie stood in front of her, hands on ample hips, her face a blotchy red. "Lay a hand on me again, Miss Hoity Toity, and I'll snatch you bald-headed."

"Unless I do you in first," Ocean retorted and, prepared this time, easily dodged Jillie's lunge.

Missing her target enraged Jillie so much she must've figured another drink from her flask was in order. Finding it empty, she flounced off and entered the ramshackle cabin. In a few seconds, she appeared in the doorway, a jug in one hand, her flask in the other. Shaking a bit, she poured contents from the jug into her flask, spilling as much as she saved.

Peckham came around the side of the cabin then, and quick as a weasel, Jillie hid the jug inside the cabin and stowed the flask in a skirt pocket.

Interesting. Ocean's eyes narrowed. So Jillie was sneaking the hooch, or at least the quantity she drank, evidently because Peckham didn't approve. Not of her drunkenness, at any rate. Or maybe he just wasn't willing to share his liquor. Very interesting.

Something, perhaps, to use to her advantage.

16

"You ride on up that hill, Ash, and pick up Peckham's trail while there's still a sign to follow." Sheriff Welburn gave orders no different than what Ash already itched to do. Planned to do, whether Early agreed or not. But he was glad the sheriff had the same opinion.

They stood aside from Judge Fedderer and the Vogel woman and spoke in quiet voices. Neither of them wanted Marta Vogel to overhear their plans considering her smirk when Patterson, the stage driver, told about the way Ocean had been dragged from the coach. Ash burned when Judge Fedderer didn't defend her.

Welburn glanced over at Judge Fedderer, who ate up the Vogel woman's attentions as if it were his due. "I'll have to stay here and help get the judge and Miss Vogel back to Clovis Creek. Plus, Patterson ain't gonna be able to mend this harness by himself. We'll have to jury-rig something to get the coach over the pass."

Ash didn't like the idea. Seemed to him the judge

could manage what with the woman hovering over him like he was some kind of hero. A hero who hadn't even gotten his pistol out to protect Ocean like he'd bragged about before they left town for the trial.

Ash knew that prior to Welburn being elected sheriff, he had made his living as a harness maker. His most lucrative business had been in saddles. The one on his own horse would've been beyond his means if he hadn't created it for himself. It made sense for him to be in charge of getting the coach horses back into a cobbled together rig and on their way. All four animals had been retrieved by now, Patterson having returned leading the last missing horse shortly after they arrived.

"I'll raise up a search party as soon as I get back to town," he assured Ash.

Ash had been thinking. Seemed to him a search party running willy-nilly all over the mountains might just put Ocean in more danger.

If she wasn't dead already. He couldn't stop the thought from banging around in his head.

A better plan would consist of just him and Early taking to the hills. They'd move faster, quieter, with more authority than a mob of men on more of an old boys get-together than men bent on rescue. He'd been on a search party before, and that's what it had been. A party. Only finding the body of the missing youngster had quelled their gaiety. And even then, when sobered, they'd been proud of their efforts.

"We don't need a big bunch of men raising a dust and making a racket." Answering Early's questioning look, he explained. It didn't take Ash long to present his idea. "Remember the Hasslebeck kid?"

Early, his lips clamping vise-like under his bushy

mustache at the reminder, nodded. "I do. He might've lived if we'd found him sooner. He hadn't been dead more than a couple hours."

"Too many men riding at the pace of the slowest horse. Too many arguments to settle."

Gritting his teeth, Early nodded. "All right. You've convinced me. I'll leave Ned in charge of the jail and come by myself. Me and maybe Lloyd Carson, if he's available. He's quiet, steady, and a dang good tracker. And he has a hound he swears will track whoever or whatever Lloyd tells him to track."

Ash had seen the dog in action and agreed. Delaying only long enough to check over his ammunition supply and make sure his canteen was full, he mounted Ranger.

"We'll meet up sometime tonight. Or in the morning at the latest," the sheriff promised. "And Ash, don't you take any unnecessary chances. We'll find her."

Yeah, but in what condition? The possibilities chilled Ash.

"Fair enough. I'll leave a sign for you." Nudging Ranger, he started up the hillside. It was a simple matter to follow where the three horses in Peckham's bunch had fought their way to the top. On the other side. That's where the going became slower, the sign harder to follow. He didn't look back.

DEFIANCE DIDN'T SERVE her well. Ocean discovered as much the next time Jillie decided to show-off her strong left hand. It left an imprint on her face and a trickle of blood at the corner of her mouth, a fact remarked upon by Peckham when he noticed. It had also nearly knocked her unconscious. The woman was as strong as a billy goat.

"What do you care if I have a little fun with her?" Jillie demanded sourly. "I don't know why you didn't up and kill her back there with the judge. She's slowed us down all day."

"I told you I got plans for her." Peckham's expression indicated he didn't like being questioned. The thing is, Ocean would've liked to know those plans, too. Or maybe she wouldn't, except necessity demanded she learn what to expect, for better or for worse. But as long as he kept delaying, she still had a chance to live. To get away. Or so she tried to convince herself.

Tonight. The word kept running through her mind, although it was hard to concentrate over the ache in her head and lingering pain in her hip. She'd have to escape tonight. And meanwhile, buck up and take the abuse. Avoid Jillie's anger, if possible. No more back-hands. Wait. Let them think her cowed.

"Look what you done to her purty face, Jillie. Scab her up too much and we'll lose out. Could be I'd have to substitute you for her. Quit fooling around and fix us some supper. I told you I'm hungry." Peckham lost his jovial mood and became serious.

His plan? Ocean could only think of one thing that might require her to be unmarked.

"Purty, huh? What plan?" Jillie glared. Even she seemed to realize she might've gone too far, that Peckham's suggestion might become reality, but she wasn't one to give in. "Why don't you make her cook? She can be our slave."

Peckham seemed to consider the suggestion, but just for a minute. He shook his head. "Naw. I don't want her getting ahold of a knife. And you," he scowled at Jillie. "Make sure you don't leave the knife where she can get at it. Next thing you know, it might be stuck in you." His eyes bugged. "Or me."

The prostitute complained loudly, arguing about cooking not being her job, although Ocean had yet to work out exactly what Jillie's job was—aside from abusing her. Somehow, with blonde hair streaming down her back and sweat dripping down a face red from leaning over the campfire, Jillie managed to cobble together a mess of scorched fried potatoes and charred venison steak. The steak had nearly made Ocean vomit just looking at its green tinge, especially since even after a few minutes in a frying pan, the inside remained raw.

Stomach heaving, Ocean moved away to sit on a stump, away from the pair as they ate. Peckham gobbled down the meat with good appetite; Jillie, less avidly. They talked, Jillie's glance landing on Ocean with a slowly brightening expression. Whatever Peckham planned for her, he was telling Jillie. And she liked it.

Ocean crossed her fingers in hope that the food made him sick, until considering her escape plan would be ruined if one of them got the heaves or squirts and the other didn't. Although otherwise, it would serve both of them right.

At least the tainted meat gave Peckham an excuse to, as he put it, "Settle his stomach before bed with a little alcoholic medicine. You though," he pointed a forefinger at Jillie as if it were a gun barrel, "you lay off the booze. You been sopping up more than my old pa used to do afore he drank himself to death."

Peckham's father must've been a wonderful example of manhood.

Meanwhile, Peckham had his orders ready. "You got to stay awake and keep an eye on her, Jillie. That's all."

As an extra precaution, he yanked Ocean's hands behind her and had Jillie tie them. "Good and tight."

Jillie nodded her satisfaction at the job. "She ain't getting loose from that."

"Make sure she don't. But you still got to keep an eye on her. Hear me?"

"I hear you. But I ain't staying awake all night. You can just get up your own self and take a turn watching her."

"Then I'd better sleep now if my gut will let me. You ain't much of a cook, Jillie. That fried venison didn't agree with me." Peckham got up and, walking sort of curled over his belly as if in need of that medicine, started toward the cabin.

At first, Ocean thought he was going to go on past her, but then he stopped. Giving her, then Jillie, a sharpish, distrustful look, he yanked Ocean to her feet. "C'mon with me."

Heart leaping with fright, Ocean cried out. "Take your hands off me." Despite her resolve to not argue, Ocean did. She fought him, too. Whatever he had in mind, she didn't want to find out. If he tried... She didn't finish the thought.

She had the use of her legs. Knee him in the nether parts. That's what Papá always said to do. Then, when the man was bent over—as he was bound to do—smash him in the throat, the nose, or mouth with all her might.

"Smash him with what?" she'd asked, bewildered.

"Your fist," he'd said, demonstrating the correct way to fold her fingers into a fist. "Or if you can't use your hands, use your head. Or even your shoulder. Whatever you can. Just never stop fighting, daughter. Never stop."

But Peckham didn't give her the chance. Worse, she had sort of given up. She'd let them take her, hadn't even tried to escape when considering the odds against her. Made plans? Yes. Moved on them? No. She'd even let Jillie whack her around without retaliation. And now this, Peckham telling her to shut up as he dragged her toward the cabin by her hair.

Jillie, standing by the campfire, laughed at the sight. "Better you than me," she called to Ocean. "That meat is bound to give him the runs."

"Mind your own business," Peckham shouted back. "You ain't any better off. Damned old whore." But those last three words were spoken under his breath.

Inside the cabin, Peckham tossed a filthy, moth-eaten blanket onto the rough dirt floor and pointed. "Lay down."

Ocean refused.

The single room—if one could legitimately call this dark, empty interior a room—reeked of mice with a hint of skunk. He shoved her down onto the floor and prepared to join her, except a huge gaseous miasma burst from his bowels just then, making him moan.

Ocean's stomach heaved. "God in heaven," she muttered, even as Jillie, still outside, yelled, "I heard that."

The outlaw pushed her away, roughly enough that she fell over onto her bound hands. "Changed my mind," he gasped. Clutching his belly, he ran for the door, leaving her to lurch awkwardly to her feet.

Now? Run now?

No, because Peckham, even as he dashed out, called to Jillie to mind the prisoner.

"Yeah, yeah, don't I always?" Jillie said.

To Ocean's ears, the prostitute sounded as if she weren't far off from being in the same condition as Peckham. Feeling downright gleeful, Ocean didn't even try to keep a crooked little smile from breaking through. The illness served them right for eating tainted meat. Any idiot taking a single look, let alone a sniff, ought to have known better. Maybe, and there was a tiny bit of hope in the thought, they'd go to sleep and never wake up.

But just in case they didn't, resolve rising once again, she started a search of the cabin.

Despite hands tied behind her, she absolutely had to find a way to get loose. With her hands tied in front when riding, escape had seemed easier. Softly, she gave a little huff. Who would ever have thought her father's lessons would, in more ways than one, stand her in good stead. First, the proper way to make fists, and second, the way to strain and puff her muscles so the ropes binding her wrists gave a little slack when she relaxed. Not much, but enough to keep her fingers from going numb. Enough, if she could find an exposed nail, a rusty blade, or even a stout splinter, to saw at the rope until it loosened and freed her hands.

Peckham managed to barely get a couple feet beyond the side of the shack. Ignoring the sounds of him being sick on both ends of his body, the only thing Ocean found that might help was a small rock with a fairly sharp, toothed edge half-buried in the floor. She had managed to sit and secure the stone between her fingers when she heard him coming back. Quick as one of the mice, she clenched her fingers around the stone and scooted up against the cabin wall. Settled in the dirt, she huddled into a ball. From here, head lowered to knees, she had a clear field of vision out the door.

Jillie, still sitting beside the campfire and not lifting a finger to clear away the used utensils, spoke to Peckham when he tottered over to the warmth. Her question to him lacked sympathy. "You done raising that gawd-awful stink?"

He groaned. "I dunno."

She huffed. "Me neither. My guts are tying in knots."

"You damn near poisoned us, woman. I'd kick your ass if I could raise my foot."

Turn about seemed fair. He had no sympathy for Jillie, either.

Jillie's lip curled in a sneer. "That ain't all you can't raise, which may be to the good. This way, you ain't spoiling the business deal. Virgin, that Marcus Streeter feller said, huh? That's what he pays for."

"If she is a virgin. She's old enough she might've been used." Peckham groaned and stiffening, tottered off into the woods again as fast as his feet would go. Meanwhile, Jillie doubled over, rocking back and forth until Peckham, without pausing at the fire, staggered into the cabin and, without further ado, collapsed onto the blanket.

He didn't spare as much as a glance for Ocean. She doubted he even glimpsed her sitting there.

Time passed. Ocean sawed at the rope with her edged stone. Outside, Jillie jumped up and rushed off in the general direction Peckham had gone, coming back minutes later with her face gleaming ghostlike under the moonlight. She glanced into the cabin, no doubt able to hear Peckham snoring with a roar like thunder, and spot Ocean now lying on her side. She then took a blanket from a saddle bag and spread it on the ground. Presently, she settled back. Her snores were not much softer than Peckham's as both of them slept.

The moonlight moved away, leaving Ocean in shadow.

Time passed. Minutes. Hours. Ocean kept sawing, until the rope split apart at last. She hardly believed it, at first.

Now. Afraid even the rustle of her skirt might disturb the sleeper—Peckham's body expelling nauseating gas every now and then, although his eyes remained closed and his snores unabated—Ocean's movements rivaled the mice as she crept past him.

Once outside, allowing herself a deeper breath of clean air, she edged toward the campfire. Jillie slept with her mouth open, drooling just a little. Ocean had intended on taking Jillie's revolver, but not only did the whore keep it right next to her, one hand rested on the butt. But for the first time, Ocean had cause to be grateful for the woman's slovenly ways. The camp knife, the one Peckham had feared she might take hold of, lay right where Jillie had dropped it at supper. Ocean picked it up as she drifted past.

She was almost to the picket line where the three horses stood dozing when one raised its head. The young mare, noticing the human, nickered a soft greeting. Not loud, but Ocean, on the verge of stepping from behind a tree into a patch of moonlight, froze.

"Whaaa?" Jillie raised up on an elbow and stared

around. Checked on the horses first to find them all standing placid and calm.

Thank goodness she hadn't taken that last step, Ocean thought.

Jillie turned to look into the cabin then, peering hard. Ocean held her breath as if, even at a distance, the woman might sense trouble.

But the shadows were deep. Peckham's noise remained loud and unrushed. Jillie shrugged, sighed, and lowered herself onto the blanket.

On the verge of moving, something about Jillie's form under the blanket warned Ocean to remain still. To wait.

And although Ocean had intended on taking a horse, she didn't quite dare. Not now. Jillie wasn't sleeping as hard as she'd hoped. The horse might not cooperate, she might be caught flat-footed if she delayed. Anyway, she didn't know if she had the strength to saddle the horse and ride away. Her ribs, her hip, even her empty stomach, all fought against her. All she had for protection was the dull kitchen knife Jillie had used to hack the poisoned beef.

It would have to do, Ocean decided. The knife and her own two feet, carrying her down the mountainside toward Clovis Creek. In the cold and dark.

All because she spoke Polish and Greek. And French and German.

Careful where she placed her feet and silent as a wraith, she slipped away from the camp. Gradually, Peckham's snores faded to nothing behind her.

Until Jillie's screech split the night only minutes later, echoing amongst the surrounding hills. "She's gone. That damn woman is gone."

17

ASH LOST THE TRAIL AT THE SCREE SLOPE. THE rock fall hadn't been here last time he hunted up this way, but he surmised snow melt had dissolved the soil and brought down a good half of the hillside. Fairly recently, too, judging by how unstable the fall still looked. Unwilling to take Ranger across for fear of starting the slide again, he cussed a little and thought about what to do.

He patted the horse's neck. "Don't worry. I won't ask you to risk a crossing. At least I can see the fall didn't happen today, so either they made it across, or they took a detour." He took another look at the scree, its rocks sharp enough to cut and ruin a horse's feet and legs. To one side, a canyon had formed, cutting off access on that side. "I think a detour, so that's what we'll do. All it'll cost us is time."

Time, he feared, Ocean might not have to spare. What Peckham's intentions toward her might be is what had him worried. The outlaw already had a woman traveling with him, one who'd helped him escape arrest once already. He didn't understand. Why had he taken Ocean?

Or, a thought occurred to him, might Vogel have put the outlaw up to this as retribution for her help in ferreting out the truth about their court cases. One thing for sure, Judge Fedderer hadn't been paying her enough.

Peckham's tracks showed up about midway when the route steepened and their horses had scrambled for footing. Ash took the safest route he deemed passable up the hillside. He doubted the outlaw would be so considerate of his mounts. Even so, Ranger's hooves slid out from under him once, until Ash thought he'd fall over backward. Stepping from the saddle, he went by foot after that, letting Ranger determine the pace as they scrambled to the top.

How had Ocean fared, he wondered, panting as he caught his breath. This had turned into a rough ride for anyone, and she wasn't a seasoned rider. He'd been able to tell as much during their ride to rescue Dzik's kid. Plus, Judge Fedderer had admitted she'd been hurt in the mob's riot. Hell, his own lungs and chest were heaving, and he didn't have busted ribs. The surge of his anger no longer took Ash by surprise.

They reached the top and stopped while Ash took stock of their surroundings, hoping that from this vantage, he might catch sight of the riders. Both he and Ranger needed a breather after the climb. The horse huffed his dislike of the whole process in short grunts. Ash didn't like it any better.

The rockfall having cleared the mountainside of trees and brush, he had a clear view as he checked his back trail. He hadn't expected to see anyone, and he didn't. Early hadn't had time to catch up and probably wouldn't until morning. He saw no one ahead of him, either. Peckham must be driving the horses hard. Horses and women.

He lost the trail an hour later. All he could do was follow his instincts. After a while, as the sun began its dip to the west, the landscape flattened. Mountains turned into hills, and the going became easier. It was as Ash, hearing the splash of water nearby, guided Ranger in that direction and finally came upon the tracks of three horses.

He had a leap of satisfaction. "Found them," he breathed. Ranger, with his nose dipped into the shallow rivulet of snowmelt, snorted into the water.

OCEAN, standing paralyzed as Jillie's high-pitched caterwauling sent small animals to their burrows and birds into the dark sky, later figured she should've known her escape had been too easy. Too lucky. The slipping out of the cabin part, she meant. Away from the stench of Peckham's bursts of incontinence, as well as the fact his normal personal hygiene lacked finesse.

But then, she reminded herself, she hadn't exactly escaped as yet. No more than a couple hundred yards separated her from her captors, but a mountain range lay between her and safety. A sinking feeling in the pit of her stomach provided an overwhelming answer. No. She had not escaped. And from the way Peckham's roar joined with Jillie's screech, they were already hot on her trail.

If she'd left a trail. She was slight, and she'd been

careful where she placed her feet so as not to make noise by rattling bushes, breaking sticks, or rolling pine cones underfoot. She had a hunch their noise stemmed more from an attempt to avoid owning to their carelessness and, maybe, a try at scaring her into showing herself.

Well, she was scared all right, but she still had her wits. And she'd pit her own intelligence against theirs any day.

But escape depended on whether she was able to backtrack the route they'd taken to this place, otherwise, she had no chance of getting away. On the other hand, even if she did backtrack, isn't that exactly where they'd be looking for her? Why didn't they just give up and go on their way? She didn't understand why they were so determined to take her.

A memory of something Peckham, or maybe it had been Jillie, had said popped into her mind. Something about a man named Marcus Streeter paying good money for her. And Jillie saying Ocean was kind of old to be a virgin and Peckham shrugging and saying, "Forget it. It ain't any of our business what he wants to do with her." A second or two later, he'd added in as thoughtful a tone as he was capable of having, "Maybe Streeter wants her because she can talk Polish. And whatever lingo the feller they hung talked. Streeter gets all kinds of girls, you know."

Jillie had answered with a surprised grunt, as if, for once, he'd impressed her with his logic. "Maybe so."

That, as Ocean thought about it now, meant only one thing. One thing she was never going to let happen.

Feeling and motion jolted back into her. Peckham was yelling at Jillie to bring him his dadburned—only he used a stronger word than that—horse, whereupon Jillie told him to get it himself, that she planned on searching around the clearing for Ocean.

The two called back and forth, their voices coming clearly to Ocean. Every once in a while she caught a glimpse of one or the other through the trees.

"I don't figure she's been gone long," Jillie said. "She can't have got far, a city girl like her. Besides, she's hurt. That there lynch mob in Colville shoved her around pretty good. I'll look around here while you ride out. If you find her, fire off a couple shots. If I find her, I'll do the same."

Peckham stomped around a bit, making plenty of noise as he grudgingly agreed to Jillie's plan. "I'll ride as far as the scree. If we don't find her by then, I figure she's lost."

"Maybe we should just leave her go. We don't need her, do we, Peck?"

"We do. Streeter' is paying me to bring her to him. Streeter, he's a dangerous man, and I don't want to cross him. We do need her. We gotta find that girl and find her fast, you hear me, Jillie? Because we'll be in deep trouble if we don't."

Jillie said a very bad word. "Well then, I suppose we'll just have to find her. Then run like hell so's that sheriff and his deputy don't catch up with us."

"Yeah, them or Marcus Streeter, either one."

Her answer came slowly. "I hear you."

They didn't say anything more. A minute later, Ocean shrank behind the too-small trunk of a pine tree as a horse and rider thundered past. They were going too fast for the horse's safety, running in the dark, although she couldn't help but be glad of it. Peckham, concentrating on the vague path ahead of him, didn't spot her as he spurred the horse, although Ocean was certain her skirt, if not her body, spread beyond the tree.

Then he was out of sight. Back at the cabin, Jillie was slamming stuff around as if she thought her prey had taken cover in spaces too small to hide a cat, let alone a full-grown woman. She looked behind a low woodpile stacked helter-skelter off to the side. Peered inside the empty cabin, where she didn't stay long, no doubt because of the lingering outhouse stench. She might've believed Ocean stupid enough to run off into the deep forest behind the cabin since every once in a while, Ocean caught sight of her flitting in and out of the clearing as if realigning her bearings. Once, she called out. "Hey you, speaker lady. Ocean. That's your name, ain't it? He's gone. You can come out now. I won't hurt you. I'll help you."

Ocean almost laughed. Almost.

Frankly, and this was a bit of a puzzle, it didn't look to her as if Jillie was looking terribly hard. What she did believe was that Jillie would shoot her dead if she got the chance, no matter what Peckham said about needing her.

Keeping her eyes peeled, in case Peckham doubled back or Jillie widened her search area, Ocean skinned out of her skirt and wrapped it around her waist. Clad now in her drawers, her favorite blue ones made of lightweight muslin, she'd never been so grateful they weren't shining white. But at least now she had more freedom of movement, and a quieter way to move.

If she should move.

Because Jillie surprised her when she stood stock still beside the campfire embers, her arms akimbo.

Jillie's head tilted to one side as if thinking. Then she picked up what looked like a bridle and stalked off toward the broken corral where the remaining two horses were hobbled.

"What is she doing?" Ocean mouthed the words to herself.

With Jillie out of sight, she wasted no time in second-guessing herself in what her next move should be. Unhampered by skirts, she dashed—and Ocean, accustomed to darting nimbly around a crowded café dining room, was mighty fast on her feet no matter how much her hip hurt—back toward the cabin. Jillie had left her pistol sitting on the stump near where she'd bedded down. It took no more than a few seconds for Ocean to snatch it up and grab one of two canteens.

She had no chance for more. Jillie, already leading the better of the two remaining horses to camp, blocked her from running across the bare area at the front of the cabin and into the woods. What now? Panic rising, she leapt for the woodpile and flattened herself behind the chunks of wood. Face pressed almost into the ground, she opened one eye and focused the slender line of sight on Jillie.

Jillie made short work of saddling the horse, showing she'd had a lot of practice. Made short work of rolling her blanket into a tight bundle around a few personal items, as well. She stopped once, briefly studying the stump where her pistol had lain. "Damn him," she said. Quick as a mink, she snatched up the remaining canteen and clambered aboard the horse. Pulling its head in the opposite direction Peckham had taken, she heeled it hard in the flanks, crossed the meadow, and rode out of sight without looking back.

Apparently, she'd looked for and found a trail to follow, one taking her north.

Slowly, when she was sure it hadn't been a ruse and Jillie had truly gone, Ocean rose to her feet and brushed herself off. "Well," she said. "Well. How about that?"

The sound of her own voice speaking out loud startled her. She cast a guilty look around, with the thought she'd best keep her mouth shut. What if somebody, meaning Peckham, sneaked back and heard her?

Ocean picked up the other bridle, thinking to take the remaining horse and ride away. Then she changed her mind. In the first place, she'd never saddled a horse for herself. Someone had always been there to do it for her.

Second, her hip hurt badly enough when walking on her own two feet. She wasn't sure how long she'd be able to ride up and down the hills. Not after yesterday. For a third, and possibly most important argument against taking the horse, Peckham would have no trouble following its tracks.

What struck her as a better idea was to turn the horse loose. Encourage the animal to follow Jillie's horse, the same one he'd patiently followed yesterday. Then, when Peckham came back, the tracks of two horses would likely send him in the direction opposite she meant to go.

Ocean made short work of lugging off the ratty old saddle some distance into the woods and dumping it there. Last of all, she shooed the horse away with a slap on the rump. Setting off down the trail, she went slowly at first. She didn't want to trip and fall in the dark. Resolved to keep a close watch for Peckham's return, although she didn't expect him for some time yet, she felt almost cheerful.

Hours later, the sky lightened. Birds sang, the sun promised warmth when it finally broke over the eastern hills, and though her stomach growled with hunger, some of the pain from previous days eased as her muscles warmed. All was well.

Until along about full light, storm clouds blew in, and instead of sunshine, rain began to fall.

An hour before daylight, Ash's weather sense let him know rain was on the way. Moisture in the air settled down, coating the ferns and bushes with heavy dew. The damp penetrated his jacket and made Ranger hump his back when he went to saddle the horse.

Ash cursed his luck. Even if a short-lived storm avoided a gully washer, rain would soon wash away the tracks he'd discovered just as dark fell. He'd camped the night there and considered staying at the stream for Welburn and Lloyd Carson to arrive so they could coordinate the search into a grid. The weather changed his mind and he didn't think it wise to wait. He didn't worry about the pair catching up. Carson's hound would follow the scent.

Meanwhile, he supposed Ocean must be scared out of her wits. Except, according to Ned Hazenberger, she didn't scare easy.

Wise to inland northwest spring weather, he'd

packed a slicker. He put it on before starting out, mounting Ranger and pulling his hat down to shield his face as the wind picked up.

A beastly day, and if he remembered right, Ocean hadn't taken much of a coat with her. She'd been wearing a short jacket over her dress when traveling to Colville for the trial, more for fashion than for warmth. He supposed she'd been wearing the same outfit on the return trip. Cold. She'd be cold if she was out in this.

AN HOUR OR SO LATER, as it happened, he had cause to be grateful for the wind and wet weather. Rain had begun falling shortly after sunrise, blowing directly into his face. It blew into Ranger's face also. Something he either scented or heard caused the horse to stop, throw up his head, and prick his ears.

Ash, who'd mostly kept his face lowered while watching the trail to make sure he didn't stray from it, lifted his head, too. The trail had a lot of switchbacks here, and while he couldn't see but a few yards ahead, it didn't mean someone farther up the road was blind to him.

"What is it, old son?"

Although he waited, he neither heard nor, squinting into the wind, saw anything moving. Visibility had grown worse as the rain thickened. He put his trust in the horse's instincts.

They listened in silence, the woods surrounding them quiet, except for the patter of rain. Finally, thinking the horse had heard a deer or some other animal, now fled, he was about to nudge Ranger on when a voice called out. It sounded pitiful and weak, like a person calling for help.

He still didn't see anyone. Ranger heard the voice and took a step forward of his own accord.

Ash drew on the reins. "All right. We both heard. But take it slow. This could be a trap." Most likely *was* a trap, he figured. Because he couldn't think of a single reason anyone but outlaws or lawmen would be traveling in these parts during a rainstorm.

Holding Ranger to a walk, they proceeded slowly. "Whoa," Ash said sharply. The horse stopped.

So did the rain, as if his word had commanded it. An excellent happenstance in view of the previously hidden rifle barrel poking over the top of a large boulder. The trail took a jog around the stone, hiding who hid behind it. The one in charge of the weapon pointed toward him. Off to the side, Ash saw a bay horse carelessly tied directly under the drip-line of a fragrant cedar tree. The horse held one foot off the ground and looked miserable. And familiar.

"Come to give yourself up, Peckham?" he called.

"Me?" The owner of the rifle kept himself hidden but didn't try to deny his identity. "Hell, no, lawman. I..." he stopped.

"I heard you call for help." This is what had Ash wondering. It was almost as if Peckham had been expecting someone else to appear. But who? And where was Ocean? Or the woman who'd been helping him at the stage? From Judge Fedderer's description, it sounded like the same whore who'd rounded up the horses at Sleeper's ranch the day the other one, Belle, shot him and the sheriff.

The outlaw didn't answer. Uneasy, Ash kneed

Ranger, causing the horse to leave the trail for the more sheltered verge. "Peckham?" he called. "What's up?"

Peckham remained silent as the rifle did a slow slide over the top of the boulder and fell to the ground.

Distrustful and aware Peckham might be trying to tease him into barging in closer to investigate, Ash stayed put. The outlaw still had a pistol and a clear field of fire. Finally, Ranger, no doubt curious about the other horse, shifted and took a step.

Ash dismounted then, drew his gun, and slipped from tree to tree until he reached the horse. It had a swollen fetlock, he noted. Sore, but probably not broken. The saddle bore smears of mud. And blood. If he had to guess, he'd figure the horse had fallen and taken Peckham down with him.

Leading with his .44, he charged around the boulder.

18

OCEAN'S TEETH CHATTERED BEYOND CONTROL. Wet muslin drawers clung to her legs like slimy, wet snakeskin. The skirt wrapped around her middle where she'd hidden Jillie's pistol was the only thing on her even halfway dry. Her hands were numb with cold. Tormented muscles hurt so badly that she inadvertently let out whimpers every now and then. Even so, she stubbornly kept moving. Her feet, clad in Sunday-go-to-meeting shoes that would never be the same, slipped and slid when she hit steep spots in the trail. Some of the worst of them she remembered from the ride up the mountain.

The rain kept falling.

Once she fell, landed on her side, and kept sliding, fortunately on slippery bear grass instead of mud, for at least three feet. Also fortunately, she fell on her good hip and was able, after a time, to get up and trudge on. The fall frightened her, though. What if she'd broken a bone? What if she lay there until she died?

She didn't find it easy to shake those dire thoughts away.

Every now and then, she'd spot a deer or some other animal browsing on the new grass, oblivious to the wet. Once, she thought she saw a wolf, but it ran from her, and she saw it was only a coyote hunting rodents.

"Lucky coyote. You have your breakfast," she called to it, willing to be friendly. The coyote slinked away into the underbrush and disappeared. Her own belly growled loudly enough to sound belligerent. She supposed there were things in the forest she could eat, if only she knew what they were. Some of the ferns, perhaps? Wasn't it the season for fiddlehead ferns? But she had a notion they needed to be cooked before eating. Even if she'd known a fiddlehead when she saw it, she had no way to make fire.

Sighing, she struggled on.

Perhaps she was hallucinating, but when the wind stopped for a moment and created a queer emptiness, she thought she heard voices—more than one—echoing far off in the woods. But though she cocked her head in that direction to listen, she heard nothing more. Just the rain.

Her heart had raced at the thought of finding help, until she had second thoughts. What if, instead of help, she met Peckham. Or the Streeter person he'd mentioned? Truthfully, she'd have been mortified for anyone, even him, to see her like this. Limping, hair streaming down, nose dripping. Clad in drawers, her legs splattered with mud from above the knee to her poor, clogged shoes. Her hip stained green from the fall in the grass.

Reminded of Peckham, wondering if he'd reached

the scree and started back by now, Ocean resolved to keep closer watch. Her hand went to the revolver. If necessary, she'd shoot him before she let him take her again. With the gun, she wasn't helpless.

Years had passed since she'd done so much as shoot a bottle off a board, but she didn't think she'd forgotten the process. Check the loads, use both hands, take aim, hold steady, and squeeze. And she'd grabbed that man's shotgun at the jail and quelled a mob, hadn't she? Acted with authority?

Putting her head down, she slogged along. Her heartbeat pounded in her ears. Her limbs were leaden with weariness.

"Keep going," she whispered to herself. "Fast as you can, Ocean. You have to keep going." *No matter how much it hurt. How hard the trail.*

She had no idea when somehow she veered off from her vaguely familiar direction. Probably at one of the steeper parts while trying to find an easier way. Or maybe when a sudden gust of wind almost blew her off her feet and she found a place out of the wind long enough to catch her breath.

But how could she not have noticed when the trail the horses had used yesterday became a narrow deer trail? How could she not have realized the rain struck at her from the side instead of right into her face?

When she did realize, she stopped. Gazed around. The lowering sky overhead, the variety of trees as far as her eyes could see—at first, all seemed the same. But then she realized the forest looked different now. The trees smaller. The sky more open. Timber had been cut here, the stumps oozing great beads of sap. Limbs on the ground were fresh and green and smelled strongly of pine.

There'd been no logging when they rode to the cabin yesterday. A cry burst from her before she stuffed her fist in her mouth and put a damper on the panicky sound. Without thinking, she collapsed onto one of the stumps.

Somehow, somewhere, she'd gone wrong.

Lost.

Awareness flooded through her. Lost. And she was no woodsman, able to find her way home. Men, for there were a lot of lumberjacks and sawmill men in Clovis, talked as they gathered in the café. They spoke of their work, of going into the woods. She overheard snatches of conversation while serving them. They drank gallons of coffee and ate heartily, talking about this logger or that one. They spoke of Abe Shepard, who'd been crushed when a mighty tree twisted the wrong way under the saw and fell on top of him. The details were gory, but it had occurred to her they'd almost relished repeating them.

"Crushed his head so's you couldn't even recognize him," a man had said. "Brains splashed six feet away. We're taking up a collection for his widow."

As Ocean remembered, the collection had not been munificent. Times were hard, donations few. And every man knew, at any time, the same thing could happen to him.

"Found a skeleton up on Freer Mountain last fall," another had chimed in. "Figure he'd been there a couple years. Feller had a pocket watch on him engraved with a name. Turns out he'd been timber cruising for the sawmill owners and got lost. Since he'd been talking about quitting when the snow came, everybody just figured he'd taken off."

A grizzled man, old for a lumberjack, had another story. "There was that cowhand from the Sleeper ranch, too, I forget his name, but he got throwed from his horse and a cougar got him. Got the horse, too. Reckon the cat smelled the blood and found easy pickin's."

The first man had snorted. "Cowhands, huh. What do they know about working in the woods?"

"Not much, from the look of things." The men had laughed.

Apparently, the Sleeper ranch fell victim to bad luck quite often.

Remembering now, Ocean thought there'd been a whole lot of ghoulish delight in these stories. Men speaking with bravado to show they weren't afraid of the mountains. But it was easy to tell they were cautious of and, most of all, respected them.

So did she. In fact, her respect grew with every minute she spent here. But enough was enough. Rising from the stump, she made herself walk again, because while sitting there, she remembered something else she'd heard the lumberjacks say.

"If you get turned around while you're up there," said the one who'd told the story about Abe Shepard, "find a stream. Any stream, even if it's just run-off. It still goes downhill until it hits a bigger stream. Right up until you reach the bottom of the mountain. Nine times out of ten, you'll find a road, and a road will lead you somewhere, even if it ain't where you started out for."

"That cowboy," another man said with all the

wisdom of Solomon, "he shoulda let his horse go. Horse woulda found his way back to the barn."

"Unless it busted a leg," the first man said.

They'd all nodded, just like Ocean nodded as she set off. And when at last she looked up, she finally saw a break in the clouds as the rain slowed to a sprinkle, then stopped.

ASH CHARGED around the boulder in a crouch. Expecting to find Peckham at least docile, if not collapsed, he found...no one. Before he had time to straighten, a heavy blow struck between his shoulder blades. Staggered, he slid on the scattering of wet leaves underfoot. Fighting to recover his footing, he failed to fend off the loop of rope that sailed over his head and settled around his arms just above the elbows. A tremendous jerk yanked the rope tight. His .44 dropped from nerveless fingers to the ground.

He made as if to reach for the revolver, a witless effort as another jerk dragged him onto his butt.

At least he could still move his body. Twisting around, he found Peckham standing behind him, a wide grin on his lips. Head down, Ash lunged toward his attacker.

Sidestepping before Ash knocked into him, Peckham moved fast. He dragged Ash close to the tree and circled around them, lashing man to the tree with a tight loop. Once bound, Peckham took a spraddle-legged stance in front of Ash and tilted his hat back, grinning like the face on a scarecrow. "Well now, Deputy Jones, that was just too easy," he said. "Hardly even any fun. I expected a fight. Guess you ain't as sharp as you let on."

Ash felt the blood flooding his face. He had to agree, not as if he'd say so. He hadn't been sharp. He'd been tired, rushed, and drawing conclusions based on misjudged evidence. Peckham had fooled him by letting the rifle slip over the boulder as if too weak to hang onto it. The part about his horse falling on the rain-slicked trail and coming up lame appeared true. But, seen close up, nothing appeared wrong with Peckham except for a scraped hand and face, hence the bit of blood on his saddle. And he was afoot. Ash got a bad feeling about that. Another thing. He was alone. No second whore. *No Ocean.*

Another idea struck him. What was Peckham even doing here? Had he figured Ash—or maybe Sheriff Welburn—would be after him and deliberately set up an ambush? If so, the outlaw was smarter than he'd figured.

"Pretty good acting," he said, grudging the admission. "Now what? You gonna gun me down like you did Roy Sleeper?"

"Thinkin' about it." Peckham studied him.

"I'm surprised to see you here." Ash flexed his fingers, already feeling numb from the tight rope. "Figured you'd be long gone by now. You and the whore. And the woman you kidnapped. Why did you do that, anyhow? Seems like an awful lot of trouble to a man wanted for murder. You could've been in Canada by now, you and both those sporting women."

Peckham grinned again. Pulling on the rope, he made another wrap around Ash's middle that felt like it cut him in half. "Wouldn't you like to know?"

Trying to ignore the painful squeeze of the rope shutting off both his breath and his circulation, Ash nodded, casting a glance at the .44 on the ground only a few feet away. A broken tree branch lay there as well. He figured the outlaw had used it to club him. "That's why I asked. Where is she?"

Peckham wasn't paying attention. Another jerk on the rope answered, this time strong enough for Ash to let out an involuntary yip when the snag from a broken-off branch poked into the back of his rib cage. At this rate, Peckham wouldn't have to shoot him. The snag would dig a deep enough hole to do the job.

"That outta do it." Peckham made a knot in the rope and brushed his hands together in a satisfied way.

"Where is Miss Galliard. And why?" Ash demanded again. "Why take her? She didn't do anything to you."

"Miss who? Who's that?" Peckham's squinty eyes opened wide.

"Don't be coy. The woman you kidnapped."

"Oh. Didn't know her name. But what do you mean, she didn't do nothin'? The hell. That damn woman is how come you're out here huntin' me, ain't she?"

"Only because you forced me. I'm out here hunting you because you kidnapped her. I want to know why." Ash snarled the reply, but Peckham didn't seem to hear.

"Yeah, Vogel told me about her when...well, you ain't hearin' about that part from me."

"No?" Ash protested. "What about Vogel? You might as well tell me." And if he got out of this, Ash determined Vogel was going to answer for whatever he'd done.

Shrugging, Peckham gave in. "What the hell. You ain't gonna live long enough to spread the news. Seems as if Günter seen us one night when Fuller and I were subtracting a few head from the roundup count. Said he wouldn't tell nobody if I'd give him a few calves. So I did. Tit for tat, as the sayin' goes.

"Anyways, she's the one what got you and the sheriff to wonderin' about that Russkie being innocent when it turned out she could speak whatever gibberish he talks. Hell, I'da ended up with the whole Sleeper ranch sooner or later otherwise. Roy's nephew or whatever he is don't know nothing about a ranch. I'da just took it away, slick as—"

Ash interrupted. "You're not giving the sheriff or me enough credit. We were figuring it out. Just tell me where she is. Make it easy on yourself."

"Huh." Peckham snorted in an unbelieving sort of way, hitched up his britches, and headed over toward Ranger, ignoring his own horse standing with its head down.

"You'd better not hurt her," Ash shouted. His hands hidden from Peckham's view, he did his best to break them loose. Quick, before Peckham got away. Didn't work. All he did was twist his thumb. The outlaw had tied a good—depending on whose viewpoint—knot.

"Hurt who? The horse."

Ash scowled. Ranger being a gelding, Peckham just wanted to goad him. Succeeding, too.

"Miss Galliard. You'd better not hurt her. Folks don't look kindly on a man who causes a good woman harm. A decent woman like her, there'll be a reward on your head, and every lawman and bounty hunter in the country will be after you. Take warning."

Peckham studied Ash's saddle, tried the cinch, and nodded satisfaction before mounting. He paused to shake out the reins before looking down at Ash from Ranger's back. "I ain't gonna hurt her, deputy. Not much, anyways. I'm gonna sell her."

"What?"

"Sell her. Already made the deal. That'll learn her not to meddle in what don't concern her." He chuckled. "Adios, deputy. Hope it don't take you too long to die." He gigged Ranger in the ribs, making the horse jump.

Ash knew there was no point in trying to dissuade the outlaw from taking Ranger, and though it chafed fiercely, he closed his mouth.

He'd get him back, he vowed. He'd get both Ocean and Ranger back if it was the last thing he ever did.

The thought was what kept him going for the next couple hours. That and the strange idea he'd have the last laugh on Peckham when he caught up with the outlaw and told him the way he found to free himself.

When Peckham broke off the dead tree limb he used to club Ash, the snag now poking his ribs remained. As it so happened, his arms were roped very near the snag. Thinking about it, Ash figured his grunt of pain had worked out for the good. Peckham had enjoyed the idea of tormenting him and deliberating tied him there.

But Ash, straining every muscle, managed to finagle sideways far enough to scrub, a quarter inch at a time, at the rope. When, with his shoulders aching and at the end of his endurance, the hemp frazzled enough for a final lunge to break him free, he ended on his knees.

He looked up, his bare head—hat lost somewhere in the bushes—just about even with Peckham's horse's lowered head. The horse whuffled. "Howdy," Ash said. "Bet you're glad you're rid of him."

The horse shook his head up and down. Ash took it for a yes.

"Pity poor Ranger. He's not used to the spur."

Five minutes later, his .44, which had been left behind, had been wiped free of most of the mud and shoved back in the holster. His wet and out-of-shape hat was retrieved and back on his head. Ash took off walking, then, following Ranger's tracks. Peckham's horse followed along, limping only a little.

After a while, the rain stopped.

19

PROMISING NEVER TO THINK OF THE LUMBERJACKS simply as an unruly bunch who caused her a great deal of extra work cleaning up after them, Ocean not only found a larger stream than the one she'd been following, but a trail at the bottom of the hill. Just as they'd said she would.

She came very close to weeping. The trail wasn't much. Any trees in the way had been cleared down to low stumps but not leveled. Grass and barely leafed huckleberry bushes were crushed and bent, showing where big-footed horses had skated chained together logs. Recently, too, as even she could tell.

"Hallelujah!" Ocean's shout echoed through the trees. Exhaustion dogged her, making her legs feel weak. Finding an old downed log, she sat to catch her breath while deciding which way to go. Left or right? So turned around, she had no idea where to find north, let alone south, or east or west. She wondered if the direction mattered. It wasn't as if she knew where Clovis Creek lay, or Colville, or even the main road the stage had traveled. But this trail must end somewhere. A safe place, where she'd find people other than Peckham or Jillie.

Or, it occurred, a sense of dread flooding over her, this unknown man who'd supposedly bought her.

After pondering, she resolved to follow the horse's tracks. Something any fool could manage by paying attention to the direction the hoofprints headed. Even a woman like her, who spent her time working in a local café. Maybe some of these loggers would be men she'd waited on. They'd recognize and set her on the right track. Or at least to a place with people.

"Hallelujah," she hollered again, and then, with a bit less volume, "Help." Useless noise, she figured. Except for birds, insects, and the susurrant murmur of the trees, it was silent here, her voice an intrusion.

But she was so tired. Best to rest a bit and start out again when the ache in her hip subsided.

The sun had come out a while ago, and with the forest canopy opened up, her bones warmed, and her clothing dried. Perched on a log that had lost most of its bark, unable to help herself, Ocean slumped and went to sleep sitting up.

The next thing she knew, something—a bird maybe —was pecking the top of her head with its sharp beak. It hurt. Flinging up her arms, she batted at the bird. "Shoo," she said and opened her eyes.

A set of beady dark eyes squinted at her. Not, she realized after a bewildered second, a bird's eyes. They belonged to a human, one she couldn't, at first glance, decide was male or female. Whoever it was had a beard-free face but looked quite masculine. No softness appeared in either the wrinkles or the eyes the wrinkles surrounded. Gray hair clubbed behind a thick neck left her no wiser, especially as the person wore britches, clumpy boots, and a shapeless sheepskin vest over a flannel shirt. A grubby, sheepskin vest. And, Ocean noted, she—or he—didn't smell much better than the sheep who'd previously worn the fleece.

"So you are alive. Wasn't sure there for a bit. Didn't think you were breathing." Ah. A woman's voice and sweetly melodious at that. "What are you doing here? Are you lost? Where do you belong? How come you are not wearing a skirt? Or britches?"

Was that disapproval Ocean heard?

"Are you sick?" the woman continued. "Lost?"

Ocean stared dumbly at the woman, barely able to keep up with the questions. A hooked forefinger remained poised over her head, its broken fingernail bearing a sharp point ready to poke her again.

Ocean flinched and picked just one question to answer. "Yes, I am lost. And tired, not sick. Can you help me?"

The woman's gaze sharpened. "Where do you come from? How did you get lost?"

Ocean wasn't of a mind to keep the event secret. "A man and a woman, not a decent woman, kidnapped me when they held up the Colville stage. They shot Judge Fedderer." A second later, Ocean thought maybe she should have left out the *decent* part of the description. There probably weren't too many people who'd judge this woman decent in her male logger attire.

The woman didn't appear to notice. "Kidnapped? Colville stage? That is thirty miles south of here." She looked off in what may have been a southerly direction. Good to know. "How did you get here?"

"I..." Ocean broke off. She hadn't realized it until this very minute, but from the first word, the woman had been speaking Greek. How odd, she couldn't help thinking, to run up against two people who spoke Greek when she hadn't heard the language in years. And even odder when the woman seemed to take their conversation for granted. "First, they made me ride a horse. Then I escaped and walked." She looked behind her. "Walked a lot."

"Get up," the woman said. "I will take you to the camp. Yes?" Mouth twisting, she ceased her harsh study of Ocean's features. "You are hungry, yes?"

Ocean nodded. Her stomach growled a response. "Yes." Two tries later, she made it to her feet. Her hips felt as if the bones had been pulled apart and were now being drawn up tight. The knees weren't much better. She couldn't stop a groan.

The woman scowled at her. "What?"

"My feet hurt, my legs hurt. And most of all, my hip and my ribs hurt." Ocean didn't care about dodging the issue.

"From walking?" The woman's overgrown eyebrows rose in wonder. "Huh. Soft. You come. I will not wait." Her snort gave a definite opinion as she turned, picked up a knapsack with a bunch of fresh greenery poking out, and started off. To the left, as it happened, in the aforementioned southerly direction.

Limping, Ocean took a couple halting steps in an attempt to get the blood flowing. Better. Hobbling, she forced her legs to obey her commands to move. She was afraid the woman would leave her behind if she didn't keep up. "My feet and legs do hurt from walking. I don't usually trek up and down mountains for pleasure. The hip and ribs are from getting beat up and kicked."

"Kidnapper do this?" the woman asked over her shoulder.

"No. A mob in Colville when they lynched Mr. Galanos."

At this, the woman spun around to face her, weathered face going white. "What did you say? Galanos? Dimitris Galanos? Lynched? In Colville?"

"Yes." Hmm, Ocean thought. A reaction she hadn't expected. But the Greek. Perhaps she should've known there might be a tie. There weren't many Greek immigrants in this corner of Washington territory. "Did you know him?"

The woman's eyes, a sort of hazel color, grew wet. "Dimitris Galanos is my brother."

"Your brother? I'm so sorry."

"Who did this?" A sob caught as she peered closely at Ocean. "When? Why did a mob beat you up? You Dimitris' woman?" She had switched to English.

Ocean, appalled, shook her head. "His woman? No. Absolutely not. I barely met him. I was his interpreter, for the trial."

"Trial?"

Ocean had to explain as the woman frowned. When she finished, the woman jerked her head for Ocean to follow, turned, and began walking again. Slower, this time, as if to allow Ocean to keep up. "Why a mob do this? What did my Dimitris do?"

This was an odd conversation to have, Ocean thought. Walking under a now cloudless blue sky with the smell of trees and fresh greenery all around, only to have the peace broken with a tale of violence and death.

The woman's name was Melia, she said. Melia Galanos, the last name same as her brother's. She'd never married, and really, Ocean sort of had a hint as to why. Dimitris had been Melia's only relative. They'd arrived in America fifteen years ago and spent the last couple of them in Washington. Dimitris had built up his saloon, which he'd dubbed the "Parthenon," and Melia had taken a job as a lumber camp cook. The job kept her from being stared at in the towns and derided for her mannish appearance. The lumberjacks appreciated her for her cooking. They had no other designs on her, which suited her very well. She had no designs on them, either.

Ocean learned as much from Melia.

Melia learned much more from Ocean.

For instance, the pure stupidity of Galanos when he wounded the dead man and showed no remorse when he died. The fellow had had friends. Apparently, the Greek had not, being of the closed-fist, argumentative sort. What he did have—according to the rumors, which he hadn't denied—was a great deal of money hoarded in the Parthenon's safe. That also proved an incentive to violence. Once started, the rabble became a mob out for blood—and treasure—and included pointing fingers at the people who defended Galanos at his trial. Their ire had surrounded the woman hired to interpret at the trial when the people who should have protected her abandoned her to the mob instead.

"When I translated what your brother said into English, they blamed me for his words." Ocean shook her head, still baffled by the way the trial had gone to pieces.

"Why?"

"Why what?"

"Why speak for Dimitris? He speaks English. Speaks it good. Better than me."

Ocean had suspected that. And she'd wondered why he insisted. Perhaps with the intention of delaying the trial?

The woman shook her gray head in bewilderment. "Why beat you? Don't make sense."

Ocean couldn't have agreed more. "But I survived that, only for Peck Peckham and a prostitute named Jillie to hold up the mid-week stage, shoot the judge, and kidnap me. Peckham said," she added, her anger increasing with the telling, "he planned to sell me to some man."

Melia shot her a glance as she strode along. "It happens more than you know, lady. Sometimes, it is good not to be so pretty. Nobody wants to buy an ugly woman."

"Oh."

"Men want a good cook. I am a good cook. I cook, but they pay me." She waggled a hand. "That is all."

"It sounds..." Ocean said, "...peaceful."

After another thirty minutes, they entered a clearing. A wagon more elaborate than a cowboy chuckwagon was parked in the center, where three large trees had been left uncut. They provided shade and a place to lift, via a simple pulley apparatus, supplies higher than a bear would be inclined to reach. Several tents were scattered here and there, empty now because the men were out working.

Melia pointed. "That tent is mine." Her finger moved to a larger one. "That is the boss'." She looked down on Ocean. "You will sleep in the cook shack."

"Oh, but I can't stay. I've got to get back to Clovis Creek before I lose my job."

"You know the way? You said you are lost."

"I am lost, but maybe...I can pay." Her savings might be used up, but at least she'd still have her job. Probably. If Elsie didn't use her absence as an excuse to fire her.

But Melia shook her head. "No pay. Bill and the boys, they will take you home on Sunday. No cost. You wait." She grinned, big teeth gleaming. "You will help me until then. Earn your keep."

Ocean, her heart sinking, didn't see that she had any choice.

THE COOK SHACK turned out to be more of a kitchen on wheels than a chuckwagon. A real stove with an oven took pride of place, a dry sink, real cupboards so implements didn't rattle around when on the move. And they moved frequently, Melia said. To wherever the forest needed logged.

"This place is good," she told Ocean, handing her a bunch of whatever she'd been carrying in her knapsack. "Is handy to water, only one hundred steps there and back. Here, these are fiddleheads. You can help. We must wash and cook them just right. They make people sick if not done right."

All the brown on the fern heads had to be scrubbed away, washed at least two times with fresh water, then cooked for at least a quarter of an hour.

"Lots of work to pick, clean, cook," Melia observed. "But the men like them."

Ocean was just happy to sit down and keep her hands busy, even if it gave her too much time to think. To speculate as to whether Ash—Deputy Jones—was out here somewhere, looking for her. Or wonder if he and the sheriff had given up hope of finding her. She wondered if Peckham had discovered Jillie had gone off without him. And she hoped, if he had, perhaps he would chase Jillie instead of her.

And the judge. What about the judge? Had he died? Did she even care? The man had left her to the mercies of a mob. And hadn't paid the slightest attention to her when she survived.

At least the jovial crew appreciated the cook's work, she discovered at supper. While some might've made moon eyes at her, they treated her with respect. Due, Ocean suspected, more to Melia's watchful eye than natural inclination. When told of Melia's brother being hanged, and the way she'd been treated, they growled disgust.

She recognized one fellow who'd been present at the hanging. Unwilling to let Melia know about a man she thought of as a friend, Ocean kept the recognition to herself.

THE NEXT DAY passed in a blur. She helped Melia, who baked the best bread in the territory, or so the men said, and Ocean agreed. She learned the proper way to pummel the dough and put in just the right amount of yeast—when she wasn't making sourdough instead.

On Friday, Ocean already had a speech to Ollie prepared. She anticipated showing him what she'd learned. Maybe he'd even be impressed. But she forgot all about Ollie when an unexpected rider came into camp.

Melia, who'd taken those fifty steps to the water and was carrying a full bucket in each hand the fifty steps back, spotted him in time to warn Ocean to get in the cook shack. "Stay there. Hide. Do not come out until he leaves."

Worried by the Greek woman's alarm, Ocean obeyed. "Why? Who is it?"

The rider, spurring his horse, gave no time for a real answer. Melia thumped the water down and reached inside the shack for her shotgun. A bucket tilted, splashing over her boots.

"Be silent and do not let him see you," she whispered through the shack door, then sat on the top step of the wagon with the gun across her lap.

Ocean stood behind the door, which had a narrow crack in the wood, so she could listen and even see a little. Oddly enough, she was trembling. But not enough to keep her from reaching for the pistol she'd taken from Jillie. Melia had approved of the gun and showed her a conveniently handy place to put it. Gripping the pistol, she stood rigid and listened as the rider jerked his horse to a standstill.

Melia's boots squished from spilled water as she stood up. "What do you want, Marcus Streeter?"

Ocean smothered a gasp. *Streeter?*

"You heard about your brother, old woman? I hear they worked him over pretty good before they hung him. Wisht I'd been there to see it." The man had a voice like gravel gritting underfoot when he laughed.

Melia didn't say a word. As far as Ocean could tell,

she didn't move at all, standing as still as one of the tree stumps in the clearing with her shotgun at the ready.

The man waited in vain for her to speak. After a few moments, he said, "I'm looking for a woman. A young, pretty woman. I hear she walked off from a camp and disappeared. You seen her?"

How did he know? Ocean frowned.

"A young, pretty woman? Why you asking? What would a woman like that be doing in these woods?"

"That's none of your business, Miss Galanos. I asked if you seen her, and I expect an answer. That's all." He sounded impatient.

"I have not seen her. That is your answer. Now go. You are not welcome here, Marcus Streeter."

It may have been the wrong thing to say, Ocean thought, since instead of driving him off, Melia's unfriendly words seemed to make him determined to stay.

"I'll go when I'm ready. What you hiding, old woman? Maybe I'll take a look inside that contraption there and see for myself."

"You will not. Is my cook shack. My kitchen. This camp belongs to Mr. Skellinger. You want a look, you talk to him."

Ocean's nerves hummed with fear. Something about this Marcus Streeter's intensity frightened her for Melia, as well as for herself. And his name. She'd heard it before, from Peckham's loose-mouthed talk. He'd said a man named Streeter had bought her and, seeming at least halfway afraid, he hadn't wanted to do anything to disturb the man.

This man.

20

Ash had no special trouble following Peckham. For one thing, he could pick Ranger's hoof-prints out of a hundred other horses by a variation in his hoof wall. For another, the outlaw hadn't counted on Ash freeing himself and wasn't bothering to hide his tracks.

On the other hand, Ash, afoot and with a shoulder strained from his escape effort, was slowed by leading a lame horse. He couldn't bring himself to leave the critter tied to a tree as prey for a hungry cougar or bear, which meant taking shortcuts was the only way to make up time. And he did, some tactics working better than others. He cut across areas where loggers had cut zigzag trails to make it easier to skid the logs downhill, going from the zig directly to the zag. Followed by the horse, he smashed through berry bushes and trampled spring wildflowers, their fresh scents rising from underfoot as he and the horse stumbled around half-buried debris and rotting tree trunks. For the most part, Peckham took the longer, easier way and just followed the road—more just a path—through the woods.

Ash soon guessed at Peckham's ultimate goal. He remembered a run-down cabin higher up the mountain and surmised this was where the outlaw had taken Ocean. Ash'd thought the place uninhabitable. Peck had probably been hiding there since he'd escaped, the ruined cabin being just the kind of place he'd know well. Him and the two prostitutes.

While he didn't know why Peckham had separated from the woman and been at the stream, he felt sure of where the man was bound now. And that he would find Ocean there.

"C'mon, horse," he said to the critter, pulling the reins. The horse, staying close, draped his head over Ash's shoulder to the point he felt as if he carried the animal. As the land gradually straightened out, they both picked up the pace. A couple miles farther on, the small meadow Ash recalled opened up, and the old cabin appeared. As he'd speculated, signs pointed to people in the vicinity, though he didn't see anyone now.

At the edge of the timber, Ash stopped and tied the horse out of sight. Even at a hundred yards distance, he noted where a few things had been piled in front of the cabin, as if someone had packed in a hurry and abandoned stuff where it lay. Moving easier without the horse walking on his heels, he trod soft-footed as he approached, slipping longways around the meadow to come up at the side of the cabin. But nothing stirred. Nothing and nobody. His prey had fled.

Disappointment flooded him. Since part of the building had caved in, apparently the group had set up their camp outside. A tarp had been rigged to sleep under. The remains of the campfire in a fire pit were recent, though burned down to cold dead coals.

A makeshift corral stood empty, and nothing remained in the filthy cabin but a fallen ceiling, a couple partial log walls, and a dirt floor. A motheaten bedroll, a saddlebag with a broken latch, and a frying pan turned black with burned-on food sat outside on a wire grill. Staring down at the pan, Ash guessed the contents had been so bad even the camp scavengers feared to touch it. What about Ocean? Though sturdy, she was a dainty lady. She must have been disgusted. And afraid.

Best not to think of that now.

Wasting no more time, he searched the meadow's perimeter. Tracks of three horses led away from the cabin and went north, toward Canada. Turning Peckham's horse loose in the corral, he found Ranger's tracks and, walking fast, jogging some, followed them. A few hundred yards beyond the cabin, he discovered a possible reason for Peckham's careless attitude. A brown bottle smelling strongly of rotgut moonshine had been tossed to the side, an indication Peckham was indulging himself. Celebrating besting Ash back at the stream?

Maybe. But if so, he'd better think again. The outlaw hadn't won yet.

Ash toiled on, careful to scan the timber for signs of an ambush. He followed for an hour, then two. Sometimes, when the footing leveled out, flat-out running and making good time. Eyes fixed on the way ahead, he ignored the sweat dripping from under his hat brim and the way his eyesight blurred. Almost blinded by the effort, he almost went past the lone horse quietly grazing a few yards off the trail. The horse, having thrown up his head, had caught Ash's attention. The horse wore a halter, but no saddle and no bridle.

What the...

His innards lurched as he examined the hoofprints. Hoofprints he'd been following since he'd left the cabin. Why had it been abandoned now?

He approached slowly so as not to spook the animal. "Whoa, horse," he said softly. Undisturbed, the sorrel stood like the stolid cow pony Ash knew him to be. Having gotten a good look at him previously, Ash recognized him as one of the horses the three outlaws had fled on, stolen from the Sleeper ranch after the prostitute shot Early and himself.

There didn't appear to be anything wrong with the horse, regardless, he'd been turned loose here in the timber. Though it galled to ride bareback, Ash lost no time in rigging a piece of the rope Peckham had used to tie him to the tree onto the halter latch. Reins, of a sort. He climbed aboard.

For a while, he rode, worrying he'd find a body somewhere, one belonging to either the whore or Ocean. But he didn't. Logic insisted the women must be riding double, though for the life of him, he couldn't figure why. He hoped Ocean was fighting her captors and this was their way of containing her.

He didn't want her contained. He didn't want her hurt.

The day warmed, then as dusk closed in and night insects began their song, the air grew cooler. A lot cooler.

"We'll catch them soon," he whispered to the horse, urgency driving him on. "And then we'll see."

AN HOUR AFTER FULL DARK, he caught the glimmer of firelight some distance ahead and knew he'd caught up. This time, he didn't try to hide, riding to the edge of their camp before pulling the horse to a halt. Ocean was nowhere in sight. His heart pounded. What had they done with her?

The pair, to his wonder, proved ignorant of his arrival. A loud battle, consisting mainly of yelling and name-calling, held their undivided attention. A blonde woman stood toe to toe with Peck, her fists clenched and her face flushed.

As for Peckham, his fists were also clenched. His face was as dark as a blackberry under a growth of inch-long whiskers. He loomed over the blonde in a threatening sort of way. But if he expected her to cower, he was sadly mistaken. Maybe due to his unsteady balance, his head weaved as if trying to catch up with his shoulders. The woman eyed him, her lips curled with scorn.

At a guess, he was suffering the vestiges of his earlier drinking spree and didn't care for her expression.

In turn, she didn't care what he thought. And neither did Ash.

He only cared about what they had done with Ocean.

Ash had the impression the two had been at this argument for a while now and that it grew more heated as time went on.

Their shouts turned the air blue with cursing and proved plenty loud enough to cover any small sounds

Ash made as he dismounted, walked over to Ranger, and gave him a pat on the rump.

Ash had a notion Peck might be wishing he'd gone easier on the hooch. The timbre of Jillie's screech was plenty to make a man's head pound as if a half-dozen blacksmiths were at work in there. It made Ash's head hurt, and not only had he been here less than a minute, he hadn't been drinking.

"You let her get away, Jillie," Peckham yelled. "You're nothin' but a stupid no-good whore who can't even follow orders." He thunked his hands down on her shoulders and gave her a violent shake, her neck bobbling like a dandelion on a stem.

"Who you calling stupid, you igorant sot. I don't take orders from you," the woman, Jillie, yelled back.

Ash supposed she meant ignorant. And she wasn't wrong.

Peckham shook her again. "Then the pair of you run off. Gonna take Streeter's money and leave me out, hey? I figure you two bitches cooked this up between you. I know women. Can't trust a single one farther than a tick can fly. Where's she hiding, huh? Tell me."

The blonde wrested herself away and spat in his face. "Don't you be calling me names, buster. You're the idiot, and nothing but a damn drunk besides. She's gone, I tell you. Get it through your thick head. Ran off while you was passed out from all that hooch. You're the one let her get away. Only thieving you're good at is stealing cows. Cows! Hell, that there horse you stole from the deputy has more brains than you do."

Hearing Peckham's accusation and Jillie's counter-accusation set Ash's mind to racing. Ocean gone? Did the woman mean Ocean wasn't with them? Then where was she? His gaze flicked from side to side around the camp. No Ocean. And no sign she'd ever been here.

Peckham let out a bellow at Jillie comparing him to a horse. He hauled back his arm and walloped her across the cheek, knocking her off her feet. A kick to the gut followed. Gagging, she glared up at him from the ground, her eyes watery and unfocused. Ash suspected she'd lost her wind and seeing double after the blow.

Time to interfere. If he let this go on, Peckham might end up killing her, and while he didn't have a whole lot of sympathy for the woman, he did have questions he wanted answered.

The outlaw had already fooled him once today. He wasn't about to let it happen again. Settling himself, Ash put fingers to mouth and emitted a shrill whistle around them.

At first, the pair ignored it. Then Peckham whirled, staggering sideways.

"You." The outlaw gawked at Ash as if an apparition stood before him. "Where'd you come from? You're supposed to be dead. I seen a grizzly. Saw its hump, plain as day. Figured you'd be et." He stopped. "How'd you get here? Why ain't you dead?"

Ash suspected the only grizzly Peck had seen was lodged in whiskey hallucinations.

The blonde, Jillie, sat up and huffed. "What I said. Stupid. Don't know your ass from your pec..."

A corner of Ash's mouth quirked upward. "She's right, you know. You are stupid. No, I'm not dead. Can't say as I'm sorry to disappoint you."

Peckham made a grab for his six-gun. The .45 was only half out of the holster when he fired into the ground at Ash's feet. He shot again as the revolver cleared leather, the bullet driving a hole through the bottom edge of Ash's vest.

Ash didn't just stand still and make himself into a target. Coolly, as Peckham blundered, he drew his .44, sidestepped, and fired once.

Peckham clutched at his chest, the .45 dangling from his fingers, before dropping to the ground. He stared at Ash, his mouth moving but the words silent. Very slowly, he bowed down until he was kneeling, as if making his respects to royalty. The Colt lay scant inches in front of him.

Ash watched, but he hadn't forgotten Jillie, sitting only feet away. Her eyes were more aware now.

"Oooh, Peck," she chortled, "he's done got you good."

"Kill him, Jillie." Peckham's last words came out on a bloody bubble of foam.

It was enough to draw Ash's attention, but not enough to worry him. Just as well since Jillie, making a face as if she'd hurt her ankle when struck down, bent to rub the offending limb. But when her hand reappeared, it held a small revolver, maybe one of the new lady's firearms Ash had been hearing about, and her finger was on the trigger.

She was fast. And maybe too fast since, not much of a surprise, due to her firing angle and the jump when she jerked the trigger instead of gently squeezing, the bullet hit somewhere around knee high. Ash stepped forward and kicked the pistol out of her hand. Wasn't too careful about how he did it, either.

Jillie let out a squeal like a sow with an arrow in its rear, and Peck, somehow still alive and moving, reached for the gun laying in front of him. Ash turned and clubbed him down with the .44's barrel.

Could be he struck a time or two more than necessary to quell the feeble attempt, but—though he'd never admit it out loud—it felt good. Ash figured he'd already had more than enough of Peck Peckham and his prostitutes. The outlaw was as good as dead anyhow. And with a couple of the woman's fingers already swelling past the ability to navigate the trigger guard on her baby pistol, he felt no remorse.

"Steady is better than fast," he told her. "You should've learned that from your friend just now."

Now he needed to shake some straight answers out of them because he had one important duty left. To find Ocean Galliard wherever she might be.

He needn't have worried about what to do with Peckham. As expected, the man stopped breathing before Jillie even got over her caterwauling spree. Ash figured death may have been the better alternative to listening to the woman screech.

"Shut up!" He didn't care how roughly he handled her when he tied her wrists and hobbled her like a horse. He shoved her down on a nest of smelly blankets and hunkered across the fire from her. "Now then..." The pause was just long enough to raise her apprehension. Ash could see she feared him, and while he wouldn't usually enjoy scaring a woman, he'd had enough of this one. She'd shot him once. Him and Early both. Had tried again just now. If she got the chance, she wouldn't stop trying.

"Now then," he went on. "I expect you know there's enough evidence against you to justify a hanging. Best you can hope for is a nice long prison sentence. I hear

Walla Walla has rooms on the second floor set aside special for women like you. Tell me about Miss Galliard. Why you took her. Where she is." He paused. "It's not a good idea to travel at night in these mountains. Accidents can happen. Which means we've got a night to get through. Plenty of time for a long conversation."

Ocean didn't know the mountains. Out here alone, she'd be terrified. Didn't the ladies always worry about being eaten by a bear or a wolf or something? Regardless of the wildlife, other pitfalls awaited. *Out here, accidents can happen.* Ash's own words haunted him.

Jillie's voice shook. "I don't know where the fool woman is. Like I told Peck, she ran off last night. Or maybe this morning before daylight. I dunno. I didn't see her go."

Her story had the ring of truth.

"From the cabin?" Ash asked, just to be sure.

"Yeah. Gawdawful place. Peck didn't even have a decent tent to shelter us, Belle and me. Listen, we might just be hard-used women, but he ought to have treated us better. I dunno why we went with him, except he said he had money." She turned her head and spat. "He lied."

"We'll go back to the cabin in the morning," Ash said. "I'll see if there's something I missed. Something to show which way she went."

Jillie just looked at him.

Sometime later, her voice came out of the darkness. "The Galliard woman, she played it pretty smart. Acted mild as milk. Fooled us both into thinking she was too scared to do anything. But when she ran off from camp, she knew Peck would expect her to run back the same way we came."

Ash stirred. "Didn't she?" It's what he would've figured, as well.

"No. She left tracks, then doubled back and waited in the woods until Peck rode off looking for her. By then, I'd had enough of the business. We figured you'd caught Belle, and I gave up on Peck for a lost cause. So, quick as he rode off, I packed my stuff and headed out on my own." She snorted. "Damn Peckham caught up with me. He thought I had her."

Jillie was silent a moment, then had one thing to add. "She tricked me. She came back while I was saddling my horse. I'd left my pistol—my other pistol—on a stump. When I got ready to go, the .38 was gone. I thought Peck had it, then I remembered where I'd put it." She paused. "She sneaked back and took my gun."

Ash grinned.

21

"Git," Melia told Streeter again. She stood like a stern Greek goddess, legs spread, in front of the cook shack door, barring the way with her shotgun raised.

But, undeterred, Streeter didn't 'git.' Through the crack in the door, Ocean caught a glimpse of his horse clopping back and forth as if it were performing a minuet. In all her life, Ocean had heard of only one breed of horse that naturally pranced in triple time, and this was not one of them. They were not allowed out of their own country. Which meant Marcus Streeter was torturing the poor animal into the restless dance.

"Now, now." Streeter chuckled. "I'll leave when I'm ready. Just let me get this horse under control."

The horse squealed. A pained squeal, and Ocean winced. For two cents, she'd throw open the cook shack door and shoot the man down where he sat. Or she would if Melia and Mr. Skellenger, owner of this operation, weren't the ones who'd have to pay the price.

With her eye glued to the thin crack, Ocean

watched as Streeter showed off. He was, she supposed, a handsome enough man, regular features, slick-shaven except for long sideburns, well-dressed—over-dressed— for an area where most men wore duds suitable to a laboring job. Evidently, he didn't *labor*. She hated him on sight. Him and his showy spurs with cruel Spanish rowels.

"Oh, by the bye," he said. "Just so you know, I plan on buying your brother's saloon, lock, stock, and barrel, just as it stands. I don't suppose you will have any objection. See, when I made my intentions known, the other bidders changed their minds, thinking the work might be too dangerous. After all, look what happened to Dimitris."

Melia gave a tiny jerk.

"So whatever I decide to pay, that's what you'll get, assuming, of course, you are his heir." He clouted the horse alongside the neck before adding, "And after the bank loan is paid, of course. Oh. I'll rename it as well. Parthenon is ridiculous here in the Washington wild country."

He waited for her to say something, but Melia, blinking, didn't. And when she remained silent, he refused to let the matter rest.

"You see, Melia—I'm going to call you Melia. That's your name, isn't it?—it sort of behooves you to be polite to me. Do you understand?"

"Git." Melia sounded as if she were gagging. "Before I run the barrel of this here shotgun up your behind and pull the trigger."

Streeter's eyes flashed. His face went turkey red; his hand settled on the gun riding low on his hip.

Terrified for the woman who'd befriended, and very

possibly saved her, Ocean cocked Jillie's .38 and prepared to fling open the door.

Saving them all, the horse Streeter had been tormenting gave a shrill neigh and, tossing its head, settled into a few hops just short of real bucking. His rider, attention diverted into keeping his seat, jerked the horse around once, twice, until again facing Melia.

"That," he said flatly, "was not very wise. Have a care, woman," his eyes drifted over her, "if that's what you are. Your mouth may be the death of you."

Melia raised the shotgun.

"You see or hear of the woman I'm chasing, it will be best if you let me know," Streeter continued. "I don't take it kindly when people interfere in my business."

He let the horse go then, urging him into a run until he disappeared down the mountain trail. Not until he was out of sight did Melia relax her stance and Ocean come outside.

Ocean's heart bled for her. For the insults, for the news Streeter had brought—if any of it was true, which she feared it was—for the seeming power he had over her. Melia's face, drawn into tight lines, showed pain.

"It is not true," she whispered.

"Which part?"

"Dimitris had no bank loan. The saloon, he owed nothing. I know he left the Parthenon to me. It is not for sale. Not yet, anyway. He—Streeter—he plans to steal it from me."

"I wish you'd done it," Ocean burst out.

"Done what?"

"Run your shotgun up his behind and pulled the trigger." The quote didn't sound quite as real as when Melia had first said it.

Line by line, Melia's face smoothed. "Well, now," she said after a while, "I may have been exaggerating. I don't know as a double-barrel shotgun would fit there. Not even on a man like him."

Somehow, the woman went on with her dinner preparations, raising Ocean's opinion of her higher than ever. Neither mentioned the other thing. The part about Streeter looking for her.

Rain poured down on Saturday morning, turning the forest floor to mush and making the footing precarious for the draft horses. Too precarious. Released for their Sunday day off, Saturday at noon, most of the men opted for a visit to town. Not Colville. A much smaller settlement that lay between the mountain and the town. Hooperstown had saloons, the criteria these men were looking for. But, as one of the lumberjacks told Ocean, if they ran out a flag, the stage to Clovis Creek would make a stop for her on its way through early-Sunday morning.

Before she left, Ocean had a question for Melia. "Shall I tell Sheriff Welburn what Streeter said to you? What he said about your brother's property going up for bid, for instance? He not only threatened you, but admitted intimidating other parties interested in buying the property, if selling is what you want to do. That's a punishable offense."

Melia gave her a startled glance. "No. Don't you say nothing. Not yet. Later maybe if..." She broke off.

"If what?"

"I'll talk to him again. Maybe he changes his mind."

Something about the way Melia's jaw knotted up and her face blotched with red convinced Ocean that her friend was lying. Melia had something in mind, and whatever she intended, it probably didn't bode well for Streeter—or for Melia herself.

But how, she wondered, could she possibly voice the idea that ran through her brain and made every muscle in her body suddenly knot. What did Melia plan?

Probably best if she didn't know.

Stepping forward, she gave the woman who had saved her from being lost on a mountain, as well as abducted a second time by a madman, a big, warm hug. "I'll never be able to thank you enough," she said and then couldn't stop herself from whispering so the men couldn't hear, "Please don't do what you're thinking. It's apt to turn out badly."

After a moment, Melia returned the hug. "Don't you worry about me."

Shaking her head, Ocean forced a smile. "I will worry. I don't want you hurt."

———

THE LUMBERJACKS SAW her stowed on the hard seat of a buckboard while they piled in back. With a jerk, they set off, Bill driving the team. Ocean, having believed she was lost miles from anywhere, was astounded when, only about an hour later, they reached a small cluster of buildings.

The stage had passed through Hooperstown on the way to Colville, she remembered, though she hadn't known the settlement's name at the time. They hadn't stopped then, and she hadn't supposed it a real named town. There were only a few buildings. Two, of course, were saloons, one a small store that sold bits and pieces of about everything, and one a blacksmith's shop. The stage, the men told her, would stop in front of the store where the proprietor would let her sit and wait in a sort of gallery, really only a wide hall, on the store's upper floor. A couple rooms for rent also served as a sort of hotel. Bill let her off there.

The arrangement, she found, was twice as uncomfortable as she expected, and cost a whole fifty cents. Highway robbery, in her opinion. At least she had the wherewithal to pay. From habit, a holdover from days she traveled with her father and stayed ready to run at a moment's notice, all her skirts had inner pockets sewed into them where she kept a little traveling money. Neither Peckham nor Jillie had bothered to search her, so she still had it. Definitely a cause for gratitude now.

Seated on the gallery bench, Ocean gathered her jacket close around her and shivered. The shoddy store building had been thrown together in a hurry at its advent and let in a great deal of cold air. After a while, she drowsed off. Then, later still, with her neck in a crick, she jerked awake, wondering what had roused her. Maybe a gunshot, she had a second to think. A disturbance of some sort, anyway. She opened her eyes.

Marcus Streeter was bending over, staring into her face.

Ocean froze, speechless.

Streeter chortled. "Here you are," he said, whispering. "I've been looking for you."

She could've told him to go ahead and shout. One "*hotel*" room was empty. She figured the second one was where Streeter had been staying. They were alone. The storekeeper had gone off to wherever he lived, telling her to throw the lock when she left on the stage. But those details struck her as something best not mentioned.

Which begged the question. How had Streeter found her? On the other hand, did it matter?

Ocean gathered her courage. Play dumb. Don't let him know she knew about him. "Looking for me? I'm sorry. I don't know you. You can't be looking for me. You have me mixed up with someone else."

He straightened and reached down to grab her shoulder. "No. You're the one. Don't matter if you don't know me. I know you. Peckham told me you've got the darkest eyes he ever saw on a white woman, and he didn't lie."

"Peckham? Who's that?"

"Yeah. Peck Peckham. He also said you were a little beat up but you'd heal. I see the remains of bruises. And I also see a woman dressed in soiled garments who looks like she might've been wandering around lost in the mountains for a few days." He chortled again. "Oh, yeah. You're her. And I'm claiming my property."

The grip on her shoulder tightened enough to hurt. Ocean winced. "Let go of me. I'm nobody's property. That's ridiculous."

"Not when money has exchanged hands, it isn't." He grinned at her. "Get up, Miss Ocean Galliard. There's no stage ride in your future. You're coming with me."

"I most certainly am not. Go away." She gripped the edge of the wooden bench with both hands. He could easily rip her away. She knew that. And he would. But she had one more thing to say, so she said it, coldly, with ice in her voice. "And you mispronounced my name, you ignorant clod."

He struck her, no surprise, lashing out with an open hand. Thankful he hadn't struck with his fist, the blow rattled her even as she pretended to be hurt worse than she was. Let him carry her out. She'd be damned to Hades before she walked with him on her own two feet.

Obligingly, although he didn't know it, he swooped her up and carried her down the stairs. But not to the front. They went out the back. Eyes slit, Ocean saw the door's latch hanging free. The noise from the Saturday night hoorah at the saloon down the street must've masked any sounds he made as he entered. Funny that he'd taken the trouble to avoid being seen.

Lying slack, Ocean wondered how he'd guessed she was here. Had he posted someone to keep an eye out for her and let him know if she showed up? She might never know. Not that it mattered as she didn't intend on going anywhere with him.

Streeter, breathing hard under the burden, carried her into some trees behind the store. His horse, appearing as if he'd been ridden hard, was tied there. What next, she wondered? Did the man expect her to run beside the horse? He stood her on her feet, one hand clasped around both her wrists.

"This isn't going to work." She let herself waver as if still unsteady from his blow. "You should let me go while you have the chance. You won't like what happens if you don't."

According to his laugh, she must've sounded as preposterous to him as she did to herself. "Yeah? What are you going to do about it?" He tossed her lightly up on the horse.

For a moment, it was all she could do to stay mounted as the poor creature hopped and sidled, more as if to get away from the man than disturbed by the rider on his back.

"Slide forward," he snapped at her. He untied the reins, gathering them in one hand and jerking hard as he prepared to mount behind her.

He looked away, seeking the stirrup with his foot and pausing to shove aside her skirt, which had fallen over the stirrup.

The rest was easy. Ocean didn't even have to think as she reached into her skirt pocket, drew the pistol she'd taken from Jillie, and shot him. The bullet passed through the left side of his chest, just about exactly where she'd been told the heart lay. He had just a second to look up at her in astonishment before dropping to the ground at the horse's side.

"Told you," she said.

Thankfully, he fell backward and sideways, which allowed her and the horse to avoid the resulting blood splatter.

Instantly, Ocean slid from the saddle a second before the horse made up its mind to run. She felt like doing the same, running, that is, but knew how unwise that would be. The horse took off into the woods and kept going.

The saloons, which stood across from each other on opposite sides of the road, were still doing rowdy business. An ill-tuned piano tinkled from one, voices raised in song. At the one on her side of the road, judging by the noise, a shooting contest of some kind was going on.

"Luck," she whispered to herself.

Shaking, careful to keep her skirt from dragging in the dead man's blood, she took the .45 from his holster. At the saloon, what sounded like another round of shooting began after a pause where pistols were reloaded.

A shot, followed by whoops and hollers. Another shot, more yelling.

Ocean cocked the .45, pressing it against the hole already in Streeter's chest, and at just the right moment to synchronize with the other shots, fired. Very carefully, while the spectators at the saloon were still yelling, she placed the gun beside the dead man's hand.

Let them make of that what they will, she thought wryly.

Slipping back through the door into the hotel, Ocean didn't look back. She mounted the stairs and, primly, knees together to stop them shaking, sat on the bench in the gallery. After a lengthy amount of time, the Saturday night fun faded to silence. She refused to let herself think. What was done, as they said, was done. She couldn't change it now. Didn't *want* to change it now. And Melia would be safe. So would other girls. Other women. And so would she.

At four in the morning, dark still overhanging the narrow mountain valley, the stage came through and stopped for her. Ocean was the only passenger aside from a youngster sent from Colville on a visit to his grandfather in Clovis Creek. She smiled at him, certain he never noticed the way her lips quivered.

Ocean slept all the way to Clovis Creek, and so did the boy.

22

ASH TIED RANGER TO THE RAIL OUTSIDE THE sheriff's office, giving the horse a pat on the neck before going inside, where Early was waiting for him. He knew the sheriff had been watching him. Watching and worrying. This was the fifth day Ocean had been gone. Folks were beginning to lose hope she'd be found. Most had drifted away from the search.

Most? All except him.

Drawing in a deep breath, Ash composed his features before he entered the building. He had a good guess at what Early was going to say.

Took the sheriff a while to work out how he wanted to voice his thoughts. Time Ash could've used to make tracks back to the mountain for another day of searching. He tried not to let his impatience show.

"It's been too long. We looked, Ash," Early said. "You know we did. Me and Lloyd Carson and some of the others. Hell, even Ollie went out on his day off. There comes a point where it's no use wearing out men and horses. Cussed rain," he added. "Might've been a different story without that. And we don't know but what Peckham found and buried her before you caught up with him."

Brutal, that last part.

Ash shook his head. "Jillie says not."

"Can't believe a word the woman says. Could be she done it herself."

"Could be..." Ash heard his voice getting louder and, with an effort, toned it down. "...but I don't think so. Or it could be Ocean is out there trying to get home. Waiting for us to find her."

Early shook his head. "Be a miracle after this many days. And don't forget, she was already hurt. A slip, a fall, a— God knows what's happened to her. And don't forget this other thing Judge Fedderer told us about."

"I'm not forgetting." Ash's teeth clenched.

They were back to that.

Ash couldn't deny his surprise at the story the judge told once they got him back to Clovis Creek and under doc's care. In plain truth, for a while, he'd thought the judge was wandering in the head. But later, bits and pieces of what he told them began to make sense.

None of which made him consider stopping the search for Ocean. Made him more determined to find her, if anything.

"You have to consider the judge's friend—"

"Colleague."

"Colleague," Early corrected, "from Chicago, had the right of it when he told the judge to be on the lookout in case her father shows up. And that he said the old man still has some very angry men who'd like to get their money back from him. Those men could be trying to use the girl as a way to persuade him."

"I know, I know," Ash said, weary of the whole business. "Kind of depends on if he knows where she is. The Chicago feller said Galliard swears he lost all the money gambling, and the ones he bilked say he's got the money socked away waiting for him. I wonder if Ocean even knows the truth."

"And I wonder if there are some who're watching to see if her pa shows up here." Welburn sighed. "One thing's certain, the girl sure ain't been living real high on the hog since she's been here. Who'd want to put up with Elsie Seibert, or for that matter her landlady, the Mercer woman, if she didn't downright have to."

"Wouldn't matter. It wasn't her that conned the money from those men."

"No, but according to the Chicago feller, young as she was, she managed to pay his bail a few times. Shows she knew what he was doing and where to get hold of the wherewithal to pay."

"Maybe so," Ash conceded. "Also shows she was just a kid and loyal to her father."

The sheriff sighed again and gestured to the door with his thumb. "That is true. Can't argue. Go on. Get out of here. Do your looking. One way or another, you won't be worth a damn until you've either found her or are satisfied nobody can."

They walked out into the morning together, Ash rueing the late start. The sun was well up, the day warming nicely. Folks were already out and about. Over at the café, the scent of coffee and bacon carried into the street. Butch Seibert had taken on a new girl, but she wasn't proving satisfactory. Not even half as fast on her feet as Ocean, she scowled most of the time and mixed up orders. Hardly anybody got served what they'd ordered. Some had been passing plates back and forth on their own until they were satisfied.

Even as Ash checked his cinch one more time, he heard a man bellowing for more coffee. Over at the store, an older couple were standing on the boardwalk, peering off toward the west.

Early pointed at them. "Harrison and Bevita Murphy are waiting for the stage. I hear they're taking their grandson in, and he's supposed to be on it. Their son's wife just died, and the son is taking a ship to Alaska. Thinks he's gonna find gold up there."

Ash snorted. "Hard on the boy."

"Yes."

Ash gathered the reins and mounted, looking down at the sheriff. "Wish me luck."

"Luck. Find her, Ash."

Nodding, Ash clucked to Ranger. At the edge of town, they met the stage racing along as if slowing down for the town was the last thing on the driver's mind. The six horses and coach rumbled by so fast Ash barely had a glimpse at the occupants. In fact, he rode several yards farther before his brain caught up with his eyesight.

"Whoa."

Ranger stopped. A rein against his neck told him to spin in his tracks, which he did. Then he was lifted into a lope, following the stage to the scheduled stop. The hostler from the livery where the stage line kept their spare horses rushed over to hold the team while the driver came around to set the step and open the stage's door.

Heart thudding fast, Ash watched as the first occupant emerged. A boy, dressed in what Ash figured his best clothes, hung his head as he hit the ground. The grandmother rushed forward to gather him in a hug, though the boy leaned out of it. Stiff and formal, he shook his grandfather's hand. An uneasy meeting.

When this tableau ended, the driver again stood ready to lend a hand.

Almost unable to believe his own eyes, Ash blinked as Ocean Galliard stepped out. An Ocean sadly worn and thin looking; cheeks hollow, dark circles under her beautiful dark eyes. Her clothing was so bedraggled the hem of her skirt had been shredded to rags. The jacket he remembered as bright and fashionable showed traces of a fall, with one bare elbow showing through a hole. The hat she'd worn when she left last Monday had gone missing, and the boots on her feet appeared to have walked a hundred miles.

But when she looked up and saw him, she smiled.

He didn't remember dismounting and, leaving Ranger to find his own way to the barn, sweeping Ocean into his arms.

"You're alive. Ocean, you made it off the mountain."

"I am." She laughed shakily. "I did."

He gripped her tighter. "I've been looking everywhere for you. Every day since Wednesday I've been out on the mountain."

Her dark eyes rose to his, a sparkle appearing in their depths. "You have?"

"Every day. Are you all right? The judge..." Ash spat. "...the judge said the mob hurt you. Then he let Peckham take you. Pshaw. Judge Fedderer and that Vogel woman."

"Ah. So that's who she is." She hesitated and gritted

her teeth. "Ash, I've got things to tell you. Things..." Looking around to where a few people, most aware that the lost had now been found, had gathered, Ocean stepped out of Ash's arms.

That is, she tried. He grinned down at her and held on. "Later."

People murmured. News of her return spread quickly. Up at the sheriff's office, Early Welburn rushed out and strode toward them. Ned Hazenberger appeared outside the hardware store, took off his hat, and waved it exuberantly. Ollie, the cook, flung open the restaurant's front door and flapped his stained apron. Elsie and Butch Seibert peered around his shoulders. Elsie, maybe for the first time in her life, wore an almost pleased expression.

Ocean looked into Ash's face, a reminder he hadn't shaved in a few days and he'd have to be careful if, by rare chance, she allowed him to kiss her. *Please, Lord*.

The idea struck him as doubtful when she said, low, so no one else might hear, "Better let me go. Your reputation will be ruined by consorting with a woman like me."

"A woman like you?" He laughed. "You're the very best kind of woman." Then, brow creasing, "What reputation?"

"As a lawman."

Ash had to take what seemed like the ideal opening. "I'd rather be known as something else."

She blinked those beautiful eyes. "Like what?"

"Your husband?"

A wave of soft pink suffused her cheeks. Her mouth rounded into a perfect O.

Looking down at her, Ash thought the shape just

right for what he wanted to do. So he did it. He kissed her. Carefully.

And Ocean did more than just let herself be kissed. She kissed him right back. Thoroughly. As if she meant yes.

IF YOU LIKE THIS, YOU MAY ALSO ENJOY: THE WOMAN WHO BUILT A BRIDGE

THE WOMAN WHO BOOK ONE

Shay Billings is pleasantly surprised when he discovers a new bridge over the river that cuts several miles from his trip into town. Quickly ambushed and left for dead, he has even more cause to be grateful when the bridge-builder saves his life.

When Shay's savior turns out to be a mysterious young woman with extraordinary skills, and—more importantly— acts as a strong ally when he and a few other men are forced to defend themselves and their ranches against a power hungry rich man, Shay is floored.

Nobody has ever stood up to Marvin Hammel, a man determined to own everything in their small valley with intentions to gobble up not only their homes and their livelihoods, but the water that flows through the very land itself.

But all January Schutt wants is to be left alone to hide her scars. She's rebuilt the bridge that crosses the river onto her property and lives like a hermit in a rundown old barn. Now, though, she's in the middle of a war over water rights. Has she picked the winning side?

AVAILABLE NOW

ABOUT THE AUTHOR

2019 Spur Award winner for *The Woman Who Built a Bridge* and 2020 Spur Award winner for *The Yeggman's Apprentice*, C.K. Crigger lives in Spokane Valley, Washington, where she crafts stories set in the Inland Northwest.

She is supervised by a feisty little dog with a Napoleon complex and ignored—except when he wants to lay on the keyboard—by a reclusive cat. Not satisfied to write only of the historical west, she also writes contemporary mysteries and dabbles in the speculative genre.

A member of Western Writers of America, she reviews books and writes occasional articles for *Roundup* magazine. *Buried Under Books* also features her book reviews.